VIRGINIA FOX

ROCKY MOUNTAIN KID

DRAGONBOOKS
PUBLISHING HOUSE

DRAGONBOOKS
PUBLISHING HOUSE

Names: Fox, Virginia, author.

Title: Rocky Mountain Kid (Rocky Mountain Romances, Book 4)/ by Virginia Fox.

Description: First Edition. | Boulder, Colorado: Dragonbooks, 2023.

Summary: When a nosy reporter catches wind of a child being adopted in Independence Junction, Colorado, the town is thrown into an upheaval, including love connections, legal battles, and four-legged friends saving the day.

Subjects: BISAC: FICTION / Romance / General. | FICTION / Romance / Contemporary. | FICTION / Women.

ISBN 979-8-9862800-7-3 (Paperback) |
ISBN 979-8-9862800-6-6 (eBook)
LCCN: 2023901151

Editor: John Palisano
Associate Editor: Eric Guignard
Cover Design: Juliane Schneeweiss
Interior Design: Jennifer Thomas

JOIN ME!

ROCKY MOUNTAIN KID

CHAPTER ONE

Paige Nilson stared down the biggest cinnamon bun she'd ever seen. It competed directly against the Rocky Mountain Diner's famous, freshly ground, steaming hot coffee. She looked back and forth between the two, taking stock, and sighed. *What came first? The chicken or the egg?*

Slightly overwhelmed, she stared at the dessert. *There's no chicken here. Or eggs. Just a luscious cinnamon bun. So, I'm safe!* She shook her head. *No. No. No. I can't do carbs and sugar without anything in my stomach.* She grabbed the coffee and took a big sip. Before she realized it, she promptly burned her tongue. *Great. Just great.* Her streak of bad luck seemed to continue splendidly. Tentatively, she nibbled on the thick sugar icing. She closed her eyes and groaned loudly. The sweetness made her taste buds stop hurting. Maybe the gods weren't totally out to get her, after all. A cinnamon bun had *never* tasted so good.

"That's one lucky pastry," an amused, deep voice boomed behind her.

Embarrassed, she turned and stared right into the broad chest and perfectly pressed fabric of a man's uniform. Her mouth watered. At first, and of course, she salivated because she'd taken too long between bites. Why else? A half-dozen other scenarios came to mind on the spot as she slowly lifted her gaze over his broad shoulders and stopped on a handsome, square-jawed face. He possessed the bluest eyes she'd ever seen, military short-cropped dark hair, and a smile that required a gun license. Maybe two.

"So, do you like what you see?" he flirted. He put his hand on his hip and leaned like he was modeling for Michelangelo. His gaze roamed all over her. Paige suddenly felt a kinship with her cinnamon bun...knew he was objectifying her the way she had objectified *it*! She always figured whenever she'd been eyeballed, it was mainly because of the way her strawberry blond hair framed her heart-shaped face. She was sitting, so she knew there was no way he could really check out her body.

"I don't know. Maybe it's just that coffee here has mind-altering properties," she said, raising her coffee like she was giving a toast. She caught the name stitched onto his lapel.

Ace O'Neil.

Ace stared at her coffee as if what she'd said wasn't a joke. Had she really been talking about drugs in coffee? Did she imply he only looked good because she was medicated? Had she accidentally insulted him while trying to flirt?

Paige noticed his confusion. Based on his looks, he was probably used to women throwing themselves at him. She pictured him checking himself out in the mirror, thrilled with himself. Then she pictured herself behind him, sliding her hands around his full chest, reaching for his chin to turn his face to hers, their mouths opening in anticipation.

She shook her head like a wet cat shaking water out of its fur to try to shake off the image.

"You all right there?" he asked.

Paige snapped out of it, forced a smile, and blinked several times. "Yeah. Sorry. Just got the chills."

"Miss Minnie's coffee ought to fix that, especially with the trippy sauce," he said with a wink. "But duty calls. So, see you around." He saluted goodbye and turned away.

"Bye," she called. "Nice, *uh*, meeting you?"

Paige looked unabashedly at his well-sculpted rear end as he left. "Speaking of nice buns," she remarked. She peered down at the cinnamon bun remnants on her plate. She put the coffee mug down and went right for the goodie.

Mid-bite, someone interrupted. "Girl? If you're going to advertise our secret coffee to the fire chief..." a voice said. Paige nearly jumped out of her seat. "You need the real stuff."

Fire...*chief?* She turned and was startled to see the waitress hovering nearby. The woman reached under her apron, pulled out a flask, and poured a generous sip of its mystery contents into her coffee before she could say a peep. Miss Minnie was her name if Paige remembered correctly from last evening's round of introductions, made during her bed-and-breakfast's check-in.

She was about to protest the unsolicited alcohol spike, but thought adding high-proof alcohol was a splendid idea, all things considered. Weren't all the famous journalists drinkers, anyway? A quiet voice in the back of her mind reasoned such "sloshed genius" consisted mostly of poets and writers, weren't usually journalists, and were mostly male. Paige ignored the voice. *Anything they can do, I can do better.* Determined, she reached for the cup and emptied the spiked coffee in one go.

Miss Minnie raised an eyebrow. Poured another cuppa. "How about you chase that with some coffee?"

Paige nodded and pointed at Miss Minnie's apron, mid-morning hangover be damned.

"Whiskey?" Miss Minnie shook her head and added a shot from the flask to the dark, steaming liquid.

Paige gulped it down almost as fast as the first. Smiled.

"Might need to cut you off."

Paige shook her head no. "I need it to find my writing muse, which walked out the door right before your fireman."

"Chief," Miss Minnie said. "Fire chief."

Paige put her head on the table—the booze had kicked in—and sobbed. "Everything runs away from me. My career. The fire *master*! Everything!" She realized she was slurring.

Miss Minnie gently and firmly grabbed Paige by the elbow. "Come on," she said. "No one needs to see this."

She led her into the kitchen, where she hugged Paige, pulling her crying face into her enormous bosom, and rocked her back and forth.

"There, there...it won't be so bad."

"Yes, it will!" sniffed Paige. "I'm a journalist. How am I supposed to write when I have no words and nothing to say?"

"Write about things that move you. Then the words will come on their own."

As simple as the advice was, it quickly put Paige at ease. Could it be that simple? Don't try to please some editor? Look for a story yourself—one that was written by life? Why not, actually? As of last night, she didn't have a job because of her unpredictable temper. She was literally stuck until she could figure something out. She had sublet her Denver apartment after assuming she would be a junior reporter for the Daily Mail for the next few months.

She straightened up. Miss Minnie's sister Miss Daisy stood by the stove, watching them. She silently handed Paige a paper towel, which Paige gratefully accepted.

"Better?" Miss Minnie asked, pinching her cheek.

She took a deep breath. "Yes. Better. Thank you so much. I'm not usually like this." Embarrassed, she let her face disappear behind her hair again.

"You're welcome. Crying never hurt anyone."

Paige nodded. Fortunately, in her miserable mood, she hadn't put on makeup yet, so she was at least spared from running around looking like a drowned panda.

"And the next time our fire chief flirts with you? I expect a witty response."

Paige rolled her eyes and went back to her place at the bar. She doubted whether her newfound self-confidence was enough for such a task. She could count her male acquaintances on one hand. But that didn't matter. After all, she wasn't looking for a man, but for a story. The story that would change her life.

With the Pulitzer Prize in mind, she ventured back to her seat at the bar and took a hearty bite of her cinnamon bun.

It only took a few seconds for the bite to register. Miss Minnie was right. Life was good. You just had to go about it the right way. And enjoy it along with a cinnamon bun. Her gaze wandered around the quaint diner, furnished with '50s decor.

Her attention turned to a group of people sitting together at a long table in the middle of the room. An incredible number of dogs sat around the table, too. A German shepherd watched the entire room, his ears pricked up. He seemed to keep an eye on the comings and goings of the customers like a security guard.

Two huge auburn bulldogs lay close by. Hadn't there once been a movie with a very similar drool monster? And at the end? Was that a giant poodle? Paige shook her head in disbelief. She felt as if she had landed in a parallel universe where dogs had taken over. *Like Planet of the Apes, only with dogs!* She spotted an incredibly ugly, medium-sized, dark brown dog. His physique was stocky, almost squat. She shuddered involuntarily and turned away. She hadn't been much of a dog lover since an unfortunate dog encounter in her childhood.

Uneasily, she eyed the group again. Who on earth brought so many dogs into a restaurant? Wasn't there some law against that? Although she had to admit, the animals all seemed very well-behaved. None of them barked or whined. None tugged at their leashes. *How could they?* She noticed none were leashed, either. Really amazing. At such moments, her aversion to dogs seemed ridiculous. Whenever she saw them in real life, her feelings changed and she sometimes hated to admit she might like them.

Meanwhile, she inhaled the last bite of her dessert. *NOM. NOM. NOM.*

Paige watched the group from her safe place and from the corner of her eye. *Don't make it look obvious. Great reporters blend in and gather all the details while remaining anonymous, right?* She recalled Miss Minnie's words: *Write about life,* she had advised. Paige guessed that meant she had to go where life was actually happening instead of always staying at home and behind her laptop. *Get closer. Get some quotes.* Prompted by her sudden inspiration, she mustered all her courage—with coffee in hand—and changed seats. Her courage was not enough to introduce herself to the group, but she sat at a right angle to them in the next window niche. From there she could observe them inconspicuously and listen in. Maybe she'd overhear a bright idea for her next story.

Jaz was getting excited. Paula, Leslie, Tyler and Pat, Jake, and Sam and his girlfriend Kat were all present. The Carter siblings' parents, Brenda and Stan, were about to arrive. Even Cole, Paula's youngest brother, had taken the day off and joined them. After all, there was something to celebrate.

"Do you think there's enough cake for everyone?" Paula asked, who had helped Jaz bake the night before.

"I'm sure there is," Jaz reassured her. "And if not? I'm sure the Disney Sisters have a backup plan. They always do."

The two sisters, who ran the restaurant, had agreed to make a one-time exception and allow outside cakes to be brought in. Originally, Paula and Leslie had invited everyone to the ranch. But when one of Jake's deputies had suddenly fallen ill, Jake had to cover the shift. He could still attend so long as he stayed in close proximity to the police station and, of course, on call. They improvised and moved the party to the diner downtown.

The Disney Sisters' concession was not entirely altruistic. The diner was not just any restaurant. No, it was still the only place in Independence that served hot meals, coffee, and alcohol. This made it the primary meeting place for social gatherings and the corresponding daily exchange of gossip.

To make things a little more interesting, the diner also ran a sort of betting shop. They bet on everything and everyone. No one was immune from becoming the subject of a bet.

Independence followed the mystery of what would happen to Leslie. Everyone familiar with the situation agreed the best thing that could happen to the girl was a permanent place with Paula. Recent betting centered solely on when that might officially be the case. In her infinite wisdom, Miss Minnie suspected they would just announce such an arrangement during their lunch. Why else would they be bringing in cakes? She knew it wasn't any of their birthdays, after all. She even checked her Birthday Notebook, a place where she kept track of such things. Even though she appeared to be filling coffee and bringing and taking plates, Miss Minnie hung on every word.

Brenda and Stan arrived, causing some chair-waving among the humans and tail-wagging among the dogs. After going down the line greeting folks, Brenda made her way to Leslie, who looked nervous.

Brenda was not empathetic to the child if she even noticed her discomfort. "Come here, little one. Let me hold you." She hugged Leslie in a vice grip. Leslie squirmed, so Brenda let up just enough so she could see the kid's face. "What's wrong?"

Leslie looked to the side, embarrassed. "You're not mad at me for intruding on the family?" she asked. Her palms were sweaty, and she wiped them on her jeans.

"No. Of course not, sugar. Do you think I'd be shy about saying something if I thought you were?"

Silently, Leslie shook her head.

"There you go. If that were the case, I would have said something long ago and not waited until now. Just think: I'm ahead of all my friends by having my first granddaughter. And one this big already, at that." She smirked. "No, my dear. You're not getting rid of us that easily. You've got the whole Carter family on your back now, like it or not."

Relieved, Leslie hugged Brenda back. "You bet I do. It's my greatest wish."

"Then everything is fine."

"What's that I hear?" Stan's voice sounded behind them. "My favorite granddaughter wants to get rid of us again already?"

Leslie blushed. "No way, Mr. Carter. *Uh*, Stan." She'd only recently gotten up the nerve to call him by his first name. Stan himself did not know where she had gotten the idea that he would attach importance to the formal form of address. But since his mind was usually on his inventions and calculations, it had only occurred to him when his wife had pointed it out. By that time, however, Leslie had become so accustomed to it that she found the change to Stan difficult.

Paige, sitting right next to them, followed the conversations of the various people at the table with growing interest. It seemed to be a family gathering of sorts. Family stories were good. They moved the reader and evoked emotions. She leaned forward a little, so as not to miss anything.

When everyone finally sat around the table and grabbed a piece of cake, Paula stood up and clapped her hands.

"Everyone, listen up. Leslie and I have some good news."

The entire party—and the entire diner—watched Paula intensely.

"As you know," she said, "I was approved as a foster parent a few months ago and can now officially take in a foster child." She beamed as though the sun itself shined through her face.

"And you just happened to run across one? Are you sure you want to keep the first puppy you find?" Cole winked at Leslie, who promptly stuck her tongue out at him. He liked the little one and made a point of raising her like a real big brother whenever he had the chance, even though he was really more of her foster uncle when you got right down to it.

Leslie pretended to be upset about it on the surface, but secretly she was excited about her new "big brother." The others were all very nice, too, but somehow took on different roles. With Cole, she could fool around and just be herself. Paula was more like a mother. At least that's what she imagined. While they both had fun together, too, the dynamic was quite different.

"You know that strays who make it to my farm stay there forever," Paula countered glibly.

Leslie grinned. She didn't mind Paula calling her a stray. She knew how hard Paula had fought to make the celebration possible. Leslie felt overwhelmed that Paula wanted her in her life permanently.

"What does that mean exactly?" Jake asked. He was familiar with the problems with her previous foster family.

Leslie had not run away from there for nothing. She was afraid to go back there, and so, had long kept quiet about her origins.

"We have completed the investigation against the previous foster family," Paula said, trying not to lose her breath from talking so fast. "In a few weeks, the trial will begin. Hopefully, they'll never be allowed to take in children again."

Tyler snorted. "I hope so. Collecting money for months on a kid who isn't even there anymore? A child they did not know was even alive? It's unbelievable how greedy and unsympathetic they were."

Paula nodded. "That's what the juvenile authorities thought, too. It was clear Leslie needed to be re-homed. That cleared the way for her to come to me officially." She shrugged. "Basically, they don't have enough foster homes, these days. It would have been silly and awful to rip Leslie away from what's become a familiar environment for her. Especially since she's also acclimated very well at school." She gave Leslie a sidelong glance. "School seemed to have been a...*AHEM*...not-so-unproblematic issue in the past."

Leslie hunched her shoulders and tried to hide her grin behind her long brown hair. Paula pulled her close and tickled her.

"But she promised I wouldn't have to worry, right?"

"Yes. Yes. Scout's honor. If you'll just stop tickling me already." Leslie felt she'd grown from a shy little girl and was finally embracing being a happy teenager.

"Now didn't you end up getting in trouble for not reporting Leslie right away?" asked Brenda.

"Let's just say it helped that Jake could prove, thanks to his logs, that he had been asking around at the various offices and combing through missing person reports. Having a police officer for a brother certainly didn't hurt either. And that I had already attempted to be recognized as a foster parent was also viewed positively. I got off with a warning and a minor fine. The judge will probably still keep an eye on me a bit, but not too harshly, especially after the huge scandal they've just been through. After that, there's nothing standing in the way of adoption."

Leslie looked up at Paula, surprised. She knew nothing about that. *Adoption?* She didn't know whether to cry or hug Paula.

Paula grinned at her. "You should have guessed as much. You know by now that I don't do things halfway."

Leslie swallowed. She had an enormous lump in her throat. To hide her mixed feelings, she threw herself against Paula and hugged her. Firmly.

"There, there," said Paula, stroking her back in soothing, circular motions. "You're not going to start crying today of all days, are you? After all, there's cake."

With her head still buried in Paula's shirt, Leslie giggled, even though she had been on the verge of tears only a moment ago. That was the best thing about Paula: she always knew the right thing to say.

"Now that's something to celebrate, sis!" Cole stood and raised his glass to toast. The others followed his lead.

Leslie also dared to join in with her glass of apple juice. She never thought her life would be so beautiful. She finally had a family. And a huge one at that! She patted Ranger's head, who had stood up in all the commotion and came to stand at her side. "Well, what do you think? Will I keep getting lucky?"

The German shepherd licked her hand. Satisfied she was okay, he settled down at her feet.

"I guess that means yes, handsome," she concluded, turning back to the others.

Paige could hardly believe what she heard. An orphan, a deceitful and abusive foster family, and a person who had apparently just taken the little girl in. The story had the makings of a hit. Emotions guaranteed! Every local newspaper would fight to run it, she was sure. Or would she rather run the story as a blog? Admittedly, she was still missing a few details. But she was confident she'd find them out. Not for nothing, but Paige knew she was a darn good reporter. In Independence, everyone seemed to know everything about everyone else. It was ideal for her research. She would uncover the missing information in no time. Once her name was on everyone's lips, her former boss would surely realize he'd missed out and gotten rid of her too soon.

She was in a much better mood than half an hour earlier, so she let Miss Minnie refill her coffee again. After all, she needed all the energy she could get to listen to the rest of the conversation and take notes.

CHAPTER TWO

PAULA PEERED INTO THE OVEN. The pasta bake had gotten a nice crust. She'd be able to serve the dish soon, she knew. Time to track down Leslie. The salad was already on the table. She turned off the oven, knowing the casserole would keep warm inside while she tracked down her protégé.

She stepped out onto the porch. The two blue heelers, Roo, and Barns, were lying in the grass enjoying the evening sun. Roo lifted his head lazily as she walked past them. Barns was curious enough to get up and trot after her. Maybe she'd get him a treat.

Leslie was probably stuck in the barn with the horses. Every day when she came home from school, she would do her homework as fast as possible before disappearing outside to play with the dogs, do barn chores, or spend time with the horses. This was just fine with Paula. Keeping busy kept her out of trouble. Paula smiled. She could relate. When she was Leslie's age, absolutely nothing could drag her away from the animals. If she was honest, that hadn't changed much over the years. Their shared passion for equestrian work was something that really bonded them. If she even considered it work. "Do something you love and you'll never work a day in your life," her mom used to say.

She slipped through the open barn door and stopped to give her pupils a moment to adjust to the dark. There were murmurs from the other side. She frowned. Had Leslie brought visitors? She had the horrible thought she was about to catch her foster daughter making out with some random stable hand. She did not know how she'd react to something like that and had no desire to find out.

Thankfully, she spotted Leslie a few seconds later, doing no such thing, sitting in the clean straw that served as bedding for the horses, deep in conversation with Dolly, the Shetland pony, who stood next to her. The pony's ear twitched, then her tail, swatting at a curious fly.

"...knows he can't hurt me anymore," she said. "But what if he's acquitted? And he comes looking for me?"

What was Leslie talking about? Paula crept a little closer. She didn't like eavesdropping on Leslie but the little girl was so careful, still trying not to do anything wrong for fear of being sent away again, that it was difficult to find out what was on her mind. If she had to listen in on a few bits of private conversations with an animal here and there to better understand Leslie's headspace, so be it.

"...it's like they're not giving me a choice if I don't want to make a statement, because they say it could help them and other kids in my situation. How can I say no?" Leslie sounded stressed. She leaned forward and hid her face in Dolly's lush blond mane. The pony stood still and let her without protest.

Paula didn't want Leslie to know she'd been listening. The trust between them was already on shaky ground, so she crept back to the barn door, pushed it open wide enough to let the sun in, and announced her presence with a loud, "Dinner's ready!"

She watched as Leslie wiped the tears from her face and jumped up. "I'm coming," she said. Before leaving the stall area, she gave Dolly an apple. "I'll see you tomorrow, sweetie. And thanks for listening." Dolly unapologetically devoured the apple and promptly searched for more in the girl's pockets with her nose. She laughed. "None left, my dear. There'll be more tomorrow. I have to go now. Just for tonight."

Dolly gracefully climbed through the fence separating the open stall area from the rest of the barn and hurried outside, where Paula waited for her. She was a lot like her new mother. The thought made her giddy, in a good way. Besides, there was a noodle casserole to tackle; pasta bake was always comforting.

Paula felt calm. Happiness spread like sun rays inside her. For a long time, she hadn't trusted her feelings but she sure could get used to seeing a thrilled Leslie skipping toward the dogs and her. Life didn't get much better.

The pasta casserole didn't stand a chance. They polished it off in no time. Paula cleaned up the kitchen while Leslie curled up on the living room sofa with a cozy mystery book. The last golden sun rays of the evening made the old wooden floor shine. The rolled-up blue heelers flanked Leslie on her left and right. Paula sighed. Fortunately, the couch was well-loved. An old, faded quilt served as a throw. At least she could wash it easily. After all, the dogs didn't wipe their paws clean before joining their new friend. Which made all the extra little chores worth it. Paula was glad the pooches had opened their hearts. Leslie could use every shred of affection that came her way, whether it arrived on four paws or two feet.

She smiled as she heard Leslie chuckle at a funny part. Then, frowning, she looked up when she heard an approaching car. *Who's here?* The car was still too far away for her to figure out. Paula wrapped up washing the last few dishes. She didn't want any prying, judging eyes spotting a mess. Probably just some family member who wanted to make sure Leslie was okay two weeks after the big announcement. Paula appreciated the support of Leslie's extended family. Everyone had followed her lead and welcomed the little runaway with open arms and little question. But after the steady stream of visitors over the past few days, she wondered how long it would be before they had a quiet evening all to themselves. Obviously, she thought, not anytime soon.

She hung the blue and white kitchen towel on the hook. The dogs, who had also noticed someone on the property, barked and jumped up.

"Is someone coming?" Leslie asked when Paula walked through, still absorbed in her story.

"Looks that way." Paula hurried past and went through the front door, pulling the screen shut behind her.

As the car traveled the last few feet to the house, she realized who it was. Nate, the veterinarian. *What the fork is he doing here?* She checked all her animals in her head, including the two hundred heads of cattle. All were healthy and none were about to give birth. So, what was the vet doing on her ranch?

After they'd clashed the previous year when her sister had been kidnapped with the help of his anesthetics, she doubted he was making a courtesy call. She hadn't yet forgiven him. She was too embarrassed by the whole affair, nor could she bring herself to apologize. *When you're scared to death for your sister, you're entitled to freak out a little. Or a lot.*

Sure, when one of her animals was sick, she had no choice but to call him since he was the only veterinarian in and around Independence. They kept it professional between them. Privately, she'd gone to great lengths to avoid him as much as was possible in a small town of just under twelve hundred people. *It's a shame things got that bad between us.* Paula watched him get out of his car. He was tall and strong, just as she remembered from when he'd helped her pull a calf from its mother when the birth had not gone as planned.

She eyed—lusted, maybe!—his flattering work jeans, matched classically with a dark blue and black plaid cotton shirt, exposing his strong forearms. They were very nice, Paula noted. Muscular, nicely tanned from working outside. That he could grip, she already knew. She appreciated men with such qualities, having not exactly been helpless herself. With most men, she bet she could fold them up and tuck them under her arm. Total libido killer. With Nate, there was no such danger.

Get a grip, she scolded herself. Heavens, what was wrong with her? With effort, she tore her gaze away from his forearms and tried to follow the conversation. She fantasized at what he'd feel like snug against her, his tight body against hers. The most tempting part, however, was his smile. It brightened his entire face and made his eyes sparkle. Not that she would tell him that. Deep down, she feared he was making fun of her. As far as she knew, there was no good reason the man should be happy to see her after she was always such a jerk to him. She kept to it, disguising her feelings.

"What brings you here?" she asked. "Pretty sure one of my animals didn't call you themselves, but who knows?" She tried to sound cool and nonchalant.

His smile turned...somehow...into an even bigger grin. "That would be Dolly. After all, she's the only one who would be smart enough to pull that off."

Paula laughed, despite herself. Why did he also have to be so attentive and remember the endearing quirks of her animals? He made it hard to hold a grudge. And she liked her grudge list. Easier and safer. He was yummy, but men? Nothing but trouble in the long run.

Nothing was further from Nate's mind than making fun of Paula. On the contrary. He liked her brusque manner and the way she never hid her opinions. After breaking up with his overly shy and reserved wife a few years back, he found Paula's directness refreshing. With her, he didn't have to guess where he stood. She let him know in no uncertain terms.

What he didn't know, though, was why she always seemed to be annoyed with him. Sure, they didn't have an ideal start the previous year. No sooner had he taken over the practice from old Doc Grant than his Ketamine, which he used to anesthetize animals, had been stolen and misused to kidnap Paula's sister. He was still sorry about it, even though he couldn't have prevented it. The practice had been locked and the drugs secured in an extra cabinet. Still. If something similar had happened to his daughter Shauna, he wouldn't have been okay around the person the drugs had come from, either.

But that was more than six months ago. Her sister was alive and well, and they had worked very well together on various occasions since. He thought a lot of Paula and her vast knowledge of animals. Most of the time she didn't really need him at all and treated her animals just fine by herself. All good. But when she found herself outside her element in a medical situation and called on him, she was prickly every time.

Which was too bad, he thought, as he couldn't help but eye the tall, slender woman with moss-green eyes as she climbed the porch steps. He wished for a little variety in his life. A balance between work and being a single father would be nice. Paula would be a wonderful change of pace. Maybe he would break the ice a little.

She glared at him, impatient.

Nate held out a bottle of liniment to her. "Here. Remember, I told you about this high-potency gel last time?" He beamed his biggest smile, trying to flirt.

Paula accepted the bottle. "Okay?"

"For Rufus," he jogged her memory.

"I understand." She lifted her eyes from the formula and looked at him suspiciously. "So, you expect me to believe that just to bring me this stuff, you drove an extra ten miles? That doesn't make sense. There's got to be something else."

Amused, Nate nodded and propped his forearms on the wooden railing. "No. Of course not. I heard it's going to be official soon with Leslie and you." He pointed at Paula, then at the house.

She nodded. "Yes. So?"

"I wanted to wish you good luck in person. And congratulate you on your decision. Kudos to you. Not everyone would have made such an uncompromising commitment to someone else's child."

Speechless for a moment, she just stared at him. *Had that just been a compliment? From Nate?* She took a deep breath, shrugged, and averted her eyes. "It's not a big deal. Whether it's puppies or children, it really doesn't make any difference. They both need to be taken care of until they're big and strong enough to handle the world on their own."

"I hope you worded that a little differently when you were negotiating with Child Protective Services," he said with a grin.

Paula giggled. "Sometimes I'm too logical, but I can bring the emotion when I have to."

Nate laughed out loud.

"It's true. If I had brought the puppy comparison, I never would have gotten custody of her."

"Which would have been a crying shame. For both of you. Because you're very good at caring for others, with a heaping side of love and affection."

She nodded. "I do what I can." Suddenly, she frowned. "Although I have no idea how you know that. After all, you only know me from working with the animals...and that other unfortunate situation."

He laughed, nervous. "I guess that's true." She swore he let his gaze travel down her body and back up to her face before catching himself. He raised an eyebrow and stared at her lips.

Paula did not miss the ambiguity of his statement. Only that didn't help her at all. But hey, two could play this game.

She studied his beautiful mouth. *Beautiful?* Where did that thought come from? She sensed a heat wave spreading through her body. *Ah, not helping, subconscious. Do something, quick, to stop this!*

"Great! So, if that's everything? Let's wrap this up." After a deliberate pause, she continued in a friendly tone, "I'm giving you exactly two minutes to get off my property!"

He grinned. "Or else?"

"I bet you remember Betty, my shotgun. She hasn't seen action in a while."

He raised his hands in mock surrender and slowly walked backward toward the wooden stairs. "I'm going, all right. I'm surprised it took you this long to mention Betty. By the way? If you ever need someone to talk to or have questions, holler."

Irritated, she waved her hand as if trying to scare away a pesky insect. "Why should I ask you of all people?

Are you suddenly a family psychiatrist, too? What could you possibly know about kids?"

Astonished, he shook his head. "How could you not know I have a daughter, too. Shauna. She's nine now. Everyone in this town knows everything about everyone."

That gave Paula pause. "Really?" she asked. "Of course, I remember, actually. You have a daughter." She would have liked to bang her head against the doorpost a few times. But alas, she couldn't with Nate right there. Embarrassed, she nodded. "Actually, I didn't know that. Okay. You probably actually know more about kids than I do."

"I didn't mean it that way at all." He shrugged. "I just know that I often have questions and wish I could pick up the phone and call someone. Not because the other person will have all the answers. Sometimes just to exchange ideas. Just a friend."

Perplexed, Paula eyed Nate. Was he serious? Friends? Was that even possible? After all, most of the time she wanted to either kill him or roll all over him. She hadn't found anything close to a happy medium. And yet that was exactly what he was suggesting. For the life of her, she didn't know how to respond. Everything she could think of was extremely sarcastic, which he didn't deserve after such an honest offer. Even she recognized that as he was walking away, backward.

"Does she live with you?" she asked.

"Yes." He smiled, turned around, and waved goodbye.

"Thank you," she called after him, lifting the bottle of liniment.

"You're welcome."

Ask him for advice? Ten minutes ago, he'd been one of the people she avoided, so the concept was quite… foreign. To put it mildly. But she could try it out. There was no harm in getting another opinion on things once in a while, right?

She decided she'd better say something and rushed off the porch and down the driveway.

Nate was already in the car when she knocked on his window. "Wait!"

He lowered the window.

Paula bit her lower lip. "Were you serious about your offer?"

Nate said. "Sure. I wouldn't have mentioned it if I wasn't."

"I would like to run something past you about Leslie. I overheard her in the barn this afternoon telling one of the horses that she's scared to testify. She's so insanely brave and eager to do the right thing. What do you think? What would you tell her to do?"

Nate sighed. Nodded. "I'm sure you're a better judge of that situation than I am."

Disappointed, Paula took a step away from the car. That was his expert advice now? She could have told him as much.

"Stay here," he said. "I wasn't finished."

Skeptically, she approached again.

Nate ignored her expression and continued. "If it's so important to her to do right, I think it helps her more if you support her in doing so instead of trying to prevent it. Otherwise, the only thing she learns is to stop when something scares her. She has backbone. She never would've made it this far without one. Look at her. She made it all the way to Independence instead of joining a gang or doing so many other bad things. Now she lives here, she's opening up to you, she's an outstanding student, and she's doing great. It would be a shame if she suddenly gets the impression you don't trust her to make her own decisions."

"I'm not doing that at all," Paula roared, ready to defend her bear cub to her last breath.

Nate laughed softly. "I know you aren't. After all, it's largely thanks to you she's settled in so well. But you're feeling parental instincts, too. It makes sense the longer she's with you."

"A little bit. I am." She put her hands in her pockets and drew patterns in the sand with the toe of her boot. "And having my support?" she asked abruptly. "How can I do that? It's not like I can hold her hand on the stand. Or make her former foster father disappear completely."

"I wouldn't put it past you to find away!" He laughed. "Seriously, though? I don't know. Maybe she can take a dog for support?"

"A dog? Roo and Barns, for example? They'd stir up the entire court. Besides, I don't think that's allowed."

Nate shrugged. "Just an idea. Your mileage may vary with my advice!"

"Thanks, though. Who knows? Anything's possible. I'll give it some thought. That was a pretty passionate speech for not knowing Leslie very well at all, by the way."

He gave her a penetrating look. "I'm passionate about a lot of things." After that enigmatic last remark, he started the engine and rolled up the window. "See you around," he said. "Hopefully without Betty." He winked.

Paula didn't know what to say, for once. Puzzled, she watched him drive away until the car disappeared into the dusk. Nate had been in a strange mood today. Then again, she couldn't claim to know his moods outside of work, either. She had explicitly avoided such circumstances. With plenty of food for thought, she turned and headed back into the house, his words ringing in her ears.

CHAPTER THREE

"And she just sort of found them?" Paige couldn't believe her ears when she spoke to Miss Minnie. The diner's patroness proved to be a veritable fount of information.

"Yes, something like that. But it's best if you ask Paula yourself." Miss Minnie let her eyes wander to the window. "Ah. Unfortunately, Paula isn't here, but Kat is part of the extended Carter family now, since she's been with Sam. I'm sure she knows better than I do. I'll give you a quick introduction."

Paige doubted anyone knew better than Miss Minnie. That seemed to her to be an impossibility. But she would be careful not to pass up the opportunity for a personal introduction to someone in the family. Was she talking about Sam Carter, the Colorado Avalanche field hockey player?

Miss Minnie spoke to Kat, who had just walked in. *It's amazing who you'd run into in this dump.* Paige winced a little inwardly. Maybe "dump" was a bit of an exaggeration. During the short time she had spent here, she had to admit that the breathtaking beauty of the mountains and the friendliness of the people had left quite an impression. In a few months, the Rock-the-Rockies indie rock festival would even be held here. Too bad she probably wouldn't be around. As nice as it was, she wouldn't put her career on hold permanently to just look at beautiful sunsets or young deer at dusk.

A young woman with gorgeous dark curls walked up to her, an open laugh on her face. She held a brown paper bag that contained Miss Daisy's treat of the day: an apple turnover with cinnamon, as Paige knew all too well, having already devoured two. A sacrifice she had been happy to make as part of her research. After all, she couldn't very well pester Miss Minnie without ordering something.

"Hi, I'm Kat," she said, extending her hand. "Miss Minnie said you had some questions about our family?"

Paige reached out her hand to Kat. "Hi. My name is Paige. *UM*, I don't even know how to say this."

Kat nodded. "I always think it's best to start at the very beginning. You see, Miss Minnie wouldn't tell me anything. You don't look like a long-lost, crotchety aunt, so I'm curious about your connection to the Carters."

Paige took a deep breath. "All right. I'm a journalist, and I'm always very interested in exciting stories that move people. A few days ago, I couldn't help but pick up some snippets of conversation when you were here celebrating."

Kat's expression became wary, even a little suspicious. "You mean you were eavesdropping?"

Paige ducked a little, breaking eye contact. "A little. Sorry. Occupational disease. Besides, I was there alone and had nothing to do."

"What newspaper do you work for?"

"*UM*, right now I'm...freelancing." Like that. Now she had said it. That sounded much better than *I-just-got-fired*.

Kat sat upright and she clasped her hands in front of her. She looked away as if there were a fire outside. "I see. Maybe you'd better turn to Paula. I don't have time right now, anyway. I have to go to the park, take my fresh addition for a spin."

She was about to turn away when Paige grabbed her sleeve. "Maybe I can just come with you? Please. It's important to me."

Weighing the idea, Kat eyed her. She shut her eyes for a moment, sighed. Opened them. "Fine. All right. I can't promise you'll get many answers, though."

Paige jumped joyfully from her chair. "Great. Thank you so much." She grabbed Kat's hands and shook it aggressively. Until just now, she hadn't realized how important the story was. She finally had a goal again. Whether anyone would print the story was still up in the air but the first step toward her professional rehabilitation was taken. She would show everyone.

When they arrived at the car, she asked, "What do you have to do in the park? Something about a recent addition?"

"A dog. A schipperke, to be more precise."

"*OOH*. A dog." Was it too late to say goodbye now? She just hoped he wasn't big...

"Why? Do you have a problem with dogs?"

"You could say that. They scare me. I was bitten by a German shepherd once."

Kat smiled at her sympathetically. "That's always a shame when something like that happens. Most of the time it's not the dog's fault. We should hold the owners accountable for not controlling their dogs."

Great. Kat was a dog savant who thought humans were to blame for everything and that all dogs were harmless. But she knew better, firmly convinced some dogs were just born evil.

Kat opened the trunk lid. A small black bundle of fur jumped out and ran directly toward Paige. She froze in fear. Should she run away?

When Kat noticed, she called the little dog to her. "Come away, Maybellene."

Relieved, Paige saw the dog turn to face his owner. After all, she wasn't that big. She got over herself and asked, "What kind of breed is it? Or is it a mixed breed?"

"Schipperkes are the smallest of the Belgian shepherds. They're beautiful, energetic dogs, and always up to something. But you'll see for yourself. They make good guardians. Although I have to admit, as far as you're concerned, Maybellene probably didn't get the info that you're a stranger." She giggled.

Paige feigned a laugh, too. She followed them across the street toward Independence Park. When they were in the middle of the park, Kat reached into the light green cloth bag she had slung over her shoulder and pulled out a dog toy. With a practiced swing, she sent it whizzing through the air. The schipperke ran after it like a little black ball of lightning.

"She's only recently felt safe enough to play," Kat explained casually as they wandered through the park. "And that's just with me. So, I'm making sure I find some time each day to spend one-on-one with her."

"Single? Do you have any other dogs? Were those all yours when I saw you at the diner?" Horrified, Paige backed away from Kat.

Kat chuckled. "No, they weren't all mine. In our family..." there it was again, that beautiful word, "they all have dogs. However, I actually house most of them. Although not all of them are mine."

"What do you mean?"

"I run *Safe Haven*, a sanctuary for abandoned animals. Dogs in particular, although we have a cat or a turtle with us from time to time. Maybellene here was left at a gas station. In a container, specifically."

"How mean!" Paige may not have had much of a thing for dogs herself. Still, she hated it when someone mistreated animals.

Kat nodded. "I always find it amazing what people are capable of." She bent down to accept the toy from Maybellene. The little dog gave her a wide berth and placed the slobbered toy at Paige's feet.

Paige froze. "What does she want from me? Can you call her?"

Kat called out to the dog. Maybellene briefly turned her head toward her, but continued to focus on the toy on the ground in front of Paige.

Paige retreated, even though the little dog was quite cute. Obviously, she was really only interested in the toy and not hurting anyone. *Maybe I'm overreacting to this.* She breathed out and tried to relax. Slowly, her heartbeat calmed down. Maybellene picked up the toy, took two steps, and put it back down in front of Paige.

"I know you're scared, and I'm honestly sorry about that, but for this dog this is a genuine breakthrough."

"Great," Paige said.

"No, honestly. Do you think you could bring yourself to throw the toy for her?"

"Who, me?" She eyed the chewed-up thing on the ground. "Won't she bite me when I reach for it?"

"Absolutely not. She's never bit anyone. But if you'd rather, you can let her sit first. Then her mouth will be farther away from your hand. Maybe it'll be easier for you then?"

"Make her sit? How?"

"Just give her the command. She knows it from me, so in principle, she should listen to you, too."

Paige looked doubtfully at the schipperke. Could it really work? *I guess you'll only find out if you try it,* she mockingly challenged her alter ego in the back of her mind.

She gritted her teeth. She'd soon see whether or not she had enough guts in her bones.

"Sit," she said. However, it was more a whisper.

Kat stifled a laugh. That would be anything but helpful in the current situation, when Paige was already trying so hard to overcome her fear. "Talk to her like you mean it. Assume it'll work. Maybe it'll help if you picture her sitting down."

Paige felt reminded of her childhood riding lessons. She had to imagine outcomes there, too. Not easy for someone used to experiencing the world in words. She imagined the word in bold capital letters, with an exclamation mark behind it. Maybe that could help, too.

"Sit!" she said, sternly to Maybellene.

Astonished, the dog looked up at her, then briefly over at Kat. She sat down, fixed on Paige instead of the toy. "Why is she staring at me like that? At least before she looked like she would love to eat her toys instead of me!"

Kat had to laugh. "Don't worry. Now that you've addressed her directly, she's waiting for further instructions from you. Even though these dogs are small, they have the complete shepherd personality. They love working with people. Especially if you treat them well and they feel safe. And apparently, she's decided you won't hurt her."

"She probably just senses I'm more scared than she is," Paige said. She bent down and picked up the chewed toy, her fingers trembling. Then she let it fly in a high arc. Maybellene dashed after it, delighted.

"Kudos. That must have taken a lot of courage," Kat said. "Now you've got a new friend for life."

Paige raised her hands defensively. "I hope not! I'm not a dog person."

Maybellene obviously didn't see it that way, and for the next fifteen minutes, she tirelessly returned the toy to her. Paige kept on bravely. Each time it became easier to let the pooch sit and grab the toy.

Finally, Kat had mercy and put the toy in her jacket pocket. After the pooch realized playtime was over, she followed at Paige's heels. Paige worried about getting pinched in the calf or accidentally stepping on the dog.

The trio sat down on one of the benches scattered around the park. "Now that you've become a great dog trainer, you deserve some answers."

Thank God. She had already feared they'd never get back to the actual reason for their walk. "Wonderful! Thanks. As I mentioned earlier, I overheard some things at your family reunion. If I heard correctly, the girl who was there is now officially part of your family. So, you guys are a foster family? Right?"

"Something like that," Kat said.

"Right. We can figure that out later. First, what I've learned of the story. Apparently there were problems with the previous foster family. Through some challenging interviews and paperwork, she ended up with you." She gave Kat a sideways glance to see how she reacted to the summary.

Kat's expression stayed neutral. "That still doesn't explain why you want to write an article about it."

"Can I be honest?"

Kat raised an eyebrow. "*Uh*, yeah, that would be great."

"I worked for the *Daily News* until recently. A small newspaper known mostly for its lurid headlines and gossip."

"That doesn't impress me very much."

"Nor should it," Paige said. "Believe me, I would have preferred to work at a prestigious newspaper, too. But I didn't find a job for a long time after graduation. The offer to work at the *Daily News* seemed like a godsend at the time. I thought if I delivered good ideas, I could change the paper's profile." She rolled her eyes. "I know, that was pretty naïve, huh? Anyway, it didn't work out. I kept getting into it with the editor. Which led to me having a huge fight with my boss on my last assignment, a series about celebrities in Aspen, and losing my job.

That's how I ended up in Independence. When I was listening to you guys, I was at a pretty low point. The story of your family and the girl really touched me and inspired me to think about our social system. I think others would be very inspired by it as well. That's how I got the idea to write an article about it."

"Specifically about Leslie?" asked Kat.

"I would keep it generic and change the names. But yes, from what happened, it would be their story." Paige leaned in.

"And where would you publish the article?" Kat sounded skeptical. "I alone couldn't decide that, anyway. Paula and Leslie would have to give their approval, too."

"Got it. I don't know yet. I would probably send a synopsis to various newspapers and magazines. If no one bites, I might start a blog." She lowered her eyes. She hadn't really thought about the business side much.

Maybellene's fur shone in the sun. Carefully, she reached out and gently ran her fingertip over the fur. Immediately, the dog snuggled closer to her leg. Startled, she withdrew her hand. Maybellene looked at her, pleading from big, black, beady eyes.

"She just begs to be pet more. Which is really amazing," Kat said. "I've never known her to be so open to someone she's just met."

"You sure she's not just hungry? After all, she hasn't eaten for at least an hour."

Kat laughed. "I hardly think so." Then she got serious again. "Back to your story. I can see the appeal for the reader in the story. I can even imagine Paula and Leslie would also be interested in having what happened made public in this way. But it's up to them to decide that. I can't give you any secret family information."

Disappointed, Paige nodded. "Sure. I understand. Of course. Thanks for your time." She rose from the bench to leave.

"Wait, where are you going?"

"Well, back to my room at the bed & breakfast."

"Won't you at least give me your number? So Paula can call you up to talk to you, too?"

"You would do that for me?"

"Well, sure. I can't influence Paula's final decision, but I can certainly make the contact."

"Oh, how cool? Great! Sure." Paige searched her pockets. "Wait. I should have a card around here somewhere." She finally found what she was looking for and held out a slightly bent business card to Kat. "Thanks a million!"

"You're welcome. And come by next time you need another dog therapy session."

CHAPTER FOUR

PAULA PACED IN HER KITCHEN as she dialed the phone.

"Hello, sis," Tyler answered.

"Great thing, this caller ID," Paula said. "You know it's me and not some telemarketer."

"You're lucky I have nothing to do right now," said Tyler. "I take it you need my help?"

"I can't even just call my younger sister whenever I want?" Paula asked. She absently pushed a coaster to the back of the counter.

"Can, except you never do..."

Paula sighed. "Am I really that bad?"

"Let's see? Last time it was a fence that needed mending. Before that, Ranger was supposed to help you find a calf, although I still don't know why your great cow dogs couldn't do that, then there was the incident with..."

"It's all right," Paula said. "You don't need to go on. I get it. I'll make more of an effort to just talk to you more often."

"Maybe not a great idea," Tyler joked. "I'd probably think aliens abducted you and exchanged you for someone else."

Paula laughed. "*HAHA*. So, how are you?"

"Very good. Pat and I are planning our next trip. He got an irresistible offer in California. Project start date is October."

"That's awesome. It almost makes me jealous you're escaping winter."

Tyler laughed. "Like anything would make you leave your mountains."

"Abandonment, maybe, but not exactly. Maybe I could be persuaded to take a two-week vacation in the warmth." She looked out the window at the vast backyard and shacks.

"Nothing better than that. Why don't you come visit us?" Tyler asked.

"Could happen. I'll see what Leslie wants to do. That'd be our first vacation together. Speaking of Leslie, have I fulfilled the small talk quota now so I can ask for your help?"

Paula heard Tyler sigh. "This is about Leslie? I wish you'd said that. Then I wouldn't have wasted time being nice."

"It's nice to know what a priority I am," Paula said. Deep down, though, she was glad her family had taken the little girl into their hearts.

Tyler said, "You know how it is? Little people just come first in the family. You of all people should know that," he teased.

"Exactly," Paula said. "But anyway? Leslie is worried about her testimony at the trial. When I talked to Nate about it, he said maybe she could take a dog to comfort her."

"Did I hear you right?" Tyler asked. "You're on speaking terms with Nate?"

"Yeah. That's what I just said," Paula said, irritated.

"And you aren't calling me to help you make his body disappear?" Paula was sure she was joking, razzing her. She rolled her eyes. Little sisters were wonderful. Most of the time, anyway. The rest of the time, they were a real pain.

"No. We're both adults. I think we're okay to have a civilized conversation from time to time." Her explanation sounded a bit exaggerated, even to her. She knew others had picked up on the tension between them. Subtlety wasn't exactly her strong suit.

"Uh-huh." Tyler didn't sound very convinced. "Sure. Whatever you say, sis!"

Paula cleared her throat. "Back to the subject that he suggested Leslie could bring a dog into a courtroom."

"Kind of like a helper dog? Like a guide dog?" Tyler asked.

"Exactly. The term is emotional support dog."

"Right," Tyler said. "Sure. But I don't see one of your spoiled yard dogs passing a service dog test in such a short time."

"Neither do I. Those two would wreak havoc in court. They'd be thrown out of there as fast as they came," Paula said. "On the other hand? What about Ranger?"

"Ranger?" Ranger was a former police dog. Her brother Cole had gotten Tyler the retired dog back when she faced a crazed stalker. Of course, she'd kept him, even when the danger had passed. "That's a good idea. I'm almost certain that with all his training, he'll be given an honorary therapy dog license."

"Exactly," Paula said. "That's how I see it, too. Although Ranger would also pass the test blind, one paw tied behind his back."

Tyler laughed. "My dog is just the best. I'll try to track down Cole in a minute." Their mutual brother worked undercover now and then and was sometimes difficult to reach.

"You can ask Jake, too," Tyler said. "If he doesn't know, I'm sure he can call friends at the Denver Police Department who can help out."

"Right. That's what I'm going to do." Paula felt her heart racing. "Don't tell Leslie about it for now, though. Let's wait until we know if it's going to work."

"No, of course not," Tyler said. "But I'd be happy if we knew as soon as possible, though."

"Can you ask Jake to call the courthouse and find out the regulations regarding service dogs?" Paula said. "I'll have a talk with the school psychologist and see what she thinks of the idea and if she might get us a note for Leslie."

"Is that still Martha Kindler?" Tyler asked.

Paula laughed. "No. Martha is retired in sunny Florida. The new girl's name is Karen Summers; she's just under thirty and quite good at her job. She seems like as a very reasonable person. I dealt with her when Child Protective Services reviewed my application for Leslie's care."

"It's strange that I've never met her before," Tyler said.

"Now that you mention it, that is weird," said Paula. "I've only ever seen her at work."

"You would think that people would inevitably run into each other in Independence."

"It doesn't matter, after all," Paula said. "I know where to find them during the day."

"All right," Tyler said. "Keep me posted."

"Sure. And Tyler...?"

"Yes?"

"Thank you."

"You betcha!"

Paula put the phone aside and looked at the clock. Almost three. Leslie would be home from school in a few minutes. She still had to buy supplies, get oats at the feed store, and work with Lucky, the training horse.

Maybe Leslie wanted to go for a ride.

The dogs barked in front of the house. The school bus Leslie rode every day stopped at the end of the driveway. She grabbed the car keys, made sure her wallet was in the large cloth bag that served as her purse, and left the house. She had just sent the dogs back to their places when Leslie came running up, her face beaming.

"What's the matter with you?" Paula asked. "Did you win something?"

"Better," Leslie said. "We have Parents' Day at school. You know, where the parents come by the school and talk about their work. I asked Miss French. I get to bring you. Isn't that great?"

"You get to bring me?" repeated Paula, feeling about the way her cattle must feel when she takes them to a livestock show.

"Right. I wasn't sure at first because you haven't been my mother that long, but I thought..." She left the sentence unfinished, realizing that Paula didn't seem to share her enthusiasm entirely. Leslie blushed and lowered her head so that her long brown hair hid her face.

Paula watched the abrupt change from exuberant happiness to disappointment in dismay; she hurried to make up for her blunder. She took Leslie in her arms and hugged her. "But of course it's all right, hon. I'm sorry. You know I'm a little on the fence sometimes. This parenting thing is all new to me, too. I had never heard of this parenting day before."

Leslie raised her eyes and asked suspiciously, "Didn't they have that when you were in school?"

Paula frowned. "I don't know. I'm so old and my school days were so long ago and forgotten"

Leslie gave her a peck. "Oh, you. I'll bring you your walker in a minute, grandma."

She ducked her head and blinked sideways at Paula, not sure if the joke had been too much.

Paula just laughed. She learned that they had a lot to love about each other. Still, she was often unsure whether she was doing things right or wrong. Because her previous life had been so different, she simply lacked experience. She sighed inwardly. Life was sometimes very complicated. "I like you better like this," Paula said, and tousled her hair. "Even if I have to be careful to keep up with your sassy mouth." She tickled her, glad to elicit a giggle. "I have to go shopping. Are you coming with me? Or did they stock you up on homework?"

"I'll go with you. I already did my homework on the bus."

Paula shook her head. Of course she had! How anyone could do homework on the bus was beyond her imagination. She felt sick just thinking about it. But because Leslie's grades were excellent, she saw no reason to interfere. "Good, then. Get in. We need food for us and for our four-legged friends."

On the drive, Leslie was unexpectedly talkative. She had already thought about a lot of things that Paula could talk about on Parents' Day. "We could take Dolly with us. At first I thought of maybe Fridolin." She wrinkled her nose. "But then I remembered he's so old already."

Paula bit her lips to keep from laughing out loud. Age wasn't the only thing keeping the old Longhorn bovine from going to school. Although he was extremely peaceful for his breed, hence the name, and had been fixed, he probably wouldn't even fit through the door to the classroom with his horns.

"Maybe we'd better stick to the dogs?" she asked.

"The dogs? But that's boring," Leslie said. "Everyone in my class has dogs. It's nothing special."

"Well, well, Barns and Roo would certainly be disappointed to hear that. After all, they're ranch dogs with very important jobs."

"But if I'm going to show how they work, I might as well bring some cows."

"*HMM*. Not necessarily. We could invite your class on a field trip to our farm if you'd like."

Leslie chewed the inside of her cheek, as she always did when she had something on her mind but was afraid to say it.

"Not a good idea?" Paula glanced at her from the side. "You know you can tell me anything."

"It's just..." she took a deep breath, probably gathering all her courage, "I want so much to just be a student like everyone else. And if we make it a field trip and all the other parents come to school, then I'll stand out again. I don't want that."

Paula, who vaguely remembered that it was often easier to remain inconspicuous in high school, got it. Especially since Leslie had already attracted enough attention with her story and sudden appearance in the middle of the school year.

"No problem," she said. "We'll just need to come up with something else."

"So, you're not offended?"

"Nope. Not one bit. It's your day, after all. I'm just the guest."

"You really don't think it's a good idea to take Dolly? I've been practicing a few tricks with her."

"You'll have to show me those," Paula said. "But yeah, Dolly's not a great idea. Imagine her letting go of a few horse droppings during a lecture. I don't think the class would ever let you forget that."

Leslie nodded. "Probably true. Too bad. I was really looking forward to it."

"But back to the dogs. How about we take the big exercise balls with us? Then we could do a drift ball demo. We'll have the dogs sort the balls and drift them into certain corners."

"Oh yeah! That's a great idea. We could even add cow faces to the ball covers."

"It's a good idea you take care of that. If I do, they'll end up looking like monsters."

Lesly laughed. "That will probably be better. Your strength is in drawing stick figures," she teased Paula.

"Hah. Come on now. We have to go shopping. We can plan all of this later." She reached inside her pocket and took out some cash. "Here's money and half of the shopping list. Meet me at the checkout. You get to take three things that aren't on the list. Okay?"

Leslie's eyes lit up. "All right. Awesome! See you soon."

Half an hour later, they left the mall and headed back toward Independence. The tack and feed store was on the southern edge of town and on their way home. The afternoon sun bathed the trees and mountain peaks in a golden light. A light breeze passed, drawing ripples in the tall tumbleweeds. Leslie sighed and leaned her head against the windowpane. "It's so beautiful here. Much nicer than Denver. It's all flat there, downtown and all. And I never got out of the city, anyway."

"I like it here very much, too. I have to admit, though, I have seen little else. Unlike my sister, I've never traveled much. Denver and Colorado Springs have been about as far as I've ever gone."

"Didn't you ever want to see the world?" Leslie asked.

Paula shrugged. "In a way, yes. But the animals were always more important to me than anything. And I like it here just fine, but wanderlust still sometimes hit me. Speaking of going places? The two of us were invited on vacation." She looked over at Leslie. "What do you think about going on vacation together?"

Leslie's eyes widened. "You mean you and I are going somewhere?"

Paula laughed. "Not just anywhere, but California."

"California! Sure! When? In the summer?"

"No, not until fall or winter. That way we can enjoy the warmth when it's blizzard season here in Independence."

"Will I see the ocean? How did we get the invitation?" Leslie asked. "Do you know anyone who lives there?"

"Not yet, but soon," Paula said. "Pat and Tyler are moving there for a while."

"Wow. That's super nice of them to invite us." Leslie peered outside. A girl stood in front of the feed store building, a flat structure made of rough-hewn wooden planks. "There's a friend of mine out there. She sits on the bus with me sometimes. Can I go see her while you're at the store?"

Paula pulled the key out of the lock and looked at Leslie. She appeared to be a few years younger than Leslie. "Sure. Just stay by the car or come into the store. I don't want to have to look for you later."

Leslie rolled her eyes and got out of the car, shutting the door behind her. Halfway to Leslie, she caught herself and stopped immediately. Worried, she looked over at Paula.

"What, did I just see you roll your eyes at me? Sure. I know it's annoying to have to say all this, and it seems silly, but I wouldn't be a good mom if I wasn't keeping an eye on you, right?" she asked.

"Okay," Leslie said. "Makes sense."

"Glad we're on the same page," Paula said. "See you later."

This elicited a small smile from her. Like lightning, she hopped out of the car. Paula smiled wryly. She didn't regret for a second taking Leslie in. But sometimes? She still felt like she was navigating a minefield. She hoped to do Leslie justice. She was good at dealing with traumatized animals—especially horses. But as many parallels as there might be between the four-legged and the two-legged creatures, they weren't the same. In addition, she felt a little clumsy communicating with the girl at times; she hoped her heart made up for it.

Inside the tack shop, Paula stepped up to the counter. "Hello, George, do you have any oats for me? And alfalfa?"

The man behind the counter nodded. "I've already told Luke to put it out back by the ramp. I'll put it on your tab. Anything else you need?"

"I'll look around some more." The tack and feed store was her favorite shop in Independence. It had everything that made ranch life easier: work clothes, warm jackets, rubber boots, cowboy boots, sturdy gloves, pocket knives, fencing materials, herbal supplements, grooming supplies, halters...the list was endless. Paula felt at home, unlike in the malls Tyler or Jaz dragged her to when they wanted to buy something "nice" to wear, which she only wore once a year.

She grabbed two salt licks, one for the horses and one for the cows, and turned the corner into the next row of aisles, only to stop, rooted to the spot.

Nate leaned against the shelf of chicken feed, rubbing his face, holding his cell phone.

"Trouble in paradise for Independence's successful and handsome veterinarian?" she asked, trying to razz him, but mortified she'd slipped in calling him "handsome." Not like she wanted to feed his ego.

"Not now, okay?" he said. He looked tired. Annoyed.

She wanted to say something and give him a hug. *What's getting over on me? This is not okay! Stop it!* She bit her lower lip. *Keep walking. Leave this man alone. He's got enough problems without you.* But after two steps she stopped. Looking away and turning the other cheek was simply not in her nature. So, she turned. "What's bugging you?"

"What do you care? I haven't lost any more medicines, if that's what you think."

She slid the two heavy salt licks onto her other hip. "That's good to hear. But that's not what I meant. You remember that—supposedly—we're friends now. And friends listen to each other when the other is having a crappy day."

At least she elicited a tired smile from him. He pocketed the cell phone and said, "I'm on emergency duty today. And once again, Nancy has picked this exact day to have a..." he raised his hands and drew goose feet in the air with his fingers, "...bad day." He averted his eyes. "I know she has some issues. I'd rather Shauna be with me on days like this, though. Sometimes it's just difficult. I can take her with me, of course. But she also has homework to do, and I don't know how many more emergencies will happen. That was only the first one of the day. I feel like a bad dad dragging her into all of this."

At that moment Leslie came into the store with the other girl in tow, looked around, and headed for Paula. "Paula, can Shauna come over?"

So that's Shauna. Huh. Leslie gnawed on a fingernail. *I can see the resemblance.*

"I don't think it's a good idea to impose on anyone," Nate said.

"I'm not worried about that. What does Shauna think about coming over?" Paula said. All the better if the idea came from the kids. That way she wouldn't look like a softie.

"Shauna thinks it's a great idea," Leslie assured her.

Nate's daughter nodded shyly.

Leslie looked at Paula. "We want to groom Dolly." She nudged Shauna. "You can do that, right?"

Shauna looked to her father, then to Paula, and then back to her dad.

Nate nodded at her. She lit up. "So, yes," Shauna said. "I'd love to come."

"Good, then it's settled. Wait for me by the car," Paula said. "I'll be done in a minute."

The two stormed off, leaving only the melodic sound of their joyous laughter behind.

"Thank you," Nate said.

"You're welcome."

"I'll pick them up as soon as I can."

"Don't worry about it. Take your time. The two of them seem to have a lot to talk about. You mentioned homework, too," she said. "I can help her with that. If you have a break at 6:30, come by. We'll have dinner then." Paula turned abruptly and left him standing there. She didn't want to give him the chance to say "no" or worm out of coming.

Nate checked her out as she walked; she made long strides to the cash register despite the heavy load under her arm. *Wow. She's got legs for miles. That ass is made for jeans. She can be tough, but she's got a heart of gold inside that killer package.* He thought about sharing dinner with her and the girls—a family scene he so longed to have again. *Wouldn't that just be perfect? Wow.* He thought about being her man. About them all living together, happily ever after. But he caught himself. *Don't get your hopes up, buddy. Be realistic and don't forecast too much. It's just the girls getting together. No big deal. Don't get your heart broken again.*

He knew he'd try. He knew he'd probably fail.

CHAPTER FIVE

"Look, Kat's here," Leslie said as they pulled up in front of the house. Sure enough, Kat sat on the porch. Her two French mastiffs were lying on the grass, letting the sun warm their lean bodies. Barns and Roo played greeter and rushed toward the car, barking in their best blue heeler fashion. Shauna, the vet's daughter, didn't bat an eye. *Good*, Paula thought. *If Nate's daughter isn't afraid of dogs, that sure simplifies things.*

She took her time getting out of the car. Leslie pushed open the door and jumped outside. "Come on," she said, urging her new friend to hurry. "I'll introduce you to all the dogs."

"How many dogs do you have?" Shauna asked as she climbed out of the truck.

"The two that greet you like crazy are ours, Roo and Barns. The other two are Kat's. The big one's name is Rocky, the other one is Nikita," Leslie said. "Maybe Bella came along, too. The dog Kat rescued a while back. Bella likes to hide sometimes."

Curious, Shauna followed her toward the dogs.

Kat, meanwhile, had gotten up and approached the car. "Can I help you carry something in?"

"I'd love that. If you take the bags to the kitchen, I'll stow the food in the barn."

"Will do."

"Do you want to stay for dinner? Nate might come, too."

Kat grabbed her heart and pretended to stumble back a step, startled. "Did I hear that right? Nate is coming here?"

Paula rolled her eyes and turned away to hoist the sack of oats onto her shoulder.

Kat said, "I don't know whether to run for cover or stay here to make sure I don't miss any of the spectacle."

"You're so funny," Paula said over her shoulder. "You can think about it until six-thirty. He won't be here before then. He's on emergency duty. His daughter Shauna is staying with us until then."

Paula pulled a large pot from the shelf and put water on to boil sweet potatoes. She would turn them into a soup with crispy bacon strips. A winter meal, actually. But she didn't care about that; delicious was delicious, no matter the season. Besides, it was quick to make, so she had enough free capacity to talk to Kat, who sat at the kitchen table, a large glass of homemade iced tea in front of her, while Paula worked.

"I didn't even know Nate had a daughter," Kat said.

"Thank God. Finally, someone who is as clueless as I am as to knowing every little thing and person in this town!"

"Well, I haven't been here that long."

"Long enough that if you were more interested in gossip, you would have caught on to him having a daughter."

"You're right again. How come you stay out of it so much, anyway? I always thought you Independence natives were born to gossip."

Paula grimaced. "I don't really stay out of it as much as I'd like to. If someone comes to me to discuss the latest news, I definitely contribute to the rumor mill. But most of the time, my head is completely somewhere else, so I simply miss half of it. Taking care of the animals takes a lot of time and energy."

"Oh, I see. So, back to Nate and his daughter. I thought you hated him?" Kate asked.

"Of course I don't hate him. I just find him..." she searched for an innocuous word. The last thing she wanted was for Kat to get the wrong idea. "...exhausting. Often arrogant. Insufferable."

Amused, Kat leaned back in her chair. "Exhausting. Arrogant and insufferable. Uh-huh. And these are all good reasons to invite a man to dinner?"

"Well, now that you put it that way," Paula said, laughing. "He isn't that way all the time. There is another side of him."

"I ran into him at the feed store. He had a problem, so I helped him. What's the saying? Good neighborly help. Shauna and Leslie were going to hang out anyway, and he was looking for help watching his daughter. If he doesn't have any other emergencies, he'll pick her up at 6:30. He might as well eat here, too, then. It doesn't have to be super personal. I invited you, too, after all."

"It's because of my winning personality."

"More like your irresistible dogs. You know I have a soft spot for Rocky. And Nikita. And Bella."

Kat laughed. "If you think you can distract me with well-timed compliments about my dogs, you're wrong."

Paula grinned and concentrated on chopping the vegetables. "Too bad. But seriously? Why did you come by?"

"That's right. I almost forgot with all the exciting news," Kat said. "I met a journalist at the diner today."

"So, is she from around here?" Paula asked.

"No. As I understand it, she's originally from somewhere else, but got stranded around here because of her last assignment. However, she lost her job in the meantime because she fought with her editor. Apparently, her assignment should have lasted longer, so she even lost her apartment over it. Now she's here and doesn't really know what to do next."

"What's her name?"

"Paige. I don't have a last name. Or I do, wait." She reached into the back of her pants pocket and pulled out the business card. "Paige Nilson. She used to work for the *Daily News*."

"For that tabloid? Compared to that, the folks of Independence are all saints."

"That's what she said. I guess she didn't have many options fresh out of college and she had the naïve notion she could make the world a better place at the *Daily News*."

"It doesn't look like that worked out."

"No." Kat said. "Right now, she's staying at the bed-and-breakfast. When we had that little celebration about Leslie and your successful proposal to be a foster parent for her, she was at the diner, too, and overheard a few things."

"Diplomatic wording for she was being nosy."

"Something like that. Long story short, Leslie's story, or what she's been able to glean from it so far, has made a big impression on her. She'd like to do a report on it."

Paula plunked the knife and turned to Kat while wiping her hands on a rag. "She wants to write about Leslie? Absolutely not." Resolutely, she tossed the rag back into the sink. "The kid already has been singled out at school. Media attention is about the last thing she needs. She's already under pressure because of the upcoming court hearing."

"Those were my thoughts, too. But Paige said she would anonymize the story. Only the events would be told unchanged."

"Nevertheless. And then in our newspaper to boot?" Decisively, she shook her head. "No. I don't think that's a good idea. People will be able to connect the dots."

Kat sighed. "I basically reacted about the same as you. Anyway, I felt it was yours and Leslie's decision. But she has a point that it's about time the abuses in our system became public knowledge. That's the only reason I agreed to tell you about her idea. She's already talked to a few other people. I'm a little worried that otherwise, she'll tell the story without your input. At least this way you would tell everything from your point of view."

"What do I care if anyone hears my side? I don't care what people say."

"To you, maybe. To a teenager? Not so much."

Paula had nothing to say to that. Her timer buzzed and she turned back to making the soup. She sautéed the finely chopped onions, added the rest of the vegetables, and reached for the white wine to deglaze everything.

While she waited a moment and it simmered in the pot behind her, she rubbed the back of her neck. "Yeah, maybe. Who knows? I have no idea after all. It's not my way to tell strangers private things."

"Why don't you talk it over with Leslie? See what she thinks. If she's not completely averse to the idea, you can always meet Paige without obligation and see what she's like in person." She grinned. "You'd better leave the dogs at home, though. The woman isn't exactly a dog lover. She was only willing to play with my dog after some serious coaxing."

Paula laughed. "I know it's not very nice of me to laugh when someone is afraid of dogs. But when I imagine that someone like that has to deal with your two huge mastiffs, of all things..."

Kat grinned. "It wasn't that bad. I had one of my recent additions with me. A schipperke."

"Ah okay. That's a lot more manageable. Is that Maybellene you told me about before? I thought she wouldn't let anyone touch her?"

"Yes! Her. And she wouldn't let anyone get close. Not even me! Not until today. Paige took her to heart right away."

"Wow. Crazy how that works sometimes," Paula marveled.

"Paige said the dog must have realized that she was more afraid of the dog than the dog was of her. Maybe she has a point. Anyway, Maybellene loved Paige. I had to literally carry her to get her back in the car."

"Love at first sight. Now all you have to do is convince Paige that she's always wanted a little black dog with a big heart."

"That's exactly my plan. I went to the diner again specifically and started a bet regarding this."

"Wow. You're turning into a local."

"As long as I'm not the cause of a bet myself, it's actually fun," Kat said.

Paula shook her head. "You're officially one to me, for what it's worth." She took a deep breath. "All right, then. I'll talk things over with Leslie. See what she thinks. But getting to know each other rarely hurts."

Kat put her empty glass back on the table. "Sounds like a plan. I'm sure you won't mind if Maybellene visits you that day?"

"I'm guessing you're definitely going to need someone to watch her that day."

Kat grinned mischievously. "Urgently! After all, I have a bet to win."

Barking mingled with the girls' voices. Paula checked the clock by the oven. "Half-past five already. I'd better call them in. I promised to make sure Shauna did her homework."

"Wow, were you already such a nerd in school?" Kat asked.

"*HA*. Not me. But those two are the perfect victims to pass down all of my mother's rules. Leslie doesn't give me much chance to do that, if I'm honest. The best thing for me to do is to pass on the responsibility for Shauna's homework to Leslie right away. I'm sure she'll be happy to be the boss for a change."

"You're pretty mean sometimes," Kat said, but her voice sounded more admiring than deprecating.

"Genius can't be suppressed," Paula said. She walked to the front door and stuck her head out. "Leslie, Shauna," she called.

First the dogs came rushing up and sat down expectantly in front of her. Amused, she looked at the two blue heelers. "No one called you two."

Roo tilted her head, and Barns gave his best I'm-so-hungry-dog look. She gave in and dug in her jeans for two treats. "Here." After they devoured the small morsel, she sent them off to get the two girls.

Minutes later, the two stood in the kitchen. They'd fed the horses earlier and were accordingly dusty. "You need to wash your hands," she said to them while she put some fruit and tea on the table in the living room.

"You did your homework, you said?" she asked Leslie.

"Yeah, I'm done," Leslie said. "But Shauna still has homework. I'll help her with it."

"As long as Shauna does the actual work alone, that's fine," she said.

Kat, who had been watching the exchange from the kitchen, had to stifle a laugh. When Paula rejoined her, she said, "If I ever have kids, I'll take a management class with you."

Paula waved it off sheepishly, but it was clear she was pleased. "Leslie's a great kid, too."

"That's certainly true. Still. You set that up pretty cleverly."

"Well. I'm getting to know her. And she's always been very helpful. With the horses, I don't have any work to do anymore, so to speak. Every time I want to do something, my little Brownie beats me to it."

"Handy. I could use someone like that at my house with the dogs."

"Is Sam slacking off?" She couldn't really imagine that with her brother. It was obvious how much Kat meant to him.

"No, no," Kat hastened to assure her as well. "But he's had a few advertising jobs lately besides training, and he's been on the road more."

In the distance, they heard an engine's hum. Paula got up and put the finished soup back on the stove to heat it up.

"That'll be Nate. Will you set the table for us? Placemats are in that drawer over there."

"Sure."

A moment later, Nate stood in the doorway, a tired smile on his face. Paula's stomach did a somersault. When did he ever smile like that? Was it because he was into Kat? *He never smiles like that around me!* She ignored the voice in the back of her head. When he looked at her, she scowled at him.

"What's wrong?" he asked.

Paula froze, and not knowing what to do, turned away to taste the soup.

Confused, he turned to Kat. "Did something happen with Shauna? I'll take her right now and you'll have your peace. I told you it was a stupid idea from the start."

"Everything's fine. Sit down and relax," Paula said, pointing to a chair with the wooden spoon. She couldn't let him think Shauna had done anything wrong. Besides, he looked like he could use a break and a decent meal. "Your little girl was, and is, perfect. She and Leslie had an excellent conversation. Right now, they're doing homework. Shauna can join us anytime. It's no problem at all."

Nate shook his head. "Okay," he said. "No worries."

"Did you have any more emergencies?" asked Kat, getting up to help Paula.

"Yeah. A breech presentation on a cow. Fortunately, the calf was quite small, so I could turn it." He rubbed his hand over his face. "Mother and baby are fine."

"Then it was worth it." Paula knew all too well how easily things could go wrong. She was lucky with her cattle. Because she specifically bred cattle that were small and tough, she had fewer problems than other breeders. "Still, every birth can be a risk. Are you done for the day?"

At that moment, his phone rang. He glanced at the display and answered the call. With his other hand, he signaled to the two women that he would go to the porch to make the call.

"I'll never understand why you two don't finally get it over with and go to bed together."

"Kat!"

"It's true. You squint over at him and he stares at you. You both don't think the other doesn't notice, and in between you hiss at each other like a couple of alley cats. It's a textbook mating ritual."

Paula didn't know what had gotten into her usually reserved friend. She was normally the one to make such wild statements. "What did they put in your coffee at the diner?"

When Kat just looked at her nails with feigned innocence, Paula became suspicious. "Could it be that you've made another bet?"

"Can be. While I'm at it? Makes sense, doesn't it?"

"You bet on Nate and I becoming a couple?"

"Not exactly that. But you're certainly going to have a one-night stand, if nothing else."

Paula threw the dish towel at her. "Well, thanks for the vote of confidence!"

"Hey, that's not what I meant. Just because something starts off small, doesn't mean it won't grow. And I wanted to make a safe bet first! Besides, I have to pay back all those residents who bet on my life."

"I wouldn't have expected that from you at all. I'd have thought the mountain air would have mellowed you more."

Kat laughed. "I'm often underestimated because I'm very reserved when I meet people. But that doesn't last long."

"You're very deceptive with your camouflage." She shook her head in disbelief, but laughed. She wasn't entirely wrong, after all.

"Attention. Nate is coming back. But remember what I said."

"Maybe you're going to lose your bet," Paula said. But secretly she wasn't so sure that was true. Nate looked even better when he walked in, the lights hitting him just right, his bicep popping as he put his hand up behind his head to ruffle his hair. *Wow! Why does he have to look like that! Not making this easy!*

CHAPTER SIX

Leslie packed a lunch in her backpack and glanced at the alarm clock sitting on her nightstand. She still had half an hour before the school bus came. If she hurried with breakfast, she could spend another ten minutes with Dolly. She just had to be careful that Paula didn't notice she was hurrying. Paula held steadfastly to the belief that it was important to eat breakfast properly. She smiled. It was nice to have someone who cared about what or how much you ate.

She thought about her last foster family. Food was only sporadically on the table. The family lived on welfare and the allowances they received for the children. Her first foster mother had spent the days in bed, drugged up and in a stupor. She couldn't take care of even mundane things. Her foster father was no better. Unemployed, he hung out with his drinking buddies during the day, coming home too drunk to be of any use.

In the evenings, he came home in a bad mood and took his dissatisfaction out on the children. Involuntarily, she had a memory of the stale, smoke-filled air that prevailed throughout the house. The stench of unwashed bodies, fear-sweat, and beer breath infused everything. No one cooked. The wife was in la-la land and he wouldn't. After all, that was women's work, he'd claim.

Weeks would pass where they'd only have cornflakes or peanut butter. More than once she had tried to get at least the two four-year-olds, Olav and Eva, to eat a little more. When they caught her, they locked her away from them overnight. Without food, of course. They supposedly gave her share to the little ones.

With a shudder, Shauna tore herself away from her nightmarish memories. To get rid of the horrible feeling, she stuck her nose into her bedspread. She smelled the laundry detergent Paula always used and a little of the dogs she sometimes snuck into bed at night. The smell was familiar and calmed her. She hoped the little ones were doing well. As far as she knew, they had been re-homed, too. Maybe Paula knew what had happened to them. It would be nice to know how they were doing.

Her stomach cramped more, however, when she thought about facing the horrible people again. She dreaded the court date. She didn't want to go but she couldn't let her former foster parents get another chance to abuse any more children. She'd just have to pull herself together. Close her eyes and get through it. Leslie hoped she wouldn't embarrass herself by spreading the contents of her stomach across the court. Tensely, she brushed a strand of hair behind her ear.

"Leslie? Are you ready?" Paula called from downstairs.

Leslie got up, took a last look in the mirror and took a deep breath. "Somehow I'll manage," she told herself. She made it out of her room and down the stairs, taking two steps a time.

When she got down there, Paula was busy moving about the kitchen. "Come on, I'll drive you to school today. But before that, let's meet Tyler at the diner for a little while."

"We're having breakfast at the diner?" So much for the idea of giving Dolly a few more cuddles, she thought, disappointed.

"Yes. Tyler has news for us."

"Is it really necessary for me to come? I can wait for the school bus by myself. You go ahead."

Paula narrowed her eyes and stared her down. "What's wrong with you that you're willing to give up fresh, hot cinnamon buns? Or French toast?"

Leslie lowered her head and muttered, "I wanted to say hi to Dolly."

"Why don't you do that now? We're leaving in five minutes."

Leslie's face brightened. "Really? Can I?"

"Sure."

"Cool," she said and ran outside.

Shaking her head, Paula looked after her. With a sigh, she picked up the backpack Leslie had dropped. It broke her heart every time she realized Leslie was still expecting the worst. She was happy knowing Ranger had received approval as a therapy dog. Jake had obtained the court's approval. Nothing stood in the way of Ranger accompanying Leslie. She couldn't wait to see Leslie's face when she found out.

Paula glanced at the clock. Once Leslie started a conversation with Dolly, she forgot the time, so she hurried outside, locked the door, and hustled to the car. She threw her bag into the car and got in. Slowly, she drove the car to the paddock and stuck her head out the window. Leslie lay on Dolly's belly, her head toward the croup, while the pony ate hay.

"Leslie? We should really get going."

Leslie turned with an elegant flourish, dismounted, and hugged Dolly in farewell. "I'll come back this evening. Then we can go for a walk together. I'm sure Shauna will be back, too."

Dolly shook her bright mane and mumbled; it was as if she understood every word. Perhaps she had. Paula smiled. Either way, the pony was an excellent listener and would keep all her secrets, wishes, and worries entrusted to herself.

Leslie spotted Tyler and Kat in their usual spot and dashed over to them while Paula went to the counter to order. Even though they were going to sit during the breakfast rush, it was faster to give the order herself.

At the bar, a new face caught her eye. The reddish-blond hair fell to her shoulders. The woman was not very tall, with curves in all the right places, Paula noted a little enviously. She knew already that, conversely, the other girl would probably like to be as tall or as slim as she was. We always wish something was different about how we looked. *No one's ever happy, are they?*

Miss Minnie hurried by and Paula grabbed her sleeve to stop her. *Like, I wish I could fill out a shirt like Miss Minnie!*

She stopped, tray in hand, and took a pointed look at Paula's hand on her sleeve.

"*OOPS*. Sorry. Sorry about that. Me and my impulses," Paula said, putting on her most innocent smile.

Miss Minnie just rolled her eyes. "You know that the wolf from Little Red Riding Hood looks more innocent than you?"

"Really? Now that hurts my feelings!"

"Let's get to it. As you can see, I'm slammed. What do you need?" Miss Minnie could be quite brusque if you interrupted her work rhythm.

"Just wondering who the woman at the counter is?"

"That's Paige. The journalist who wants to do the feature on you and Leslie."

"Thank you. I was hoping it was her." *How nice that once again all of Independence knew about all the plans before she even talked to the woman*, Paula thought dryly and pushed past other guests to where Paige stood.

Paige looked up from the newspaper she was reading.

Paula reached out her hand. "Hi, I'm Paula. I think you were looking for me?"

Surprised, Paige pushed the newspaper together and stood. Enthusiastically, she shook Paula's hand. "Right. I have to admit, though, you surprised me. I was expecting a phone call rather than meeting you in person right away."

"It's not like Independence is that big. Since we still only have the diner here to get decent meals, I'd run into you eventually. So, what's the point of making a phone call? Besides, I like to meet in person."

Paige laughed nervously. "Okay, how am I doing?"

"So far, so good. We'd be happy to sit down and discuss your idea sometime."

Her eyes lit up. "Really?"

Paula narrowed her eyes warningly and said, "That's not a commitment yet, just so you know. I don't know enough about the reportage for that yet. But just come by the ranch tomorrow at four o'clock and we'll see."

"Oh, okay. You don't want to meet here?" Paige broke out into a sweat and wiped her wet palms on her jeans.

"No, I'd rather not. We have more peace and quiet at home. And fewer curious listeners," she added with a wry smile.

Paige looked to the side in embarrassment, but couldn't help smiling, too. "I guess I deserved that."

"Don't worry about it. Eavesdropping on conversations is a national sport in Independence. So, you'll fit right in. I've got to get going, though. Miss Daisy can give you directions." Paula grabbed the drinks Miss Minnie had placed in front of her and turned away.

"Sure. See you soon," Paige hurriedly called after her. "And thanks."

Wow. She was a little odd, wasn't she? Paula thought. *Yup. She's definitely one of us!*

When she returned to the others at the table, a mug of cocoa in one hand and her coffee in the other, Leslie was already beaming all over.

"I see you've already heard the good news." Too bad. She would have liked to tell her herself.

"Yes! Just think, Ranger gets to accompany me to my court date. And not just to the courtroom, but also when I have to go up front to give my testimony!" The good news really bubbled out of her.

"So, does that help?"

"Very much!" She stood up and wrapped her arms around Paula's stomach as she pressed her face against hers. "Thank you."

"You don't have to thank me. Ranger is on loan from Tyler." She stroked her hair. Leslie never sought physical contact. That made it even more important for her not to startle her. But she couldn't stop what she imaged were golden tendrils from spreading inside her and twining around her heart. She loved the little girl. She knew that. It always amazed her how much her feelings increased each day.

"French toast for the princess," Miss Minnie announced, placing the plate in front of Leslie with an elegant bow. Leslie giggled, embarrassed by the salutation.

With far less fuss, she placed Paula's plate of bacon, eggs, and potatoes on the table. "Hey, am I invisible?"

Miss Minnie laughed out loud. "If you're invisible, Paula Carter, then I'm going to win the Miss World contest."

"Did she just elegantly call me a narcissist?" Paula asked.

Leslie and Tyler nearly choked on their drinks while Kat desperately tried to hold back laughter.

"Of course not," Miss Minnie said smoothly. "I only meant your inner greatness and incredible charisma."

"It's okay, it's okay. Story time is over." Paula gestured toward the counter between bites. Her phone rang. She looked at the display. *Nate.* What did he want from her? "Yes?" she answered.

"I'm really sorry to bother you. But I'm at an emergency and...holy cow is it difficult!"

"What do you need?" she cut him off and got right to the point.

"I'm up to my elbow in a cow trying to turn a calf that wants to be born breech," he said.

"And now you need someone to tell you which way is up and down?" Paula asked. The others at the table were trying not to listen in, but the phone was loud.

Despite the stressful situation, Nate had to laugh. "No. I can still do that. But Nancy, my ex-wife..."

"I know who Nancy is."

"Oh. Good. She called and said she couldn't make it to take Shauna to school. Of course, she didn't think of it until five minutes after the school bus left."

"Give me the address. I can take her."

"Really? That would be great."

"Sure. No problem. I'm taking Leslie there, anyway."

"You're the best. I owe you one."

"That's right." *A favor from a veterinarian was nothing to sneeze at*, Paula thought. Wholly inappropriate ideas flashed through her mind about how he could pay his debt. What was the matter with her? If it kept up, she was going to sign up for one of those dating sites Tyler always mentioned when she ranted about the lack of suitable men in Independence. If her sister knew, though, that she resorted to it only to get a certain vet out of her head, she'd probably laugh herself to death. She tore herself away from her muddled thoughts and refocused on Nate, who was just giving her the address.

"Why don't you text me the address?"

"Haven't you been listening to me?"

Paula rolled her eyes. So much for the *I'm-in-your-guilt thing*, she thought, and couldn't quite decide whether to be annoyed or amused. She tried to save face. "Sorry, it's so loud in here." That wasn't even a lie. All around, guests clattered silverware and shared the latest morning gossip. She couldn't tell him the real reason she'd missed half of it—daydreaming about him!

"You remember, the cow, my arm, and a gigantic mess?"

"Right! For heaven's sake, just have the farmer send me the address," she growled into the phone and hung up. Men! Just couldn't delegate. However, secretly fearing the calf might throw a wrench in the exchange, she stood and looked around for Miss Minnie. She must have known someone who knew where Nancy and Shauna lived.

"Do we have to go?" Leslie asked.

She nodded to Leslie. "In a minute. We have to pick up Shauna on the way. I just need to find out where she lives."

"Right behind the church," Leslie said.

"Are you sure?" Paula remembered there being an apartment building close by. "In one of the apartments?"

"Yes. She told me when I asked her if she had an animal at home."

Paula raised her eyebrows. "Well, does she?"

"I guess her mom doesn't like animals. But her father has this big black dog."

"Right. The Newfoundland." She'd noticed that one, too. "Beyond me what Nate would want to do in the middle of the mountains with a dog that's been bred to work in the water, but hey, to each his own."

"Good, let's go then. I'm sure Shauna is already waiting."

As they parted, Tyler winked at Leslie. "I'll bring Ranger by in the next few days. Then you two can get acquainted before the trial."

Leslie grinned. Ranger and her knew each other very well already. "Gladly. Sure won't mind adding another four paws to the dog pack at home. We can never have enough *fur-sonalities* around."

He giggled at her joke. "For you, always," Tyler said, hugging her tightly. Leslie ducked in embarrassment and waved goodbye to Kat.

Kat waved back.

Paula said goodbye and hurried to catch up with her protégé.

Nate passed the cell phone to the farmer. Paula sometimes put his patience to a real test. For example, when she cut off the call without warning. But he had to admit he could really rely on her when it counted. Like how she agreed without fuss to take his daughter to school. Simply great. It was well worth having patience. He smiled and concentrated again on ushering the stubborn baby cow into the world.

CHAPTER SEVEN

"PAIGE IS COMING OVER in a few minutes. You remember? The journalist," Paula said.

"What does the woman want again?" Leslie asked in a huff. Sitting on the floor next to the stove, she frowned and stroked Roo intently. Whatever it took to avoid eye contact with Paula.

She'd had a bad day at school. Some girls had made fun of her during recess. Afterward, she hid among the trees at the edge of the playground. She couldn't take their taunts anymore.

At the ranch, it was easy for her to be happy—to hope that everything would be all right. But at school, when the others called her a freak no one wanted, her fragile self-confidence crumbled. Doubt spread like black poison through her veins. All she wanted was to belong. To have a family. But no one had ever wanted her in her entire life. So why should this time be any different? And Paula wanted her to talk to a stranger about her screwed up life? Right. That would only cause the woman, and probably even Paula, to look at her with disgust. She was just waiting for the day when Paula realized what she had gotten herself into, anyway. She swallowed and tried to get rid of the lump in her throat. Roo pressed against her legs a little more. At least she could rely on the animals. They were always there for her, no matter what her mood. Seeking comfort, she buried her hand deep in the speckled fur.

Paula eyed Leslie. Her grumpy days had become fewer. But today was not one of them. *I wonder if something had happened at school.* She resolved to call Nadine, the principal, later and ask her to keep her eyes and ears open. It was always better to know and be able to intervene before a difficult situation took on a life of its own. *And God knows Leslie has enough other problems to deal with. Cat fighting's the last thing she needed.*

"She's heard about our shared history and thinks it would be important for other people to hear about it, too." Paula eyed her, looking for any signs, but Leslie kept stroking Roo.

"Just great. The great rescuer and the dirty runaway no one wants." Her voice, muffled by the dog's fur as she buried her face in it, sounded defiant.

Paula winced at the accusation. *Ouch. That hit home.* She took a deep breath. This was not about her. It was about this girl with the deep psychological wounds. About a girl who could not believe she was lovable. Paula went to Leslie. Somewhat awkwardly, she stroked her hair. "The story is about you and me. We're kindred spirits."

Suspiciously, Leslie blinked from behind her curtain of dark hair. "Kindred spirits? That's bull-doggy!"

Paula raised an eyebrow. "Is it really? If you find, say, an injured baby bird that's fallen out of its nest. Or a deer that's been abandoned by its mother, what do you do?"

"I'd take it home and nurse it back to health," Leslie said.

"That's right. You care. I care, too. About you. And you care about me."

Wide-eyed, Leslie stared back. Finally. She'd hit a nerve. Leslie cleared her throat and averted her eyes, embarrassed. "Okay. If you say so."

"I actually mean it. Now come on. Eat something before Paige gets here."

"Did you bake chocolate chip cookies?" Leslie lit up.

"Unfortunately, no," Paula said with a laugh. "But I made you a smoothie with banana, strawberries, and coconut milk."

"Well, that's almost as good as cookies," said Leslie.

"You see," Paula said with a sideways glance, "now you've taken care of me. It was important to you that I not be sad. And now I'm not! Empathy is what you call it when you're good at putting yourself in someone else's shoes. That quality will serve you well in life."

"*HMM*," Leslie muttered from behind her tall glass.

"Hello! Am I late?" Kat stuck her head in the doorway. Barns and Roo jumped up to greet the new arrivals, as she'd brought Maybellene with her. They all jumped around excitedly.

"No, no. Paige isn't here yet. So, you came just in time to put your plan into action."

"What plan, then?" Leslie looked from one woman to the other.

"Oh, Kat met this Paige by chance when she was out with Maybellene. It was during that encounter that her little schipperke decided Paige was going to be his future forever home."

Kat grinned. "There's just one teeny problem."

"And what is that?" Leslie asked.

"Paige is not a dog person. She's actually afraid of them."

"Oh." Leslie perked up.

"Right, 'oh.' Maybellene peeled away some of those dog-hating layers with her never-ending charm, but she still has a lot of work to do." Kat picked Maybellene up and gave her a quick kiss on the nose.

"That's why you brought her over today, when you know she can't leave?" Leslie said.

"*UM...*"

Kat looked to Paula for help, but found her of no help at all, just standing there, leaning against the table with her arms crossed, amused and eager to hear how Kat was going to talk her way out of this now. Fabulous.

"That's pretty genius. Nasty, but genius," Leslie surprised her with a response. "I take it her fear won't ruin the interview?"

"No, no," Kat said. "If that were the case, I would never consider such a thing. She's already played with Maybellene in the park." She put Maybellene back down and he ran right to Leslie.

"Yes, then we'll hope for the best, won't we, Maybellene?" Kat asked.

Enthusiastically, the black dog lapped his pink tongue across Leslie's face. "Ugh. You can save that for Paige." She pushed Maybellene off her and stood up. "Shouldn't she be here by now?"

"She should be. I'm sure she'll be here in a minute."

"I'll be going now," Kat said goodbye and hugged Paula. Leslie stroked her over the head on the way out.

As Kat walked to her car, Paige was just pulling up in a red Honda. Probably a rental car, she bet.

Paige turned off the engine and got out. She waved cheerfully at Kat. "I didn't know you were going to be here, too."

"I'm not. I was just about to leave," Kat said.

At that moment, the dogs in the house kicked up, and Paige turned chalk white. Kat was convinced the woman was about to pass out. "Brought the dog over," she said, adding fuel to the fire.

The front door of the house opened, and three dogs and a girl nearly somersaulted as they rushed down the stairs. Paige took a step behind Kat.

"Safe is safe," Paige said. "Don't care if that makes me a coward. Better to be a coward than to be eaten by a dog."

Kat felt bad for making Paige's life that much harder.

The two dogs Paige didn't know were close when the little black lightning bolt named Maybellene kicked it up a notch and rushed in front of the other dogs.

Paige peeked out from behind Kat. "What's she doing?"

"Well, it looks like you have a personal bodyguard for the duration of your stay here."

"Bodyguard?"

"Yes. The little lady here has made it very clear to the two yard dogs that they are to leave us, and specifically you, alone."

"I'm sure she didn't mean *me*. She doesn't know me that well at all."

"Obviously, she does. She just ignored them when they greeted me inside. She knows you're nervous."

"You really think so?" Furtively, she glanced at Maybellene, who was still keeping the other dogs at a distance. Roo and Barns seemed to confer, the way they ducked their heads and sniffed the air.

"But she's so much smaller than the others. I hope she doesn't get into trouble because of me."

Kat smirked when she heard that. It was a step in the right direction having Paige worried about Maybellene's well-being. "Don't worry. They're just figuring out how to get out of this without losing their pride. They'll probably discover something immensely important behind the barn or in the grove in the next few seconds and need to scout it out." As if on cue, the two blue heelers raised their heads, gave one abrupt bark that made Paige wince, and ran for the barn.

"I knew it," Kat said. "You're in excellent hands with Maybellene. Just go on in. Paula and Leslie are waiting for you."

"But what about the dog? She doesn't listen to me, does she?" Paige asked.

"I wouldn't worry about that. As it is, as long as you're here, you can't even go to the bathroom by yourself."

"Oh."

Kat laughed softly as she realized Paige did not know what she was talking about. Oh well. She'd find out soon enough. "Have fun, you two," she said, getting into the car and leaving.

Stripped of her human shield, Paige peered down at the small dog sitting beside her, tongue hanging out, watching her expectantly. "Bodyguard, huh? Well, here we go." She walked up to the house, Maybellene close by her side, hoping she'd make it through the door before the other two crazy dogs came back.

Fortunately, Paula looked out the window and saw her coming up the stairs. She opened the door before Paige had even raised her hand to knock.

"Hi. I'm glad you're here. I see you brought company?" Paula said.

"Company?" Paige was confused for a moment before she realized what Paula meant. "Oh, you're talking about Maybellene. She doesn't belong to me. She's Kat's. I don't really like dogs."

"I guess the little sheepdog doesn't see it that way," Paula said. The corners of her mouth twitched in amusement. "Come on in."

Paula led her and the dog into the kitchen. Leslie sat at the table. Paige walked right up to her and held out her hand. "I'm Paige."

She might as well as have handed her a used doggie scoop bag. "The woman who wants to make a media spectacle out of my life," Leslie said without shaking.

The provocation in her voice was unmistakable. Quickly, she cast a searching glance in Paula's direction to gauge her reaction.

Paula shrugged. Paige realized she and Leslie had to deal with each other.

Paige took back her hand and examined Leslie. So, the little girl was showing teeth. Interesting. And a challenge. But that was okay. After all, she had been an angry teen herself not too long ago, albeit for different reasons. Still, she could empathize. She knew she'd have to be brutally honest to gain her trust. She pulled up a chair, turned it around, and sat down so she could rest her forearms on the back.

"Honestly, yes. What I know so far about your and Paula's history together has the potential to be a great article. That would be just fine with me. My career is pretty much dead right now and most importantly? What you experienced, what Paula experienced, it's important enough that other people should know about it. Because that's what this is all about. An honest report about foster care and where the strengths and weaknesses of the system lie."

Leslie's face flushed. "All I can think of from that time is my stepfather's raised hand. My stepmom putting down pathetic attempts at food. The vomit in the living room. Paula covered me with an old horse blanket. My four-year-old step-sister was wailing all night because she was so hungry."

Paige noticed a wide range of emotions race across Leslie's face.

She started to cry.

Paige shifted uneasily in her chair. "Are you okay?"

The girl wiped her tears with a tissue. Out of the corner of her eye, she realized Paula had anxiously taken a step forward. Shoot. She couldn't remember an interview subject crying, and especially not right away. Things must have been really bad at the previous home.

Paula let out a shrill whistle. It jarred Paige and she looked to find Paula at the back door. Within seconds, Roo and Barns stomped into the kitchen. Paige held her breath in horror. Maybellene stood in front of her, tail wagging.

The two ranch dogs paid her no attention, though, and thankfully targeted Leslie and licked her face.

Leslie buried her face deep into Roo's fur, inhaling deeply the smell of dusty dog and sunshine. She beamed.

Paige was relieved to see some color return to her face, which had turned pale as a sheet after the initial blush. *Better.* She'd continue to hold back and see how the situation developed. She was fifty-fifty of it going forward. "Look, if this is too much, I don't want you to do it. Obviously, this opened up some deep wounds." She reached out—really stretched—and offered her hand. "I'm sorry I didn't know how bad it was. I would have never..."

Leslie grasped her outstretched hand, and shook her head in a way that was both yes and no. "I'm going to do it. I have to. All right? But only if I like your questions. And I want my name changed, and Paula's. That's the most important thing of all. I don't want any of it touching my new family. I'd rather go back to living on the streets."

"Sure. Of course. That's a given. I don't reveal my sources, after all." Paige breathed a sigh of relief. "We've got you. You're safe now."

Paula set a cup of coffee down in front of Paige and sat down next to them with a cold, sweetened iced tea.

Leslie looked nervously from one woman to the other, rubbing her palms together. "So how does this work now?"

Paige pulled a small voice recorder from her pocket and placed it in plain view on the table. A pad and pen followed. "We just start talking. See where it takes us."

"Are you writing by hand?" Leslie asked, momentarily distracted by this incredible fact.

Paige laughed. "Yeah, I'm pretty old-fashioned in that aspect. But for this, I'd like to run the recorder and record our conversation, too. In case I'm too slow and miss something while taking notes."

Leslie gave Paula a questioning look. She just shrugged. "I don't know. Kind of has a police interrogation feel to it. But if that's part of your normal modus operandi, I suppose that's okay."

"It's really just so I can go back to the conversation and make sure I'm not misquoting you."

Paula grabbed Leslie's hand and gave her an encouraging nod. "You're right. This does feel like we're in an old detective movie."

"Black and white, I assume?" Leslie said.

"Sure."

Paige grinned and pressed the record button. After a brief introduction in which she explained who she was and what they'd talk about, she addressed Leslie and

Paula. "Leslie. You're thirteen years old, and you've spent most of your life in a variety of foster homes. You've been on an adventurous journey where you've ended up here with Paula on a ranch in the middle of the Rocky Mountains in the small town of Independence. Were you transferred here?"

Leslie looked helplessly at Paula. Roo, who until just now had been sitting relaxed at her feet, sat up and stared at Paige until she shifted uncomfortably back and forth in her chair. Immediately Maybellene was on her feet, licking her hand and staring venomously at the other dog.

Paige thought the little black dog was certainly cute, even if she would have loved to do without having dog saliva on her fingers. Disgusting. And she couldn't even think about the proximity of her tongue to the dangerous teeth.

"I think the question is a little too big for Leslie," Paula interjected.

Leslie nodded. She reached for Roo's ear and stroked his fur.

Paula turned to her. "Only tell what you're comfortable with. If you want to stop, we'll stop, okay?"

"That's right," Paige said.

Leslie's eyes looked enormous in her pale face. She nodded bravely. "Okay," she said. "I'm ready." She shared a knowing glance with Paula, then looked back to Paige.

"It's best to start at the beginning," Paige said. "When did your parents die?"

Leslie shook her head. "My parents aren't dead."

CHAPTER EIGHT

"WHAT DO YOU MEAN, your parents aren't dead?" Paula asked. She was taken aback by the bombshell.

"What does it matter? They just didn't want me." Leslie looked away.

"But..." Visibly at a loss for words, Paula broke off.

"But nothing. It just so happens that not everyone grows up in a storybook family like you. They give dozens of children away for foster care every day." Leslie bit her trembling lower lip to keep from crying. Not that she was sad about it. After all, she had had enough time to come to terms with that fact. But she was so ashamed to admit no one had wanted her, even then. Somehow it had gone on and on. Sure, some of the foster families had important reasons she couldn't stay with them but it still hurt.

Paula was the first to want her to stay. She dreaded the day Paula might realize what she'd gotten into and change her mind. If the interview continued as it began, that moment wasn't too far away. She lifted her chin, turned up her nose, and stared at Paula.

Paula couldn't help but admire Leslie for her strength of character. She was visibly shaken. Leslie usually hid and tried to be as inconspicuous and well-adjusted as possible. "You're absolutely right," Paula said.

"I know well that I am very fortunate with my present family," Leslie said and nodded to Paula. "My reaction is probably from being scared of not having you in my life."

Paige chimed in. "I automatically assumed that your parents left you involuntarily. My mistake. I'm sorry."

"I'm just glad I'm not being sent away again to Denver through Child Protective Services," Leslie said.

"Oh, no way. Not a chance." Paula stood up and took Leslie in her arms. "You will not get rid of me that easily. You've got a place to live here, so to speak, until you're old and gray. Just like Rufus." She tickled her, and Leslie giggled. At last she sounded like a thirteen-year-old girl again, and not a disillusioned adult.

Paige followed the interaction of the two and diligently took notes. The depth of their connection was wonderful. She wished she had someone at her side who stood by her so faithfully. She shook it off, though, because the interview wasn't about her, after all. She was surprised, though, at how many new things had already come to light—for each of them.

"No thirteen-year-old should have to go through what you've been through," Paige said.

Leslie nodded. "You're probably right. I mean, my mom gave me up for adoption at birth. The reasons were never clear to me. Growing up with that factoid? Didn't seem like there was anything wrong with it." She swallowed hard. "Probably my mother couldn't take care of me. Or she was sick. Then it's good if another family steps in," she shrugged. "Right?"

"Glad you're seeing the silver lining, when possible," Paige said. "Go on."

"Well, I wasn't adopted right away, but a foster family found me. They wanted to see how they coped with a child before actually going through with it. When foster mother number one unexpectedly became pregnant, I wasn't needed."

Paige scribbled some highlights to refer to.

Leslie continued, her voice matter-of-fact. "Since they needed to do something with me quickly, they sent me to the next foster family. They already had four children. I did okay there. Until the parents divorced a few years later, and then it was on to another new place. They were super nice, and all was good until my step-sister Emily died of leukemia. It was awful. They said I reminded them of Emily too much, so they had to relocate me again. Bear in mind, I had just turned ten. Then there were three more, I think, with the last one so bad I literally ran away. So, like six homes in four years, or something like that. Always a foster, never up for adoption."

Leslie sighed and lowered her chin. "Think I need a break," she said. "This is stirring up a lot of emotions I had buried away."

"Of course," Paige said.

"Take a break, hon," Paula said.

"I will," Leslie said. She bent down and lifted Maybellene. Despite attempts to persuade her, the journalist had not wanted to adopt a dog. Even when she'd been assured the cartoon sisters had nothing against a dog.

"The sisters that run the diner with the cartoon names might not. But I do. Believe me, the fact that I can even stand being in a room together with three dogs for more than a few seconds is something of a record for me. Granted, Maybellene alone deserves credit for that," Paige said. With affection, she petted the little dog behind the ears. She changed the subject.

"I'll get back to you as soon as I finish the article. I'm going to supplement it with some facts and figures on the subject, so I'll need a little more time to research," she said. "So, with that, I think we did good here today and I'm going to give you all back your evening."

Paula stood and shook her hand. "That's all wonderful. Thank you for coming and hearing Leslie's side of things. Before the rumor mill got out of hand."

Shaking her hand, Paige grinned. "I'd love to let you all have the rest of your night. I know this wasn't easy and I sure do appreciate your time."

"Likewise," Paula said.

"Back at you," Leslie said. "Hope you got all that you needed."

Paige laughed. "You've given me the gift of plenty," she said and went on her way.

Suddenly the dogs lifted their heads and looked toward the door. The schipperke dog fidgeted in her arms and Paula put her on the floor so she could run after the other two dogs. She thought that maybe Paige forgot something.

"Hello?" She opened the door, and who stood there? Nate. Her heart did a loop-the-loop. "Oh! What are you doing here?"

An amused smile flitted across his face. "I'm glad to see you, too."

"Yeah, yeah, yeah," she waved it off. "Sorry. You just surprised me! What's up?"

"I wanted to see you," he said.

"Me?" she said. "Did I do something wrong?" He looked...different. *He likes you!*

Nate stepped through the door without being asked, so Paula had to take a step back. That didn't suit her at all. She avoided no one. Not dogs. Not horses. And, usually, certainly not alpha males. "Did someone invite you in?" she grumbled, putting up her defenses.

"No," he said. "I'd be standing there a long time waiting for an invitation. Shauna's in the stables with Leslie, by the way."

"Shauna's here, too? Good. Maybe she's giving Leslie some support," she said. "Did it ever occur to you that I have my reasons for being so cold?"

Fortunately for her, he refrained from asking. Instead, he strolled into her kitchen and dropped into a chair. The dogs, who knew him from his frequent visits, trotted after him, the little traitors. Only Maybellene looked up at her with uncertainty, not sure whether to run after the others or stay in the relative safety of their proximity. Maybe she would just give Barns and Roo to Kat and keep the little dog herself.

Nate reached onto the table for one of the clean glasses left-over from the interview and poured himself some tea. She couldn't help but admire his audacity. She couldn't stand people who, after the fifth visit, still behaved like a rare guest and had to be served from back to front.

"I came to say thank you."

"I'm sorry, what?" Paula was honestly surprised. She hadn't expected that at all.

"Of course. I even brought you something," Nate said.

"Brought me something?"

"I see the prospect of a gift is turning you into a parrot."

"*HAHA*. So what is it?" she asked.

"Oh, now we're curious, are we?"

Paula rolled her eyes. "Of course, I'm curious. Who wouldn't be? But either show it to me now, or just put it on the table later. Because unlike some people, I should do some work today."

"Do you need help?" Nate asked.

"No."

He raised his hands. "It's okay, I'll keep it short. You really helped me out when you jumped in on the spur of the moment to pick up Shauna yesterday. I can imagine that wasn't as easy as you thought it would be."

She grimaced as she thought of the scene that had played out when she'd picked up Shauna. "Well, let's just say a little warning would have been nice." Nate's ex Nancy had made quite a fuss when she had shown up instead of Nate. Paula didn't understand why. They weren't friends. But they had met and talked a few times on various occasions. Apparently not enough, because Nancy had acted as if Nate had sent a complete stranger to take her daughter to school. Only after ten minutes of gentle coaxing had she calmed the woman down enough to stop the screaming and crying. Shauna had been terribly embarrassed. It had been obvious that she was anxious about her mother. Fortunately, Leslie had been there to give her a hug. Since the interview that afternoon, Paula also knew why Leslie hadn't flinched during the whole incident. Because of her own history, she was all too familiar with such behavior.

Nate pulled his head in. "I know. I'm sorry. The only excuse I have is a thankfully healthy black and white pied calf that was in quite a hurry to come into the world."

"That's what I assumed. Otherwise, you would have heard from me already."

He grinned. "I can vividly imagine that."

"What's going on with her? With Nancy?" She couldn't bring herself to call her his ex-wife. Idiotic, since that's exactly what she was. Yet somehow she just couldn't bring herself to think of them as a couple. Quiet Nate and this neurotic woman? She almost shook her head, but caught herself at the last moment. She didn't mince words, but that didn't mean she trampled over other people's feelings, regardless.

"She's mentally unstable. She always has been. Over time, it got worse and worse. She now takes medication. That's how it goes to some extent. But as you might imagine, there are good days and bad days. Yesterday was a bad day. Like that, she suddenly remembers that she has an urgent appointment. Or that it's basically too dangerous for Shauna to go out of the house. She also has an immense need for attention."

"And, of course, she doesn't get that when the child is in school," Paula concluded.

Nate sighed. "You got it. I try to shield Shauna from it as much as I can. She's clearly with me more now than she is with her mother. But every once in a while, there's just no other way. And, of course, Shauna wants to see her mother, too."

"That figures."

"So, you can see why I'm very grateful to you for stepping in on the spur-of-the-moment yesterday. Otherwise, Shauna would have been absent from school once again."

"You're welcome. It's what anyone else would have done."

Nate looked her straight in the eye. "That's not true. Besides, I still don't really have many friends here. After all, we only moved here less than a year ago. Between work, emergency services, and my daughter, there's not a lot of time left to make a social life, no matter how friendly people are. I know we've had a bit of a bumpy start. But I have to be honest and say that I really appreciate your friendship."

Paula, who coped poorly with such a barrage of nice things, resorted to humor. "If I interpret the extent of your gratitude correctly, I'll find at least one fresh baby horse on the doorstep. Or maybe two."

Nate laughed. "I'm sorry to disappoint you. The horses were just out while I was shopping. But I got this."

He handed her a sterile package.

Interested, Paula took it and read the label. "Wound dressings with medicinal honey. How cool is that! Thank you so much." The antiseptic effect of honey and its positive effect on wound healing, even of poorly healing injuries, had been scientifically proven for years. Paula liked to use the dressings for wounds on joints resulting from falls that were often deep. Unfortunately, they were outrageously expensive.

"Somehow, I knew these would make you happier than a bouquet."

Paula grinned. "Definitely!"

"Are we interrupting?"

Paula winced in surprise when she heard her best friend's voice. Jaz stood in the doorway, a big bright red bowl in her hand and a knowing smile on her face. She sighed.

She knew at breakfast the next morning at the diner, she'd suffer an interrogation. Ever since Jaz was her friend, her life had actually included things like girls' nights out and gossip about the male species. Not that she had much to contribute on that subject usually.

Their close friendship was unexpected and beautiful, she had to admit. She had even let Jaz ride the horses a few times and Paula tried her hand at yoga. Even though she didn't like to admit it, practicing yoga made her feel better about her body. She always noticed it immediately, which was a similar buzz when she was riding.

Paula's brother Jake stood behind Jaz. He carried a gigantic bag in each hand. Ever since Jaz's belly showed the beginnings of a baby bump, he'd been extra chivalrous. Maybe too much! It was a wonder he didn't try and tie her to the bed so she couldn't overdo it. But Jaz would be no man's possession. She still taught her yoga classes and trained regularly with Pat in martial arts. The head of the Carter family gave her support. She liked to make fun of her son's overprotectiveness. No wonder. With five children, she would have gotten nowhere over the years if she'd taken it easy every time she received good news about a new baby. Especially since she'd always been the one who'd kept the ranch running. Paula's father had always been happy to help—but the rest of the time he devoted to his inventions. He worked as an engineer or taught at the university, which kept him busy.

"Not at all. I'm just surprised to see you here."

At that moment, Kat jumped up the steps to the porch. "Hello. What're you all doing here?"

"I wondered about that, too. My kitchen is turning into a train station concourse right now," Paula muttered, which made Nate smile.

"We're bringing dinner. Today was the interview with Paige, right?"

"Yes."

"Exactly. So I thought, after a day like today, I'm sure you'd be fine if you didn't have to cook, too."

"*Uh*, yeah. Sure. I'd love that." Food was always welcome.

Nate rose from his chair. "I'd better be going. This seems to be a family affair here, so I don't want to interrupt."

"Go? But why? There's enough for everyone." As if to add emphasis, Jaz cleaned out her bags and put the contents on the table and in the refrigerator.

Nate gave Paula a help-me look to find out where she stood on his staying. She only gave him an amused smile. He had to decide for himself whether he could stand an evening in the presence of her wild family.

Jake grabbed a cold beer and offered one to Nate. "Here. Or are you on call?"

"Well then, to a beer, delicious food, and delightful company," he said. "Not today, for once. I'll gladly partake."

Kat peered over Jaz's shoulder. "Do you have enough for me and Sam?"

"Sure thing. I talked to him on the phone beforehand. He already knows."

"Very good." She turned to Paula. "I'm disappointed Maybellene is still here, by the way. I thought we agreed she belonged with Paige?" she teased Paula.

"You know that, I know that, and the dog knows that. Only Paige doesn't seem to have gotten the memo. But I'm confident that the two of you will change her mind." Paula glanced at the clock by the oven. "So, folks. While you're here preparing dinner, I actually have to work for another hour." She pushed herself off the kitchen counter. "Meat is in the big freezer in the basement."

Jaz was an excellent cook. However, as a staunch vegetarian, she refused to take care of the meat. That was Jake's responsibility.

Outside, she took a deep breath. She really appreciated the visit from her siblings and friends. Immediately following the emotional afternoon with the interview, however, it was almost a bit too much for her. There was a reason she worked with horses and cattle: they didn't chatter the whole time endlessly.

The sun had warmed the house and deck. It smelled of pine resin and summer. She had to take advantage of the pleasant weather over the next few days and ride to the river with Leslie, she decided. The horses and Leslie would appreciate the cool down. In the Rockies, the weather could change in an instant. Sudden, violent thunderstorms were common. Right now, however, things were stable. She could use the opportunity to familiarize her training horse, Lucky, with the water. If he was going to be a reliable ranch horse, he needed to learn about it, anyway. But first? Basics were on the training agenda. She reached for the carrot in her bag, which she had pocketed earlier in the kitchen, and headed toward the barn.

CHAPTER NINE

Nate leaned back against the barn wall, beer in hand, watching Paula work with the young horse. As a veterinarian, he knew the entire spectrum of trainers. He only rode rarely and not particularly well, but knew what he liked and what he didn't. Paula's way of working with the youngster made him happy. Her body language was friendly, determined, and above all, clear.

The pinto worked with concentration and eagerness. He learned that working with humans was fun. *That's the way it should be*, he thought. The horse moved sideways toward them with a hand signal.

Paula noticed Nate's presence. She appreciated he didn't interrupt her. *He isn't all that bad once you get to know him. And whose fault is it that it took so long?* she scolded herself. Sometimes she really was an incorrigible, stubborn person. Not that she wanted anything from him. Even though he looked scrumptious, with his dark eyes and rough exterior. He could probably even beat her at arm wrestling, she bet. *What are you thinking about that for? You're not interested in him just now. No way.*

She felt a tingle spread through her stomach. She was good at ignoring such things. Lordy. After all, she had been very successful at completely ignoring the man for all the last few months. *You can push this aside this...this fleeting interest-only feeling because, let's face it, it's been a while. He's a friend. Nothing more, nothing less. One could always use a new friend.*

Paula shook her head, trying to lose the thought. *Focus on the guy who deserves your attention, hot stuff!* Lucky had cooperated well. When she started, she hadn't been sure she could block out the day enough to put him at ease. He still got irritated when she wasn't on task.

She called him to her center and stroked his shiny summer coat, offering praise. "Enough work for today. Let's go find the stable elves," she said. "I'm sure they have some oats for you."

Paula headed for the exit. The horse followed her without her putting a halter on him.

On the way to the barn, Nate joined them without a word. Without her doing anything, her mouth twisted into a smile. Fortunately, he didn't comment on it, just returned it wordlessly. She would not have been willing to give a reason for that smile. Maybe she'd slept through an alien abduction? That, at least, would be a reason for her sudden change of mind where Nate was concerned. The thought was so absurd a laugh escaped her.

Amused, he glanced at her. "What's so funny?"

She had to laugh again. "Oh, nothing. I was just thinking about alien abductions and consequences."

Surprised, he raised an eyebrow, but she shook her head. "Don't ask."

"Do you want to talk about it?"

"Talk? About what?" About her inappropriate crush on a certain vet? That couldn't really be what he meant. Her poker face was too good for that. She hoped so, anyway. The man was just too sensitive. Why couldn't he be an insensitive lug like she'd been accusing him of being all along? That would simplify the situation immensely.

"Well, about the interview," he said. "Maybe you learned things you didn't know. You told me once that Leslie was pretty closed up about her past."

Relieved, she breathed out. Leslie. Sure. She could talk to him about Leslie with no problem. That was what friends were for, after all. And she had to admit, in the short time since she'd had more to do with him, he'd proven to be an excellent friend.

Lucky, who was still walking just behind her, raised his head in concern when she breathed. He lowered it again, satisfied she was okay. When Paula was safe, he could relax, too.

Arriving at the barn, she called out to Leslie.

She came running, her friend close on her heels, followed by two dogs playfully jockeying for the front spot.

When she saw Lucky, she slowed down.

Shauna did the same.

"Can you please bring me Lucky's halter and his food?" Paula tickled Lucky under the chin, which made the girls laugh. It looked hilarious.

"Let's do it." Murmurs followed. The two girls were probably discussing who got to do what. Shauna was a serious negotiator with horse stuff.

In the end, Leslie pulled the halter over Lucky's head while Shauna waited patiently with the feed bucket in her hand. Paula was glad to see Leslie's eyes were clear. Obviously she had stopped crying a while back. It was a good thing they had a ride planned soon. She always found it easiest to talk to Leslie on the trail. They were both much more relaxed when they were out with the horses.

"I could have haltered him," Shauna said to the two adults. "But since Leslie is taller than me, it makes more sense for her to do it. I have his dinner here for that." She proudly pointed to the bucket in her hand.

"Why do I see a pony in your immediate future?" muttered Paula in Nate's direction.

The latter promptly choked on his beer. "Don't. I've got enough on my plate trying to get organized in my new life as a single dad. And then there's Nessie."

Paula frowned. "Nessie? Who is Nessie? And why don't I know her?"

"Nessie is our dog," Shauna said. "She just moved in with us recently."

"And guess what? She's already got the death of five pairs of shoes on her conscience." Leslie laughed and shook her head as if she still couldn't quite believe it.

"Those are some adventurous stories." Questioningly, she looked from the girls to Nate. "Is there more info?"

"Nessie is a Newfoundland. Sixteen weeks old, yet possesses the grace of a full-grown walrus and a shoe fetish that is only satisfied with men's left shoes."

Paula laughed. "You're lucky again, Shauna. He's only eating your dad's shoes."

"I'm glad about that, too."

"I can imagine that. Leslie, can I leave it to you to put Lucky out to pasture with the others? Because then Nate and I will go back to the house already. Half the family is there. We'll have a campfire later. Just join us when you're done here. And by the way? The barn is clean enough." She winked at the little girl.

Leslie promptly rolled her eyes. She said, "Sure. Let's do it. Is Cole there, too?" she asked about her favorite uncle.

"No, unfortunately not. But everyone else is here. Sam is still missing, and Tyler and Pat will be a little late, too."

"Great. I'm sure they'll bring Ranger."

"You'd almost think there weren't enough animals on the farm without her hoping for Ranger, too." Nate sounded amused as they walked back to the house. "And what was that about the barn being clean enough? You're not going to keep them from working, are you?"

"Oh, if it were up to her, we'd have to have at least as many dogs as Kat. But she's always had a special relationship with Ranger. Even more so now that she knows he gets to come with her to the trial."

"It's great that worked out."

"That's thanks to you. It was your idea," she said, realizing it wasn't difficult to be nice to him. She always believed she was an excellent judge of character. Maybe she'd been wrong about that! *He's actually a pretty great guy and you've convinced yourself all this time he wasn't. Shoot. An apology would be awkward, so maybe make it up to him at the dinner somehow. That'd be an obvious way to show him how you feel without having to say anything. Right?*

"What about the stable thing?"

"Oh that. She actually overdoes it sometimes with work. She likes to make herself indispensable. While I appreciate her help and think it's great she has such a good work ethic, it's important she understands I don't need her to sweep the floor twice. It's not healthy!"

"I get it," he said. "She's a little A.D.D. when it comes to that sort of thing."

Paula was still struggling with the emotional chaos inside her. Somehow, it was very different when she and Nate were alone instead of when he was acting as her vet. She didn't want to let him know about her change of heart. Not yet, at least. Even a few weeks back, she saw red when Jaz even mentioned him. She'd get a real kick knowing she was now falling for him, especially as she'd been making him out to be such a bad guy.

Arriving at the house, he stopped and turned to her. "Whoa," he said, grabbing her by the upper arms to keep them both from falling over the porch steps.

Their faces came very close to each other. So close. Her heart raced. Nate's hands felt good. He smelled of sun, leather, and a hint of aftershave.

Her head spun. So many thoughts circled. *I can't like him. Can't like guys. I'm so busy. This is wrong.*

But her heart had other plans and she jutted forward and kissed him. Right on the mouth. Fire spread through her, from the bottom of her feet, to her belly, to her heart, to her fingertips, to the soft ends of her lips. *Oh, wow. This is better than I thought it could be. But the town will talk, won't they? Aren't we supposed to be enemies?*

Said enemy was kissing her back. It was not a one-way street. She couldn't believe it. *He likes me, too?*

Time stood still and it felt like they kissed for an eternity. She was lost, lost, lost.

Somehow, she summoned up all her willpower and took a step away from him to save at least a last bit of her sanity.

Nate looked at her; his eyes sparkled as his eyelids lowered just a bit. He tightened his grip around her waist. He didn't want her to stop, she knew.

I need a moment.

Paula took another step away from him, causing Nate to let go.

"Wow," was all that came out. He seemed as dazed as she was. Good. She would have hated to be the only one impressed by their explosive attraction.

So much for "it's-just-a-kiss."

"Wow pretty much sums it up." Nate didn't stop looking at her.

Not knowing for the life of her what else to say to that, she pointed to the house with a stiff movement of her head. "Well then. We'd better get inside. I'm hungry." Her voice was softer than usual, almost a whisper. "They'll be wondering where we are."

Without waiting for his reply, she skipped up the porch steps and slipped inside.

She felt like she couldn't catch her breath.

In the house, dinner was in full swing. Jake had lit a large campfire. Thanks to the unexpected nighttime thunderstorms of the last few weeks, it was safe. In Colorado, the air was often so dry that the danger of forest fires in summer was very high, and open fires were forbidden. But they'd been spared.

Paula paused at the back door for a moment, watching the hustle and bustle of her family and friends. She may not have been rich, but she was doing fine. She had her own land, her own house, and the best people in the world in her life.

"What took you so long?" asked Jaz, who had just stepped out from behind her with another delicious smelling casserole. Her eyes sparkled with suppressed merriment.

Paula groaned. "Now don't tell me you were just standing at the window."

Jaz grinned. "Yes, I was. First-class entertainment. And I have to say: lucky I did! I don't suppose you would have told me about it anytime soon."

Paula ducked her head. "No. In fact, I probably wouldn't have," she said.

"Almost had me going there."

"What were you talking about?" Tyler asked, joining them with a fully loaded paper plate in her hand.

"That friends and sisters are completely overrated," Paula said. "Especially when they're too nosy." She grabbed a stuffed mushroom from her sister's plate.

"Hey, hands off."

"You can't eat all that, anyway. After all, you don't want to get fat now that you're about to dance again," she said

"Must be important if you're trying to insult me," Tyler said, holding her plate out of reach.

"They kissed," Jaz said in an idiotic sing-song voice.

"Are we in kindergarten now?" Paula asked.

"Really?" Tyler said, nonchalantly. "It's about time."

"I agree." Jaz laughed.

"Wait a minute. What do you mean 'it's about time'?" Paula said.

They both gave her an incredulous look. "If it hadn't been for Tyler's kidnapping, it would have happened a long time ago. But since you can be pretty stubborn and anti-social, it just took a little longer."

"You guys are so well matched, it's kind of scary," her sister added. "And he's finally one that doesn't need saving. Remember that guy last year from the Indie Rock Festival?"

Tyler laughed. "That's right. Although I didn't realize it myself."

"You were busy with Pat, too."

"Exactly." Tyler sounded very pleased at this reminder. "But from what I've heard, this was another one of those starving artists looking for a temporary place to stay."

"He found that with Paula," Jaz said.

"Hey, he had a beautiful voice and his body was nothing to sneeze at," Paula said.

"Which is why Betty came into play when it became clear you shared that view with all his groupies." Jaz laughed. "I mean, who names their shotgun Betty?"

"I do!" Paula said. "He was just generous and liked to share. Including himself. Unlike me."

Contrary to what the others might have thought, she had not thrown him out because he had broken her heart. But because she realized she wasn't into it. She'd found his behavior rather amusing. He had been a good example of a nice package with very little underneath, except for his singing voice. Nice for a few nights. But in the long run, rather exhausting. She didn't enjoy listening to music that much.

"He's lucky he got away with it," Jaz said. "You usually eat a guy like that for breakfast and spit out his bones."

"Oh," Paula said, flattered.

Tyler rolled her eyes. "You're pretty weird sometimes, big sister."

Jaz nodded. "That's why we love her so much."

Paula patted Jaz's hand. "That's sweet of you to say. But please, now no more niceties. I think I've used up my years' worth of emotional pep talks today."

"Then you really need something to eat. Come with me," Jaz said and pulled her along.

Fifteen minutes later, Paula sat in a comfortable lawn chair. She had a large steak, a baked potato with sour cream, and a salad all balanced on her knees, with a beer on the stool beside her. Relieved, she exhaled. While she ate, she listened with half an ear to the conversations all around her. She was perfectly content just to listen. She had already used up her daily allotment of words. Tyler and Pat were talking about their planned trip to California. She would ask them about it in more detail at some point. She liked the idea of visiting them together with Leslie more and more. But there was still time for that later.

Jaz's grandmother Rose and her friend Nadine, the school principal, had also come. The two lived together. No one, not even Jaz, knew for sure how they were related to each other. She was pretty sure they were a couple. But it didn't matter. The main thing was that they were both happy. Everything else was a private matter.

When Paula spotted a white dog with black spots and a third French mastiff among the other dogs, she looked around for Lily. She had probably come with Tyler. The two had gone to school together and had renewed their friendship in the last few months since her sister had returned to Independence. It was nice to see everyone together again.

Lily wiped her hands on a paper napkin and threw it into the fire. Her eyes drifted to Tyler and Pat, and she sighed. They really were a dream couple. She begrudged them with all her heart. But she could not prevent a certain melancholy from spreading through her. Would she ever be so happy herself? Perhaps. But she suspected that someone like her would not find happiness in a town with only a little more than a thousand inhabitants. But she couldn't imagine moving away. She needed the rugged silhouettes of the mountain peaks, the biting cold in winter, and the abundance of nature and its colors. She would suffocate if she had to live in the city.

"Beautiful, isn't it?" Surprised, she turned to see Rose, who had joined her unnoticed. She smiled. Rose had always been very attentive. She remembered coming into her mother's flower store and knowing within minutes how everyone in the family was doing, which flowers were doing particularly well, and which desperately needed special attention. As a little girl, they had convinced her that Rose was a fairy godmother. She had to smile at the thought.

"Are you going to let me in on the secret?" Rose raised an eyebrow.

"Oh, I was just reminiscing. You were always the fairy godmother in my fantasy."

"How nice," Rose said. "Then why did you look so sad five minutes ago? I mean, if your personal fairy godmother is already present at the party, you'd think she'd take care of your bad mood."

Lily laughed. "Oh, just ignore me. It was just a moment. It'll be over in a minute, too. I just wish I could find someone to share my life with, too. Like how Tyler found that with Pat."

"Except you wouldn't be happy with someone like Pat, would you, my dear?"

Her tone was friendly. Lily took a step back and blushed. "I have no idea what you're talking about," she said.

Rose simply ignored her. "It's certainly difficult to live in such a close-knit community. When everyone knows everything about everyone, it has its advantages. You don't have to explain yourself."

Curious, Lily gave up trying to pretend she didn't know what the older woman was talking about, even though she would have liked to know how Rose had guessed. "Possibly. That's not what worries me. I'm just afraid finding my soul mate here in Independence will be nothing more than a pipe dream. But I can't imagine leaving here, either. It seems like I have to choose one or the other. That's just not fair."

Rose patted her hand in approval. "Logical. Of course, I can't promise you that. Fairy godmother or not." She winked mischievously at Lily in the fire's glow. "I don't think Tyler expected to find the love of her life here. Love always discovers you."

"*HMM.*" Lily wasn't convinced. "And what do I do in the meantime?" she grumbled.

"Well. Tourist season in Aspen or Breckenridge can be quite productive. Or you could try Internet dating. That's how Nadine and I met, by the way. Actually, 'met' is the wrong word. We had always known each other. After all, we grew up here together. But neither of us knew what made the other tick. Just think, without the Internet, we'd still be nothing more than polite acquaintances." With this last revelation, she squeezed Lily's shoulder one last time and sauntered over to Jaz, who was engaged in an animated conversation with Stan.

Stunned, Lily stared after Rose. It had been a completely unexpected conversation.

Nate looked for Paula and spotted her in her quiet spot. With his eyes fixed on her, he walked toward her and sat down. He looked at her. Without batting an eye, she returned his gaze. She read the challenge in it. Dang. She had never resisted challenges.

Fortunately, they were interrupted. Leslie and Shauna shot around the corner giggling and laughing, two yelping blue heelers close on their heels.

"Dad, can Leslie spend the night with us? Please?" Shauna asked.

Nate hadn't expected such a question. Since they had moved to Independence, his daughter found it very difficult to make friends. Not sure where Paula stood on the subject, he looked at her for a clue.

Paula shrugged. "You don't have to ask me. I don't have any experience with this kind of thing at all. Leslie, would you like to spend the night at Shauna's house?"

Leslie nodded and smiled. "If I may?"

"Well, then...if you don't mind, and she can ride to school with you tomorrow, she's welcome to go to your house, for all I care."

"You're the best." Leslie hugged her, while Shauna did the same to Nate.

Their gazes met above the girls' heads. They both smiled.

CHAPTER TEN

PAIGE SAT ON THE PARK BENCH she had discovered with Kat and the terrifying, adorable dog, her laptop on her knees. She had taken to going here every morning after a quick trip to the diner, where she picked up her daily shot of caffeine and sugar in the forms of a hot coffee and a sweet baked item.

The fresh air and views of the surrounding majestic mountain peaks lifted her spirits. The article about Leslie's story and the foster care system had just flowed from her fingers to the keys. Admittedly, that was probably because of the subject. She felt like she was finally writing something meaningful. Something that also triggered emotions in the reader and hopefully made people think to maybe lend a helping hand. *Like the people here in Independence.*

She knew Kat's story and how she'd come to launch her animal shelter, Safe Haven. The name alone gave one a feeling of security. When she had a chance, maybe she would pay Kat a visit. That would definitely be worth a story, too. However, she'd have to overcome her dog phobia. If she was lucky, Maybellene would be there...if she was still around. Paige knew Kat was always placing animals. The schipperke dog would surely find a good place in no time, as cute and loyal as she was. Surprised, she realized the thought of never seeing the little dog again made her sad. Maybe she shouldn't have been so hasty in dismissing Paula's suggestion to take Maybellene on. But no. Her and a dog? That was just ridiculous. Especially since she didn't know where she would end up.

Paige read through the final draft again, made a few final tweaks, and saved the finished version. "That's it. Done," she said. "Now it's time to put out feelers to my contacts in the newspaper world and hope for the best. Maybe send it to my old boss. Then at least he would see what he had lost in her, that slave driver."

"Hey, hard at work?"

Paige shielded her eyes against the sun. Something wet touched her hand. Startled, she jerked back and looked down to find a familiar friend.

"Maybellene! I was just thinking about you!" Tentatively, she reached out and stroked the dog's fur.

"Really?" Kat said.

Paige turned to Kat. "Hi. Good to see you. Are you making your morning rounds?"

"I am," she said. "Although I have to admit, I was hoping to run into you."

"After all, that's easy with me right now. I'm either here, at the B&B, or at the diner."

"Then you'll come to the dance, too?" Kat asked. "If you're already staying at the diner, anyway? Because that's what I was going to invite you to. We're all going."

"Dance night?" Paige asked, her throat going dry. "I don't know anything about that. And who is 'we'?"

Kat raised her eyebrows. "Really now? That would be the first time that wasn't the talk of the day."

Paige ducked her head slightly. "It's also possible that I wasn't paying much attention."

"And I thought you journalists didn't miss anything?" said Kat with a wink.

"You'd think," Paige laughed. "I have to admit, I've been pretty wrapped up in writing and reporting the last few days. That's where I'm completely in my own world and disappear."

"Wow. That's what I call focus. Is the article done yet?"

Paige held up her closed laptop. "Yeah. Just now. In fact, I think it turned out really well."

"Nice! It's an important topic, after all."

"Exactly. That's what was going through my mind. Now, all we need is for a newspaper or magazine to print it." Absently, she stroked Maybellene's head.

Kat watched her pet Maybellene—watching intently. Looked up quickly as if she were seeing something she wasn't supposed to. "It'll be fine," she said. "Do you think it'll make it to print?"

"Theoretically. I don't know exactly where yet, though, after my last boss fired me." She stowed her computer in her bag. "But enough about me. What about the dance? I didn't even know Independence had a nightlife."

Kat pulled a toy out of her jacket pocket. "Do you feel like walking with me for a bit? The little pooch needs some exercise. Then I'll tell you all about our wild night life." An exaggerated eye roll accompanied the last sentence.

"Sure. I don't get enough exercise, anyway. I actually wanted to explore the hiking trails in the area. Haven't had the drive to do that until now."

"I know how easy it is to get wrapped up in work all too well. If you want to tackle it at some point, I'd recommend taking a mountain guide. The mountains are very unpredictable."

"That's a good tip. I hadn't thought of that at all. Is there anyone here in Independence who does that?"

"Sure. Some. All of them are good. Some are a little more affordable than others. If you like something more scenic, too, I'd recommend Ace."

"Ace O'Neil?" blurted out Paige.

"Yes," Kat said in amazement. "Do you know him?"

Paige grinned. "No, no. I bumped into him on my first day in Independence. Doesn't he work for the fire department?"

"Yup. He's our fire chief. In his spare time, he offers mountain tours."

A soft smile played around Paige's lips. "Thanks for the info. The idea of having his tight rear end in front of me during the strenuous climb is immensely motivating."

Kat's mouth dropped. She pictured his butt, too. "Yes, isn't it?"

"Not that I'd tell him that," Paige added with a conspiratorial wink. "The man's convinced he's God's gift already."

"He sure does. At least he has some reason to believe that. Most don't." Kat handed her the slobbered-on dog toy. "Want a turn?"

Paige didn't have to think long. Her fingers had been itching all along, but she hadn't dared to ask after the last time she'd overreacted. "You betcha!" she said and grabbed the toy and sent it flying. To her delight,

Maybellene dashed after it and promptly brought it back. The dog placed the toy at her feet before sitting down and looking at her expectantly.

"Can anyone resist those eyes?" Paige asked.

"Well, you apparently," Kat said. "Otherwise you would have adopted her long ago."

"*HMM*. True. But I don't even know where I'm going to end up next. What if I can't take her to work with me? Or won't have enough time overall for a dog? My stay here is practically a state of emergency. I'll probably never have this much free time in my life again."

Those were valid arguments that actually spoke against getting a dog.

"It's like the decision to have a child," Kat said. "If you don't have one yet, there's never time. Why should there be? It doesn't seem necessary until you want it badly enough. Then you find a way."

Paige looked away and mulled what she said. "That's pretty spot-on. I still need to think about it, though. It's a big deal for me." She let out a sigh. "Now what was that about wild nightlife?"

"Oh yeah, that's right," Kat said. "Somehow, we keep getting off topic."

"Well, Maybellene is a magical distraction."

"That definitely. But now let me tell you, so you know. The sisters with the cartoon names that run the diner, with the help of a few volunteers, clear out the free-standing tables and chairs, creating a dance floor in the middle of the diner. There is dancing, laughing, playing darts and pool, and of course drinking. The latter is the reason Jake or one of his deputies is always present.

If they see someone drinking too much, they make sure they get home safely and don't get in their own car."

"Awesome." They really only had things like this in the sticks, Paige thought to herself. Nice, actually.

"Today it's Jake's turn."

"Jake is the sheriff and Paula's brother. Do I have that right in my head?"

"Exactly. That's why we decided we'd all go."

"Who is 'we'?"

"Well, the whole Carter clan, of course."

"Are you one of them?" Had she missed some kinship there? She must have really missed half of what was going on around her.

Kat laughed. "No, I'm not related to the Carters. But Jaz is my best friend; we used to live together in Seattle until we both made it to the Rockies. And Sam, also Paula's brother, Jake, and Tyler. All friends."

"Sam Carter? The Colorado Avalanche hockey player?"

"That's the one."

"I'm impressed. You definitely don't need an attractive mountain guide if you want something for the eye when you have Sam Carter at home."

Kat blushed as a dreamy expression entered her eyes. Paige felt an unfamiliar feeling stirring in her heart. Was it...no, it wasn't envy, but rather a longing to also have a person in her life to whom she could show such affection as Kat obviously did toward Sam.

"So," Kat said, "how about now? Are you coming tonight?"

Paige shrugged. "Sure. I'll be there. How dressed up do you want me to be?"

"Well, since we have few opportunities to dress up around here, everyone pretty much gives it their all. However, in these parts that means putting on clean boots and a little black dress. Although, if you don't mind standing out, I'm sure you'll meet plenty of men who will appreciate your efforts."

Paige snorted. "I'm sure. But I don't think I could handle that much male attention. As a writer, I'd rather stay in the background. I'll figure something out."

"Great. I'll see you then. And bring a jacket."

"Because I have such a long way home?" quipped Paige.

"A major temperature change is in the forecast. Thunderstorms with the possibility for snow at the plateau."

"Really?" Paige was flabbergasted. "Isn't it summer? After all, it was a pleasantly mild eighty degrees today."

"Even in summer, you best believe it. These mountains are known for their unpredictable weather changes."

"Okay. Good to know. I don't want to keep you."

"Yes, my mother is waiting for me. We want to go to yoga together." Kat's mother had just arrived from Russia a few months ago. Since then, she had lived in the apartment above Kat and Sam. The beginning of living together again had been bumpy. But they were getting along better every day, which she was thrilled about.

"Well, have fun." Paige crouched down and called out to the dog. Immediately Maybellene came running up and pressed against her, almost causing her to lose her balance. She laughed and stroked her silky fur. "Take care. Maybe we'll see each other again."

Kat, who had heard the last sentence, said, "You're welcome to stop by Safe Haven anytime and see her."

"Yes, yes. Until one day I drive away from there with a dog in the trunk."

Kat grinned, "That's the plan. Bye."

Paige waved goodbye. Then she shifted her laptop bag higher on her shoulder and walked back toward the bed-and-breakfast, stretching her face toward the sun. What a great day. Finally, the article was done and now she even had an invitation to celebrate. Not for the first time, she thought it would actually be quite nice to stay longer in Independence. She sighed. Enough moping. Now she had to figure out what to do next and start making inroads with her various contacts in the publishing industry.

"And you're sure you don't want to come?" Paula stood in front of the mirror and plucked at her auburn strands. Normally she wore her hair practically tied up in a ponytail. Since her sister and Jaz had coerced her into going out with them, her hair fell loose over her shoulders. For the same reason, she had applied lip gloss and nearly poked her eye out with the mascara brush. A little more practice probably wouldn't be bad. But since she couldn't keep up with her cows' eyelashes anyway, she usually refrained from making the effort in the morning in favor of a few more minutes of sleep.

Leslie rolled her eyes. "Yes. Just as sure as I was five minutes ago."

Crap. She would have loved to take the little girl with her. At least then she would have had a good excuse to leave again after an hour. She straightened her shoulders. After Leslie canceled that option because she still had to study, she had no choice but to join the darts and pool players. Brilliant, that kid. Really. But couldn't she have picked another night to discover her inner Einstein?

Paula grudgingly put on her best blouse with her favorite jeans and slipped into her nice boots. The temperature had dropped significantly, as predicted. She grabbed her jacket off the hook, looked for her car keys, found them in the fruit bowl, and said goodbye to Leslie and the two blue heelers lying on the warm floor in front of the stove. She had built another fire earlier; on such occasions, she was always glad she had enough firewood, even in summer.

"I have my cell phone with me. If anything goes wrong, call me. I can be here in twenty minutes." Since the ranch was a little out of town, she wouldn't be able to make it any faster.

Leslie shook her head. "I will. Now go. Go now before you're late and lose your place at the pool table."

Did the kid know her that well? She said, "Sounds like Tyler's been gossiping."

"It is what it is!"

Paula shook her head in mock sadness. "Unbelievable. There's just no loyalty in the family anymore."

"Jake says that in a family, you don't keep secrets from each other."

Now Paula thought that was a bit of an exaggeration. She bet Jake wanted to make Leslie feel like she belonged and had no secrets from the adults, so she let the matter go.

After a fleeting kiss on Leslie's forehead, she got into her pickup truck and drove off.

By the time Paula arrived at the diner, the party was in full swing.

"You actually came," Jaz said and hugged her. It was hard for Paula to free herself from the embrace.

"If I didn't know better, I'd guess you already have a whiskey or two in you."

"Raging baby hormones apparently put any legal drugs to shame," Jake grumbled, a bottle of beer in his hand. But he smiled lovingly at his fiancée as he did.

"He's right," Jaz said with a smile, placing a hand on the gentle bulge of her pregnant belly. "Just this morning I had to cry when I drove past a herd of goats."

"Goats?"

"I know." Jaz rolled her eyes exaggeratedly. "Idiotic, isn't it? In retrospect, I can look at it objectively and laugh about it, too. It's just that while it's happening, I can't do that at all."

"Watching this grow with you, I think it's more awesome every day my daughter has already been delivered fully grown." It still felt strange to speak of Leslie as her daughter.

"Besides, I bet twenty dollars that you would come."

"Good for you. Explains your great joy a little better than a flimsy excuse about hormones," Paula said. Jaz was a little crazy but had a decidedly well-developed business sense. No wonder her yoga school was doing so well.

"That's not the only bet that revolves around you, sis." Tyler joined in and pressed a kiss to her cheek.

"It's not? I'm surprised. I usually manage to fly under the radar, don't I?"

"If you wanted to continue to be invisible, you shouldn't have kissed the new hot vet." Even though Nate had lived in Independence for almost a year, he was still considered the new guy. That was just the same in Independence as it was anywhere else in rural areas, the only difference being that here it actually served more to distinguish him and had nothing to do with his popularity. Especially the animals of the female owners had various new ailments in one fell swoop. Paula might have been jealous if she hadn't known that he always nipped customer advances in the bud.

Paula raised both eyebrows. "And whose fault is it that all of Independence already knows?" After it took place at her home on the ranch, the circle of suspects was small.

Jaz shrugged. "*Uh*, maybe I talked to Tyler about it."

"Really? And where did this exciting conversation about my personal life take place? You'd think you'd have enough intimate details of your own to talk about. Would you like me to talk to your husband? Do a little tutoring?"

"Hey!" That came from her brother.

Jaz kissed him on the mouth. "No complaints from my side," she reassured him. Turning to Paula, she said, "That must have been at the yoga studio when I was talking to Tyler. "

Paula rubbed the root of her nose. The yoga studio—after the diner, the best source for information of all kinds. Probably one reason for Jaz's success, she thought ungraciously, even though she knew Jaz didn't consciously encourage gossip. The inhabitants of their small town already made sure they knew about everything. "I need something to drink," she grumbled.

"But I haven't even told you what the bet is yet." Tyler grinned mischievously at her.

"I can guess. Why do you think I'm so desperate to find booze?"

"You want to give me your keys right now?" Jake was relaxed and in a good mood. But that didn't mean he was going to stand by and watch someone get into the car in a drunken stupor, endangering himself and others.

"Oh, you know I never drink more than one beer when I'm out."

"True. But who knows? You might need a second beer for once when you hear the contents of the bets," he said, a suppressed laugh in his voice.

Awesome. Apparently, she entertained the entire diner for a change. Paula shrugged. "Won't be so bad."

But that was it. Except for the names of their potential joint children, just about anything possible between a husband and wife was the subject of a bet starring her and Nate. Surprised, she realized the bets weren't half as funny when she was involved instead of others. Okay, there was speculation anyway, and the bets at least served a good purpose. But did the bets have to be about her? She was a very private person. It pissed her off that her love life was being speculated about so publicly. Especially since there was nothing to speculate about. If there was, she would also like to have some of the passionate nights that had been attributed to her, she thought.

"Are the kids asleep yet, honey?"

At the sound of Nate's humorous question, she turned to him. "So, you've heard the rumors, too?"

His eyes sparkled. "Sure. The only question is what do we do with that knowledge."

Paula bit her lower lip. She hadn't thought about the whole thing that way. Of course. They could turn the tables, too. Clever. She wouldn't have believed him to be that cunning. The man had more layers than she wanted to admit. Her eyes fell on the leather jacket he had casually draped over his shoulder. The reason he had smelled of leather. Unexpectedly, she was transported back to the kiss.

"So, what is it?" he asked. "Do we dare to dance and cheer the bets a little?"

She swallowed. Dancing, of all things. But it was tempting to pay back the others in this way. Besides, maybe the money would go to Kat's animal shelter. Or new basketball jerseys.

"All right. Just let me place a few bets first."

"You can bet on yourself?" he asked.

"Theoretically, no." She winked at him. "But I know someone who owes me a favor."

In two steps, she was with Jaz, letting her in on her plan. Finally, Jaz nodded and Paula returned to Nate.

"All right. Pick a song. To be fair, I should probably mention that I have two left feet. So don't come complaining about your battered toes later."

Nate laughed. "Got it. Just let me lead. It'll work out."

She gulped. Leading was no problem. Letting herself be led was more of a problem. *Maybe it'll be fun to let go a little. Let him drive. Have someone else take care of you. Why the heck not? Might as well enjoy it.*

CHAPTER ELEVEN

NATE TOLD THE DJ what song he wanted. When he saw Paula was still standing in the same spot, he walked over to her and took her by the hand. He skillfully led his reluctant partner onto the densely populated dance floor. It truly amazed him at how much dancing there was going on among a wide variety of people.

Young and old were letting it rip to a song by Garth Brooks. He glanced over his shoulder. Paula followed him. This didn't surprise him. Jake and Sam hadn't believed him when he'd casually remarked that he was dancing with Paula. But he had known she couldn't resist challenges. She made a face like she had to strip in the next two minutes, but he was confident that would change once they were on the dance floor.

Miss Minnie did not share his confidence. She stood in their way and held a shot glass under Paula's nose. "Drink!"

Paula wrinkled her nose as the pungent smell of alcohol hit her and took a step back. "Ugh, what is this? I suppose you want me to not only dance but sing, too?"

"Don't be like that. It's your favorite poison. I need to make sure you don't chicken out. My bet is on the line."

That piqued Paula's interest. "Whiskey? Give it to me!" She emptied the glass in one gulp.

"Now let the boy here do his work and follow his lead."

Fortunately, the whiskey was already down. "Yes, yes," Paula said. It fueled her usual kick-ass attitude and she went for it. "Come on, let's get this over with."

Nate gave her a hug. "I kind of imagined this would be more romantic." Her muscles tensed under his hands.

"Maybe that will come later. As soon as I realize I'm not making a complete fool of myself. Or later when the alcohol takes effect."

"Just relax."

"*HA*! That's easy for you to say," she muttered.

"Breathing might help, too."

"Are you a dance teacher now, too? Breathing is overrated. I'm busy dancing."

Amused, and in one fluid motion, he pulled her to his chest, lowered his head, and kissed her.

Completely unprepared for the kiss, Paula lost herself completely. Her brain, which had just been trying to coordinate dance steps, shut down. Her body vibrated. The feeling of Nate's lips on hers—his powerful muscles under her fingers, the touch of his hands, and the music—it all merged into a single pulsating wave that swept her along.

It was Nate who finally ended the kiss. "Better?" he asked.

"Better?" she asked. "Better than what?" Paula's brain needed a moment before she understood what he wanted.

"Did you kiss me just to make me stop talking? How naughty!" She noticed the tension in his arms. He was into her, she realized with a primal, feminine satisfaction.

"I kissed you because I wanted to," he said, "and because I thought it would relax you."

"You thought what?" Her tone was skeptical.

"Hey, it worked out wonderfully. After all, the dancing works flawlessly now."

He was right. Apart from it going against her nature to be pushed around, she had to admit she had not stumbled once and even moved in time to the music and Nate's steps. Not so dumb, her vet Nate's strategy. Apparently, his expertise extended to bipeds as well. She found it quite attractive to witness him directing and skillfully guiding her. That stupid word again. She tensed her muscles and promptly lost her newfound looseness.

"Watch out. Otherwise, I might have to kiss you again. Purely to make the dance better, of course."

"I see. From my point of view, you can use such a tool again. Maybe I should just trip?" she laughed. The last bars of the song faded away.

"See? That wasn't so bad," he said.

"You're right," she said, "but enough is enough. We've put on a show-worthy performance. Dancing and kissing. Now it's time for fun."

"Dancing wasn't fun?"

The kissing had been the most fun. The dancing, surprisingly, had actually been tolerable. It was good to know the combination of dancing and kissing worked.

"Not as much fun as what we're about to have," she said. "Namely, beat the crap out of some of our friends at pool."

"Pool?" he asked as he struggled to follow her through the diner and the drinking and dancing patrons.

"Or darts. You get to pick what we start with."

"I get to be on your team?"

She gave him a mischievous look. "Today it is. After we're in the same boat or betting pool together, it's the only right thing to do."

"Sure. I'd love to. From what I've heard, you're very good at both."

"Oh," Paula said, raising both shoulders. But then she turned to him and grinned broadly. "That's right. I'm actually pretty good."

He liked the way she stuck to her strengths. She wore that on her sleeve.

Two hours later, they had stomped all challengers into the ground. Even her brother Sam, against whom she usually had to be pretty careful, didn't stand a chance. While a few calls for revenge went up, she grabbed Nate by the hand.

Surprised, he looked at her. Her hand felt warm and dry. She had large, slender hands, and he felt the strength and skill that was in them.

"Let's get out of here. I've reached my daily limit of exchanging niceties."

He stroked the back of her hand with his thumb. "Only too happy to. Your car or mine?"

"Mine."

Paula drove up a narrow pass road, through pine trees, until they came to a viewpoint. There she pointed the front of her car directly at the valley ahead and turned off the engine. The sky was clear. Countless stars stretched across the sky.

"I don't think I'll ever get used to this sight," Nate said.

"Couldn't you see the stars as well where you lived before? Where was that? In Denver?"

"It was no match for the spectacle you get here." He sighed.

Paula leaned back and looked at Nate from the side. He looked tired. "Is everything all right?"

He rubbed his hand over his face. "Yes. Basically, yes. But let me make a quick call to Shauna. Maybe I can get her to go to bed."

"Shauna? I thought she was with your ex-wife today?"

He grimaced. "That was actually the plan. But then something..." he seemed to search for a suitable word, "... got in her way."

"Got in her way?" How could something come between you and your own child? She would probably never understand that.

"Actually, everything should be fine. I've set her up on video chat. Now she can contact Leslie anytime. I hope that's okay with you."

That was news to Paula, that Leslie used video chat. Of course, she didn't mind. But she resolved to have an apparently much-needed conversation about the dangers of Internet use and open communication. "Sure. I'll wait outside then."

She got out and breathed in the cool night air. The temperatures had dropped precipitously. Maybe there would be a little snow overnight. She pulled her jacket tighter. So much for her idea of lying together in the bed of her pickup truck and watching the stars. Very romantic, but maybe a little too cold without a sleeping bag.

Nate stepped up to her at the railing of the lookout so that their shoulders touched. Her nerve endings tingled, and a shiver ran over her. He looked at her. "Are you cold?"

"No, no," she hurried to say, even though she obviously was. He made moves to take off his jacket. "You'd better tell me why you don't stand up to your ex-wife. After all, life's extremely difficult for you to organize when she keeps bailing on you."

Nate ran his hands through his thick hair before lowering them in a helpless gesture. "It's okay. But I told you how she was doing health-wise. I'd rather have a little stress than have Shauna with her and have to worry about what Nancy's going to come up with today."

"That's right. That's what you told me. I had completely forgotten about that." Nothing was as simple as it seemed.

Nate shrugged. "No problem. It's not relevant to your life either. And I can certainly tell it twice. I'd rather have Shauna live only with me. But Nancy won't go for that. That being said, of course, Shauna wants to see her mother too. Just rather on her stable days. She has a hard time with extreme emotional swings. They scare her."

"Understandable."

"What have you been up to today?" he asked, having run out of steam about his failed marriage.

Paula smiled broadly and propped her elbows on the railing. "Leslie and I got everything ready for Parents' Day today. I tried to convince my two no-good yard dogs that exercise balls are better cows, while Leslie designed the fabric cow covers for the balls."

"What are the dogs supposed to do with exercise balls?"

"Never heard of the dog sport of push ball?"

Nate shook his head.

"In a nutshell, you put various exercise balls in front of your herding dog and encourage it to maneuver them in a certain order with its muzzle or sometimes with full body effort into a pen or even a goal like in soccer. We wanted to simulate herding dog work on the farm this way without actually having to bring cows."

"I take it from your wording that the dogs' willingness to cooperate was limited."

"It was. I had imagined it would be easier. In the meantime, at least a certain sequence works. Now we'll just practice this one for the next few days. Then it will work out on the big day."

"I can't believe the ideas you come up with."

"Trust me, if your daughter likes to bring a longhorn bull to Parents' Day, you'll get creative, too," she said dryly.

As she had hoped, the story made Nate laugh. Immediately, her mood lifted. She moved a little closer to him and looked him straight in the eye.

Heat flared between them. His pupils darkened. Her heart beat strong and fast. What was her new resolution? Be direct? She liked that idea better and better. She couldn't imagine their third kiss would be as good as the first two. There was a good chance the chemistry between them had fizzled out. All that was left was a practical test to confirm her theory. Direct questions provided direct answers.

Paula leaned forward until she was almost touching Nate. Their breaths mingled and the attraction she hoped disappeared came to life so powerfully that she backed away a little in surprise.

This time he did not hesitate. Taking control, he put a hand on her neck and kissed her. She thought that probably they should talk about different things. Discuss how it should go on. What they expected from each other. But all those things could wait.

"I want you," he said hoarsely, close to her mouth.

Obviously, she felt it too. She pressed herself closer to him and wordlessly answered his question by returning his kiss with the same intensity.

Two hours later, Paula lay exhausted but content in the bed of her pickup under an old horse blanket in Nate's arms. It was apparently possible for them to produce enough heat to spend a frosty night outside. She snuggled closer, glad that he seemed content to enjoy the silence. Words would only ruin the moment. Her thoughts already picked apart the evening, analyzing its parts.

Of course, even their third kiss proved Nate to be an excellent kisser and lover, she thought, miffed. Not the result she had imagined. Actually, they should both keep as much distance from each other as possible, as highly explosive as they were.

Only that was impossible in Independence. She groaned. This was exactly why, since she had outgrown high school, she had sought her lovers and boyfriends either in Denver and the surrounding area or among the tourists who eventually moved on. Both options had an expiration date, which had always been enough for her. So what changed? Had anything changed at all? She did not know.

Paula had two options. Either she reverted to avoiding him as best she could, or she took advantage of the moment, enjoyed her newfound lover, and saw where it led.

That was something she couldn't decide at the moment, with his manly scent in her nose and his strong muscles under her fingers.

"Come on, let's go. I'll drive us home." To soften her abrupt words, she kissed the sensitive skin above his collarbone.

He gave her one last kiss and gathered his clothes.

Paula did the same. She avoided his gaze. She was glad he hadn't contradicted her and had followed her lead to end the night. It might have been a little harder for her to part with him. *UGH.* When had the transformation into an indecisive chick taken place? That was exactly why she preferred dogs. Their roles were clearly defined. She distributed food and petting, and the dogs warmed her feet and brought back any lost cows.

They drove in silence back to the center of the small town. In the parking lot in front of the town hall, she let him out.

He seemed to hesitate, as if he wanted to say something else. But then he left it at a simple "good night".

"Good night," Paula said.

CHAPTER TWELVE

PAULA HAD JUST POURED herself the second coffee of the morning when a car approached the house at high speed and finally braked sharply, splattering the gravel.

What's Tyler doing here at this hour? And at this speed? She only hoped that now the great inquisition would not start. She had been avoiding everyone since the dance a week ago. Even the four-legged ones cooperated and stayed healthy. She wasn't ready to discuss the deal with her and Nate. Her feelings were too new and too raw. Besides, it would become real if she talked about it. That way she could fool herself a little longer that it had only been a pleasant dream.

All these thoughts were blown away when her sister stormed into the kitchen.

"Good morning, where's the fire?"

Instead of a reply, Tyler slapped a newspaper on the table. "Did you actually give your approval to this article? Seriously?"

Keeping her eyes on her sister, Paula reached for the newspaper. "Now, calm down first. What's the big deal with it?"

"Read for yourself."

Paula laid the *Daily News* on the table in front of her and froze. Emblazoned on the front page was a blurry picture of Leslie and her shopping. Next to it was the lurid headline, *Local Animal Rights Activist Takes in Stray*. Paula broke out in a sweat. Hadn't they agreed: no photos? Filled with horror, she read the article.

"They mentioned my name. And Leslie's. I'm going to kill Paige! She didn't keep a single promise!"

The phone rang. Paula answered. "Hey, Mom. Yeah, I know. Tyler just dropped off the article for me." She listened to her mother, who was about to run Paige tar-and-feather out of town.

"Get in line." She was silent while her mother continued her tirade.

"No. I have no idea what to do now. Do damage control, I suppose. Wait a minute..." She took the phone from her ear and glanced at the display. As the beep had announced, another call was waiting on the line.

"Mom, I have to go. Someone's knocking."

"All right. Take care of yourselves. And avoid reporters like the plague."

A little late, her advice.

Nadine, the school principal, was on the other line. "Hello, Paula. I'm sure you already know about the article."

"I haven't gotten around to reading it in its entirety yet. Doesn't look great. Has Leslie found out about it?"

"I'm afraid so. Understandably, she is very shaken. As I understand, it was all arranged differently? Perhaps it would be smart to call a meeting where you can present your side of the story. That would put a stop to some of the speculation in the article."

Paula thought feverishly and went through her day in her mind. If she completed the most pressing tasks right away, she could be at school shortly before noon.

"If you call the students into the gym at a quarter to twelve, that might work. If Leslie can't take it at all, have her call me."

"I think I'm okay now."

"Tell her..."

"What?"

"Oh, nothing." Words failed to express what she felt.

"Darn it," she said with emotion as she finished the call.

"I guess you could say that," Tyler agreed with her sympathetically. "What are you doing now?"

"I would love to go to the diner right now. But unfortunately, I still have to drive water to the south pasture and fix the water tank."

"I'd offer to take that over but we know your animals would die of thirst because I always mess things up."

"Probably true."

"I'm really fuming. Paige definitely messed with the wrong family."

Leslie didn't fare any better at school. She took the school bus and was looking forward to the school day, even if that was hard to believe. As soon as she got off the bus, the girl triumvirate stood in her way and laughed.

"We knew no one would really want you. You'll see. Eventually, even Miss Paula will come to her senses and throw you out." One of them threw a copy of the *Daily News* at her feet. They all laughed.

Shocked, Leslie backed away in horror.

"Get back." Shauna came from out of nowhere and stood between the attackers and her new, older friend like an angry little pit bull.

Snapping out of her shock, Leslie reached down, grabbed the paper, and bundled it up.

"That's it," Shauna called to the trio of terror. "Get out of here or else."

Their laughs stopped and they looked like they saw the Ghost of Christmas Past. "Come on," one said.

"Better hurry!" Shauna huffed and jumped forward at them.

They screamed and scattered.

"Go, you rats!" Shauna turned to Leslie as soon as they vanished. "You okay?"

"I guess. And thanks," Leslie said. "I had no idea you had that in you."

"Like they always say—watch out for the quiet ones."

"I guess! So, now I have to see what was in this article." Leslie opened it up.

The class bell rang. "I'm going to go find someplace quiet to read this. You'd better get to class before you're super late."

Shauna's fingers dug into her arm. "I'm coming with you."

"Are you crazy? Out of the question. It's enough that I'm getting in trouble."

"That's what friends are for," Shauna said.

"Fine. Let's go to the football field. At least no one will see us there. I hope."

In a good mood, Paige went down to the diner. She hoped to hear from some magazines she had queried today. For once, she was really proud of her work. She would be happy if the article also received proper exposure from a prestigious magazine. She hopped a few steps and breathed the crisp morning air. There was fresh snow on the surrounding mountain tops. It reflected the sunlight and blinded her, so she put on her sunglasses. Life could be so beautiful. Work that was fun, gorgeous surroundings, and new friends.

Elated, she pushed open the diner door and stepped inside. As soon as she stood in the room, all the surrounding conversations fell silent. Shocked, she looked around to find out why there was a sudden silence.

Miss Minnie approached her with a heaving bosom and a steaming coffee pot. *Almost a bit like an archaic goddess of vengeance*, Paige thought fondly.

Miss Minnie addressed her, and all sense of well-being vanished. "People like you are not welcome here. There's nothing for you here. Leave my property right now. Only go to the bed & breakfast to pack your things. You have five minutes." She glanced at her watch. "The clock is ticking."

The blood rushed in Paige's ears. Did she really mean *her*? It couldn't be! It had to be a mistake. Seeking support, she looked around the guest room. Everywhere, she met hostile glances. Involuntarily, she took a step back. At that moment, she wished she had called the schipperke dog to her. She would certainly have stood by her side.

She couldn't think of anything she'd done wrong. "I don't understand?" she asked, summoning up all her courage.

"The problem?" said Miss Minnie incredulously. "The problem is you. Journalists like you, walking over dead bodies to get published. Disgusting is what it is." With those last words, she slammed a newspaper in front of her chest and manhandled her rudely out the door.

Outside in the bright sunlight, she turned the paper over. The *Daily News*. Oh no. She had a bad feeling about this. But surely he wouldn't dare!

Ten minutes later, she realized the editor of the *Daily News* had actually been impressed by her article. He had sent one of her former colleagues in Independence to research the names and take a lurid photo. Piece of cake. Especially if you already knew the back story. Then put a lurid spin on the whole thing, and you've got today's headlines.

"Oh, no," she said and hid her face behind the newspaper. Everything Paula had feared and been promised wouldn't happen...had happened. Loss of anonymity, exposure of Leslie, and a photo that violated their privacy. Who had the money to sue for that?

Worst of all, as she realized with horror, her name was above the text. No wonder they ran her out of town. She bit her lower lip. What was she going to do? She really needed to sit down with Paula, explain the whole thing to her, apologize, and work with her to do damage control. Too bad her car had been in the shop since yesterday and probably wouldn't be roadworthy until that night. She didn't want to wait that long.

She looked up and spotted Ace O'Neil walking across the street toward the diner. Probably on his way to his morning coffee. Indecisively, she watched him. He gave her a friendly wave. Could it really be that he hadn't heard about her new status as *persona non grata*? She called his bluff and stepped into his path.

"Hello? Ace? Right?" Nervously, she smiled at him.

He smiled. "Right. Where's the fire?"

"Burning? Oh, that's right. You're the fire chief." Fearfully, she glanced through the large windows of the diner. Surely someone would rush out at any moment to warn Ace off. She swallowed. "I really need to talk to Paula. But I don't have a car. I was hoping maybe you could give me a lift?"

"Me? What am I, a cab driver?" asked Ace. "Right now?"

She ducked her head. "Yes. So only if you can, of course."

Again, her eyes wandered anxiously in the diner's direction. *Whatever was happening in there?* He'd find out soon enough.

He said, "All right. Let's go then."

"Really? You're the best! Thank you!" Impulsively she hugged him.

Ace freed himself. "There, there. It's no big deal," he said gruffly.

Ashamed, she turned away and buried her hands in the pockets of her anorak. Silently, she followed him to his car.

Paige sat tense and pale in the passenger seat, staring blindly out the window. Ace glanced at her from the side. Normally, Paige was bubbling over with energy.

"Do you want to talk about it?"

Startled, she looked at him. "Talk about what?"

"About the reason you're upset."

"You can tell?" she asked, momentarily distracted by the intriguing notion he had actually paid enough attention to her to notice. Or she just had the worst poker face in the world. The latter was probably more realistic.

He did not even dignify her question with an answer. After all, she was not well.

Paige sighed. So much for her charm. "Thanks for asking. But I'd rather not talk about it. I need to talk to someone else first."

"With Paula, I assume?"

She looked at him suspiciously. "Why do you even care?"

Ace shrugged. "Curiosity. What else? Haven't you learned anything about us yet? Here, everyone interferes in each other's lives. Besides, I'm your impromptu driving service right now. Allow me a little curiosity."

She winced. He was right. Besides, he would find out soon enough. Still, she hesitated. He was probably the last person in all of Independence who was still talking to her.

"You must have heard about the report I did on Paula and Leslie. Paula had very specific conditions that had to be met for her to give her consent. Leslie only went along with it as a favor to Paula. The two main rules were no photos and I couldn't use their names."

"Let me guess. The article came out and included both."

Paige nodded. "Exactly. I made the mistake of sending the article to my former boss for review to possibly publish, among other contacts in the media world."

"And in doing so, you forgot to mention the framework?"

"Yes, of course I mentioned those. But apparently, he decided those didn't apply to him. So, seems he did a little research, took an unauthorized photo and published the article."

"And stole your work."

Paige squirmed in the car seat. "Not exactly. He stole my idea, rewrote the article, outed everyone involved against my agreement with Paula and Leslie, and finally put my name under the article."

"Oh, shizzle!"

"Exactly. How do I explain this to Paula? I'm sure she's furious as hell. Not to mention what this is doing to Leslie."

Ace brought the car to a stop in front of Paula's porch. He thought for a moment. Then he turned to Paige and lifted her chin with two fingers. "Cheer up. Paula may have a hot temper. But she's also very reasonable. I'm sure it will all work out."

Paige pivoted her head to the side. "That's sweet of you. But I don't think this thing is just going to settle. Too much trust has been broken for that." She unbuckled her seat belt. "Thanks for the ride. You don't have to wait for me. I'll find a way home."

Wherever home was, she thought and looked after the car. She didn't even know where she would sleep. A loud bang made her cringe. Guiltily, she turned around.

Paula had come out of the house. In her left hand, she carelessly held Betty. At the sight of the shotgun, Paige's eyes widened in horror, as Paula noted with satisfaction. She briefly considered shooting into the ground at her feet, but then kept that option open for later.

"Now that was a little hasty that you already sent your ride away. You are trespassing on my property! You are neither invited nor welcome."

She aimed the shotgun at Paige.

Paige ran to the nearest group of trees to hide behind a narrow aspen. Did she think she wouldn't hit her there?

"Paula. I am terribly sorry. I can explain everything! Honestly. And above all, stop pointing a gun at me!" How had it escaped her at the last meeting that Paula was completely insane? She knew Paula was within the law, but still. What civilized person actually pulled a shotgun? Surely this action was left over from the last century. Or the one before last. Her wildly beating heart was not interested in her thoughts, it concentrated solely on survival and pumped adrenaline through her veins at lightning speed.

"I'm not interested in your explanations. I'm only interested in how quickly you get out of here." She raised the barrel of the shotgun threateningly. Lightning shot from her eyes. "Who do you think you are? You ignored our agreements and then just showed up, acting surprised when I don't roll out the red carpet."

"That wasn't me. I sent the article to my former employer. To consider publishing. He must have sent someone out to get your names."

"Delightful story. Only I'm not interested. Because it's got your name under the text!"

"But...this was done without my consent!"

Paula fired a shot into the canopy above Paige's makeshift hiding place. "Sorry, squirrels!"

Bark splintered, and some leaves sailed to the ground.

Paige cried out and ran.

It wasn't until she reached the country road that led from Independence to Breckenridge and bordered Paula's land that Paige dared to slow down. Her breathing came in jerks. Her side was killing her. Completely at her wits' end, she dropped onto a large boulder. How could a day that had started so well end in such a disaster? Not only was her reputation at stake but also all the friendships she had made. She'd already toyed with looking for an apartment.

Paige was so wrapped up in feeling sorry for herself she didn't even notice a car pull up across the street.

Kat was on her way home with her two mastiffs Rocky and Nikita and the pit bull mix girl Bella. She had finally taken her three darlings on another long hike. They had been out for three hours, all the way up to the snowfields and away from all the other charges. The three were really very tolerant of newcomers. But they also appreciated it when she reserved time just for them three, the core pack so to speak.

When she saw the huddled figure on the side of the road, at first she thought of a hitchhiker on the way to larger towns. But then she recognized the reddish-blond hair. What was Paige doing here? Had her car broken down on the way to Paula's? Then why didn't she go to Paula for help? Oh well. Maybe she didn't know she was already on Paula's land. She rolled down the window.

"Hey, Paige! Is everything okay? Do you need a ride?"

Ashamed, Paige buried her face in her hands. "No, no, it's okay," she fought back. "I don't want you to get into any more trouble."

Trouble? What was Paige talking about? Was she drunk? Hardly, she realized after glancing at the clock on the dashboard.

"What are you talking about? Come on, get in. Then you can tell me everything in peace."

Tired, Paige got up, knocked the dust out of her pants, and crossed the street to Kat's car. Before opening the door, she hesitated briefly.

"Where have you been?"

"Hiking. Why?"

"Outside the cellular network, I suppose."

Kat shrugged away. "Probably. Why? Did I miss something?"

"I guess you could say that. Do me a favor, call Jaz, and get an update. If after that conversation you're still willing to give me a ride, I'd love to. If not, I totally understand."

Kat couldn't understand what was going on, but Paige obviously cared about the call. She reached for her cell phone and pressed the speed dial button.

CHAPTER THIRTEEN

Shauna tried desperately to talk some sense into Leslie. She didn't listen to her but muttered. "If I disappear into my room right after school, I can pack the most important things. I just need my thicker jacket, my favorite book, and a change of clothes. That should be enough. Food. Something to eat would be good. At least until I get to the next town."

Leslie looked up, an eerie, detached-from-everything look in her eyes that sent a shiver through Shauna. "Can I have your lunch?"

"My lunch?" the younger girl asked.

"Yes. Along with my food, it should last me a few days."

"Why does it have to last for a few days?"

"Well, because I have to go away."

"Gone? You can't just leave." She stared in disbelief.

Leslie's gaze focused, and she seemed to perceive Shauna again. Lovingly, she stroked her hair out of her face. "Don't you understand? I have to. Leaving is the only way Paula can live in peace again. But for it to succeed, I need a head start. Promise me you won't tell anyone about this. Do you hear me?" She uttered the last words with great urgency, a hand on Shauna's arm.

Shauna broke away and shouted, "No, you don't understand. Paula will be anxious. You can't go!"

When Leslie didn't reply, and just looked stubbornly to the side, she took a few steps backward.

That got Leslie's attention. Alarmed, she asked, "Where are you going?"

"To school. I hate you!" With these words, she turned and ran away.

With tears, Leslie looked after her. She did not want to leave. She'd finally found a home. Even a friend. But because of her, Paula had all the problems. Even a horrible photo was in the newspaper. Hadn't the woman from the newspaper wanted to prevent exactly that? But actually, it didn't surprise her. Adults always said one thing and then did something completely different. All except Paula. Her heart contracted. She suppressed her rising emotions and concentrated on her plan. She would have to corral the dogs when she left. Preferably with the horses.

"Leslie?" Startled, she turned around. Miss Saunders, the principal, stood there. Her brown eyes looked worried. "Are you okay?"

Leslie wrinkled her nose, hugged her school backpack tighter, and nodded.

"Paula will be here in a minute. If you want, you can go home with her afterward."

"Paula is coming?" she asked. "Why? I don't want that."

"We thought it would be a good idea for her to say a few clarifying words to your class."

"No way!" Leslie said.

"Why not? It's always better to take the bull by the horns and present your own version of events than wait for the rumor mill to take on a life of its own."

Leslie searched for a valid reason. The thought of Paula having to face the ridicule of her classmates was unbearable. "I just don't want to. Otherwise, otherwise..."

Nadine, noticing Leslie's stress, stroked her head in approval. "It's okay. If you'd really rather, we'll wait and see. I'll let Paula know. In return, go back to your class now. I'll write you an excuse for the teacher."

Leslie nodded silently. Her relief was too great. She would have to power through the last few hours of school.

Kat was still on the phone with Jaz. During the conversation, her eyes had gotten bigger and bigger, and she had kept looking over at Paige.

After the third glance, Paige walked along the side of the road. It was unlikely Kat would give her a ride. She'd better start her long trip back to Independence right away.

"Hey, where are you going?"

"Well, to Independence. I still have my things there," she answered.

"Is that so? Well then, call me when you get to the Pacific."

"Pacific?"

"Yes," Kat said. "Independence is in the opposite direction."

How embarrassing. Not even her sense of direction was reliable anymore.

"Go on, get in."

"Get in?" Paige looked at Kat. "You still want to take me?"

Kat gave her a searching look. "Let's put it this way, I'll take you with me in exchange for your version of events."

"You're the first one interested in listening to me."

"I bet Paula was unwilling to hear you out?"

"She was way too busy reloading her shotgun."

"So you've met Betty," Kat said. "Come on, now get in the car."

Paige was still standing rooted to the spot in front of the open passenger door. "*Uh*, I don't think there's room for me in there." Three pairs of eyes looked at her expectantly. The two mastiffs had heads like soccer balls, while the third dog was just...ugly. Mean, but the only apt word she could think of.

"Just ignore those three. Rocky has a soul of a dog. Nikita is just happy to finally be rid of her motherly responsibilities and Bella? Bella's a sweetheart. Just don't touch her, it always takes her a while to get over her fear of strangers."

Bella? This ugly thing was called Bella in all seriousness? And was afraid of strangers? Fascinated that the roles could also be distributed differently, she studied the dog.

"So, what's it going to be? Ride or hike?"

"Get in?" said Paige uncertainly. Maybe it'd go better if she closed her eyes? Like the three monkeys? "Too bad you didn't bring Maybellene. She could have been my personal guardian dog again."

"*HM*. But then there definitely wouldn't have been any more room for you." So slowly, Kat's patience was wearing thin. She understood Paige had a dog phobia and that it wasn't something that could just be magicked away. But she couldn't help it now that the dogs were there. She sighed and let the two mastiffs make room in the back seat. At least that way they didn't seem so big anymore. Bella banished them from the footwell of the front seat to the back of the car with others.

"Better?"

Paige's relief was clearly written all over her face. "Much better." With a relieved snort, she swung into the car. Rocky promptly sat up in the back and stretched his huge head forward to lick her once across the face. Mastiff enthusiasm, that's what. Too bad Paige didn't know that. The woman was stuck to the window in fright and groped for the door handle in a panic.

Kat forced herself to take a deep breath. In. Out. Somehow she had a feeling it was going to be a long day. Then she pushed Rocky back into place.

"You know, big guy, not everyone loves your kisses like I do," she explained, patting his large skull comfortingly.

"Relax," she said to Paige. "Now he's said hello to you and satisfied his initial curiosity. If we're lucky, it'll last until we get out."

"We?"

"Yes, we. Because now I'd like to know how come Leslie's and Paula's story appeared so publicly in the newspaper. Especially since she explicitly asked that their names be changed, that the location not be mentioned, and that no photos be taken."

Paige groaned and dropped her head with a thud against the headrest. "Right. Right. Sorry. I got distracted by those monsters for a second." She glanced back nervously as she wiped her wet sweaty hands on her pants. After another deep breath, she explained everything.

When she finished, Kat realized that although she had had her hand on the ignition key the whole time, she hadn't started the car. They were still on the side of the country road next to Paula's property. She started the engine. "Where do you want me to take you? You don't even have a room at the bed-and-breakfast anymore."

Paige stared at her hands. "I don't know. I still have to pack my things. Then I guess I'll spend the day at the park until my car is ready and then drive to Denver. I'm sure I can stay with one of my acquaintances there for a couple of nights." At least she hoped. She wasn't sure. She didn't really have any close friends in Denver. "Or I could go to a hotel. But for that, I need my car first. If the mechanic actually fixed it," she added. "If he's in on the Paige boycott, too, I'm screwed."

"Are you done wallowing in self-pity? You're not the aggrieved party here."

Paige swallowed and averted her eyes. "I know. But it's difficult for me, too. I'm not the one who created the problem. I would love to undo it. But I don't see any way to do that."

"Well. You can't actually undo it. The article is out. Period. But just throwing up your hands isn't a solution, either."

When Paige wanted to protest, she raised her hand and said, "Now we'll go get your things. Afterward, you'll come with me to my place. You can stay there for a few days and we'll figure out what to do about this mess."

"To you? But I'm *persona non grata* to all the Carters."

"So what?"

Paige rolled her eyes. "You live with another one, I understand?"

"Feel free to leave Sam to me."

Paige thought Kat sounded a little too confident. But she certainly would not try to change her mind. Not when she had nowhere else to go.

Paige was to be proven right. She was barely in the room when Sam shot out of his chair and glared at her. "You! What are you doing here? I can't believe you dare show your face here!"

Intimidated, she took a few steps back.

Kat seemed unimpressed. She calmly unpacked the groceries and stowed them in the refrigerator. "I invited her over. She doesn't have a place to stay right now."

"And you didn't think to check with me?"

"No, honestly, I didn't. She'll sleep upstairs with Mom."

Sam paced the living room. Bella followed his movements, looking worried, then hid behind the couch.

"You're scaring your dog," Kat remarked.

Frustrated, he ran his hand over his face and tried to relax. "Look, I know you like to rescue animals. But this is beyond that scope."

Kat turned to him. "You didn't really mean that now, did you, Sam?"

"Listen, guys. I don't want you to fight because of me," Paige said. "I'm sure we can find another solution."

"Good idea," Sam said.

"You stay," Kat said. Her eyes narrowed to narrow slits. "Just because my husband is too stubborn to see when he's in the wrong, doesn't mean you have to sleep on the street." She turned to him. "Unlike you and your siblings, I listened to Paige's explanation. If you must take your anger out on someone, I suggest you stick to the editor of the paper."

"Ah yes, the journalist! So innocent." He glowered at them.

"She's the only one who might put a new spin on this disaster."

"Am I?" Paige wondered when she heard that. "I'm not too sure."

"I know. Believe me, when I'm done with you, you'll have a finished plan in hand. Isn't that what you want?"

"Does it matter what I want?" muttered Paige. She didn't feel like she had any say in the matter.

Kat looked her straight in the face. "I thought you wanted to make up for your mistake?"

"Of course. Yes."

"So?"

Sam threw his hands in the air. "I give up. Get back to me when you've come to your senses." He hurried out of the room in a huff.

When he had gone, Paige breathed a sigh of relief. "Not an easy man," she noted. "I feel very uncomfortable coming between you and Sam." She stepped uneasily from one foot to the other.

"Oh, he's just very loyal. To a fault. Much like the rest of the family. He'll come around."

"I like your confidence." Exhausted, Paige dropped into a chair at the kitchen bar. As it seemed, the morning's heavy emotions had tired her out. She lowered her head into her hands.

Meanwhile, Kat finished putting away the groceries. "Just because I'm part of the Carter family doesn't mean I don't make my own decisions. But about you? I actually hadn't pegged you as someone who would give up without a fight."

"You said that earlier. And you're right. Just sitting around idly and accepting my fate is not usually my thing. On the contrary. After all, my inability to shut up cost me my job. It's just...this time I don't know how to do it."

Kat held out a plate of fruit and a glass of water. "Here. Have some food first. Then we'll sit down and come up with a battle plan."

Paige obeyed and accepted the plate. She was very relieved that at least Kat was on her side. Maybe together they could actually get back at the *Daily News*.

"Where is Maybellene, anyway?" she asked abruptly.

"Are you missing your friend?"

"Not at all. Pure curiosity."

Kat's knowing smile spoke volumes.

"Okay, okay. Yes. Of course, I've missed her. Although, I'm getting used to the rest of your pack, too."

"At least from a safe distance." Kat winked at her. "I'll get her in a minute. She's in the garage with Safe Haven's other charges."

"So, you haven't found a new owner yet?" she inquired casually.

Amused, Kat shook her head. "No. Or rather, yes. But the new owner is stubborn."

"Oh."

"Don't worry about it. It was a joke. You must feel the need to have a dog, this dog. Otherwise, I won't give her to you at all."

"Makes sense. Anything else wouldn't be fair to the animal, either. And what exactly is she doing in the garage? Guarding the cars?"

"The garage is currently housing animals instead of cars. It serves as an interim solution. The plan is to build an additional building. But funding has not yet been secured."

Paige stored this information away. Maybe she could repay Kat for her kindness and help her once the nightmare was over. Thanks to her, she had a roof over her head and was confident she would find a solution to make up for what had happened with the article.

Six hours later, Leslie finally got off the school bus. The day had seemed endless to her. At least Miss Saunders had kept her promise. Paula hadn't shown up at school. She dreaded getting under Paula's nose. How would she feel to be associated with a failure like her? Besides, she knew perfectly well there was nothing she hated more than being the subject of speculation.

She shifted her backpack higher on her shoulder and walked with a heavy heart up the long driveway to the house. Fortunately, she had her provisions together. Even though Shauna was mad, she brought her lunch at noon. All she had to do was pack some clothes and her favorite book, *The King of Narnia.* She would take her school backpack. It was the most comfortable and had the most room. She kicked a stone in front of her.

Roo and Barns jumped happily toward her. She crouched down and greeted them. "Well, beautiful ones?"

Roo pressed against her leg and wanted her to cuddle his back, while Barns immediately flung himself on his back and stretched his belly out to her. With a lump in her throat, she complied with her wishes. There was no way she could cry now. Otherwise, Paula would notice that something was wrong.

But she had worried for nothing. Paula was not there at all. There was a note on the table in the kitchen.

> *Am at Jaz.*
> *Crisis meeting.*
> *Come over if you want.*
> *—Kiss, Paula*

The McArthy Ranch property directly bordered Paula's. On foot, it was a good fifteen-minute walk without ever having to enter a road. She'd walked the route many times before. Then she knew what to give a wide berth to. Paula scribbled an answer.

Not wanting to lose any time, she jumped up the stairs, taking several steps at a time. In her room, she stuffed the bare necessities into her backpack. She had to stop and take a deep breath to prevent herself from crying. Unlike the other times when she had run away, she was infinitely sorry to leave the house, Paula, and the animals. Hope for a better future had always traveled with her. She knew everything that was to come would be worse, and she had no one to blame but herself. There was no other way out.

In the kitchen, she grabbed a few apples from the sideboard, as she always did when she went to the barn. She didn't realize she'd done so, however, until she locked the dogs in the feed room and was about to say goodbye to Dolly.

The pony was not at all pleased she wanted to leave without giving her an apple and buried her nose in Leslie's jacket pocket. "What do you want? Oh, the apple. I didn't even realize I'd pocketed any." Lost in thought, she stroked the furry ears while Dolly gleefully crunched the fruit. The little horse had grown especially fond of her. The thought of never seeing Dolly again broke her heart.

Unless that was, she took them with her. Startled by the audacity of her own idea, she took a step back. Could she really do such a thing? Maybe Paula would even understand. Or turn her into the sheriff for horse theft.

She was so afraid. Afraid if the decision was the best one. Afraid of where she would end up. But if she had Dolly by her side, everything would be all right.

CHAPTER FOURTEEN

Maybellene snored. "I have to fix this." Paige mused, sitting at the small table in a lovely, newly remodeled guest room at Kat's mom's house. The little dog lay at her feet, sleeping, oblivious to Paige's woes. Luckily, Kat let her borrow Maybellene for some much-needed emotional support.

Kat's mother Nadia, in whose home she stayed, was wonderful. She asked no questions, just welcomed her with a smile, and assured her she could stay with her as long as she needed. She knew from Kat that her mother had thrown herself headlong into a new life in Independence. There had been talk of a knitting club, and she diligently exchanged recipes with the cartoon-named sisters. She, like the rest of the thousand-and-something residents of the small town, was well aware of everything and everyone. Much like her daughter, she was willing to give her the benefit of the doubt. That would never have happened in her old life in Denver. Granted, so far, there were only two people sticking by her. That was enough. They weren't uncritical, but at least they trusted her to fix her mess. To convince the rest of Independence, she would have to work a lot harder. But she had never been one to shy away from hard work. She felt better realizing as much.

As Kat had so aptly pointed out, it wasn't like her to just give up without a fight, anyway. But how was she going to go about proving the evil machinations of the *Daily News*? Impatiently, she drummed her fingers on the tabletop as she ran through the names of her former colleagues in the paper.

Someone had to have been in town.

Actually, it was strange she hadn't run into whoever it was, since she had practically lived at the diner. Of course, the person knew Paige would absolutely disagree with her boss's plan, and had gone to great lengths to avoid her. She had to get Miss Minnie to talk to her again. She would have noticed a stranger asking inappropriate questions.

It had to be a regular paper employee who had taken the photo and found out the names. Her old boss would want to make sure he had his co-conspirator well under control.

One came to mind, after careful consideration. Peter had always been eager to endear himself to the editor. If so, why hadn't he published the article under his own name? It made no sense to go to so much trouble and end up putting her name on the byline. He couldn't take credit that way.

Unless they feared legal repercussions. In that case, Peter was probably happy to pocket cash instead of public recognition.

But it should be easy to figure out. All she needed was high heels, a plunging neckline, and a lunch date with Peter. After trying unsuccessfully to date her for the past two years, it wouldn't be hard to talk him into it, she bet. Then she'd just flirt, and he would tell her everything. She hoped. Maybe a dinner date was a better idea; it wouldn't be as noticeable if she plied him with alcohol.

Paige wasn't sure what she would do with the info if her suspicions were right, but one step at a time.

Motivated to have a battle plan, she pulled out her laptop and got to work.

Sometime later, she heard excited words from downstairs. A dog barked, and Maybellene answered with a short bark of her own, making her flinch.

A moment later, she looked out the window to see Kat and Sam rushing out of the house; the dogs close on their heels. Kat pulled on a light rain jacket as she ran, while Sam was in the car, starting the engine.

Not sure what it all meant, she glanced at the surrounding mountain peaks. Sure enough. Thick storm clouds piled up in the sky and pushed in front of the sun. That explained the choice of jacket. But where were they going? She glanced at the time on her laptop. Weren't they supposed to have dinner in half an hour? Maybe that hadn't suited Sam. That could be a good thing. Oh, dear. She hoped she hadn't caused a prolonged issue between them. Indecisive, she stared at the screen and stroked the little dog's soft fur. The pooch hadn't calmed down and was whining incessantly. She looked down at her. "You don't think they just went shopping either, do you?"

Relieved the woman finally had the right idea, Maybellene barked loudly and ran to the closed door. There she stopped and looked at the door handle expectantly, as if it would open by magic. It took Paige a moment to figure it out. When the dog stood in front of her and barked at her, her heart had almost stopped. In her imagination, she could see the razor-sharp fangs digging into her arm and the blood spurting. How absurd and unfair, after Maybellene's behavior had been nothing but friendly and protective. She let out a shaky breath and joined Maybellene. Hand on the doorknob, she said, "All right. Let's find out what's going on."

From the wag of her tail, she had said exactly the right thing.

Accompanied by a deep sigh, Paula turned off the engine and, exhausted, let her head sink against the headrest for a moment. What a day. First this article, then the corresponding questions from every single person she had run into today, followed by an emergency meeting at Jaz's. As if that hadn't been enough excitement for twenty-four hours, the water pump in the east pasture, the one without a natural watercourse, had gone out.

Seeing no way to move the two hundred thirsty cattle alone—impossible even with two dogs—she had had no choice but to go to the hardware store-slash-feed store for the spare parts, whisk her father away from his studies (luckily he had been home), and join him in mending the pump. It'd been a dirty and wet job.

At least it worked properly again, and the animals had enough water. She peered at the dark clouds gathering on the mountain slopes. The rain would fill the watering trough. She was sorry Leslie had been alone for so long. She hadn't shown up at Jaz's. She checked with her friend by phone. Paula bet she would find her in the stable, where she often lost track of time.

She would take a shower and think about what to cook. Maybe mac and cheese. Not the healthiest food, perhaps, but good soul food. They could both certainly use some.

In the house, she threw the keys on the kitchen table and poured herself a large glass of cold herbal tea. *Where are the dogs?* Busy enough with Leslie in the barn that they had missed her coming home? That wasn't like them. They always came to say hello.

On the table, she spotted the note she'd left Leslie. She reached for it and was about to throw it into the basket with the firewood when she saw Leslie had left her a reply.

I'm at Shauna's. Will be back after dinner. —Leslie

Torn whether she should be relieved that she didn't have to cook, or disappointed because she had actually been looking forward to seeing Leslie and discussing the day's events with her, she dropped the letter on the table. She'd take a shower first.

Something didn't add up, Paula thought. She rinsed the shampoo absently and turned off the shower. She just couldn't figure it out.

Finally clean again, she went downstairs to at least make herself a sandwich when it occurred to her what was bothering her: If Leslie was with Shauna, where were the dogs?

Paula reached for the phone. Two minutes later, her uneasy feeling was confirmed. Leslie was not at Shauna's.

"She's not here," Nate said. "I'm sorry. I haven't heard anything."

"Oh, no. Well. Thank you," she said, eyeing the property, desperate for any signs.

"Should I come over?" he asked.

"No, no," she said. "There's nothing you can do. You need to stay and be with Shauna. I'll keep you updated."

"Please do," he said. "Holler if you need anything."

"'Kay," she said and hung up. She slipped on her boots. Before she panicked, she would check the stable. Her heart raced.

As soon as she opened the stable door, the two blue heelers shot toward her. Excitedly, they jumped around Paula.

"Why are you two locked in the barn?" She dreaded the answers. So, she pushed them aside and looked in the run at the horses and in the feed and tack room to see if Leslie was hiding somewhere, even though deep down she already knew it was for nothing.

She was about to leave the barn when her eyes fell on the board with the hooks for the halters.

One was missing.

Dolly's. Slowly she understood nothing anymore. Was she just taking Dolly for a walk? But why the wrong message?

She hurried to Leslie's room to see if she could find any clue about what the girl was up to before jumping to conclusions.

Once there, discouraged, she lowered herself to the floor. Her worst fears had been confirmed. It looked as if Leslie had gone. Run away.

Paula wiped her face furiously as tears ran down her cheeks. What had she been thinking? Her biggest concern about the interview from the beginning had been it reflecting badly on Paula if it was associated with her. That's why she hadn't agreed to it until the names and places would be changed.

She would kill Paige, that much was certain.

But that would have to wait.

First, she had to find the child, who had apparently run off with her pony. Leslie was no different than her in that respect. If she had run off when she was that age, she would definitely have wanted a pony with her, too. And if she was lucky, Dolly would cut the trip short. How long would she be able to hide with a horse, after all? She'd get noticed soon enough. But a lot of trouble could still befall her.

She didn't want to rely on Dolly alone.

So she called Jake, who immediately organized a search party.

Within half an hour, the ranch was swarming with helpers.

Miss Daisy had brought over soup with hot dogs for the search party. Tyler was having Ranger jump out of the car. Kat and Sam were waiting for Ace's instructions. As chief of the local fire department, he was also in charge of the search and rescue team. It was a well-oiled squad. Every year enough idiot tourists came to Independence for vacations, only to get lost or crash or both on the first day.

Jaz set up a table on the porch with Lily's help. The soup and the thermoses with hot coffee would find places there.

Lily, the owner of the flower store, stayed open until eight o'clock on Friday evenings. But when she'd heard from Jaz that Leslie was missing, she'd turned the sign from "open" to "closed" on the spot, made sure her dogs had enough water, and gotten in the car to help.

Paula put her hands in her pockets and felt useless. At that moment, another car pulled up. Nate. "What is he doing here?"

Paula walked over to the car and asked him, "Did you want to go to the party here, too?" She pointed to all the people scurrying around in her front yard, looking like a busy anthill.

Instead of answering her, he hopped out of the car and gave her a searching look. "Come here," he said and pulled her into his arms.

Her first impulse was to resist. She didn't have time for this. But then her concern for Leslie prevailed. The lure of not relinquishing responsibility but sharing it for a moment was too great. With a sigh, she let herself sink against his broad chest, breathing deeply for the first time in hours. They stood like that for a few minutes. Finally, reluctantly, she broke away from him. "Thanks. I'm not usually the princess-in-need type."

Nate laughed. "Don't worry. Your reputation is safe with me." Then he grew serious. "My daughter has something to tell you." He turned toward the car. "Shauna? Are you coming?"

Lowering her eyes to her feet, Shauna approached. It was clear to see that the little girl had just been crying.

"Well, you wanted to tell me something?" asked Paula gently, even though she would have preferred to shake her.

"Leslie was going to run away," she burst out. "She's been wanting to since this morning. I tried to talk her out of it. Honestly. But she didn't listen to me." She pressed her lips together. "She made me promise not to say anything. What was I supposed to do? I didn't want to lose my friend, did I? And now she certainly doesn't want to be my friend. Even if you find her."

"Thank you for telling me, Shauna. I'm sure it took a lot of courage. I know that sometimes it's quite difficult to decide when it's okay to break your word. There are good secrets and dangerous secrets. This is a dangerous one. Leslie can get hurt if she's out there alone."

Shauna nodded and swallowed, looking miserable.

"Thank you for coming by. Did she say where she was going?"

"Just said she wanted to get away from here, to the next biggest city." She glanced to the side. "That's all I know, too. I ran away because I was so...so angry."

"Then the very first thing she'll have done is set out for Independence, hoping to hop on a truck. At least, that's what I would do. Mind you, that was probably the plan before she took Dolly with her."

Shauna's eyes grew wide. "She took Dolly?"

Leslie realized her spontaneous idea of taking Dolly along had its negative sides. The pony behaved in an exemplary manner. She didn't pull on the rope, stopped willingly when she tried to find her way in the forest's twilight, and was a noble companion. But Leslie was worried. She had forgotten to bring food. Sure, she could eat grass, but would that be enough? She had already given one apple to the pony, but she had to be sparing with her provisions. After all, she didn't know when she could find food again. Especially since she could hardly hitchhike with a horse. She didn't think the truck drivers would be happy to have a four-legged passenger and his companion.

The thunderstorm was getting closer. The sun had set and it was already dark because of the storm clouds. Where should she take shelter? She had her rain jacket, after all. But Dolly? Of course, she had a coat. She was used to being able to shelter if she needed to.

She wondered what Paula was doing right now. Rejoicing, of course, she tried to convince herself. Every time she thought about Paula, she saw the woman who had become so dear to her, who even volunteered to be her mother, pacing up and down in the kitchen, flustered with worry. At least people would finally stop talking bad about Paula. She couldn't stand it when someone spoke poorly of her.

"This little town lives and breathes gossip," said a small voice in the back of her head. She stumbled as she thought it over. The voice continued, "Whether they're talking about you and her or Nate and her doesn't matter at all. It's always someone."

Could this really be? she asked herself, drawing hope. But again and again, the blackness with its sticky tentacles expanded inside her and smothered any tiny sparks of light.

Finally, it rained. Lightning crashed to the earth to her left and right, followed by tremendous thunder and heavy rain. Completely frightened, she flinched.

She dragged Dolly into the undergrowth and huddled with her under an immense tree with enormous branches. Soaked from head to toe and completely worried about Dolly, she cried. If only Paula were there. She would surely know what to do.

The pony, who seemed to sense her despair, pushed her velvety nostrils into her face. Absentmindedly, she stroked the wet pelt and went over her options, which seemed to dwindle with each drop of rain.

Unexpectedly, Dolly gave her a friendly nuzzle. The nudge interrupted her racing thoughts. Surprised, she paused. She already knew what Paula would advise her to do. The first thing she would do was tell her she loved her. She always did that at moments when she least expected it. And the second thing she'd do is give her a good scolding and tell her to get her honorable rear end home. Where she belonged. Immediately.

Finally, the rain let up a little. The entire forest was dripping. Mist rose from the ground. Uncertainly, Leslie looked first toward Independence, then in the direction from which she had come. Her home.

She let the word roll back and forth in her mind until she realized it was true. Paula's home had become her home, too.

I wonder if it still is home? Would I still be welcome after doing all this? Could she forgive me?

CHAPTER FIFTEEN

THE SEARCH AND RESCUE TEAMS worked under Ace's guidance. Tyler led with Ranger, hoping the dog would pick up Leslie's trail. One team followed Leslie, while two other teams fanned out behind in a semicircle, covering the area where Ranger indicated.

Ace was about to join the rear guard when another car stopped at the head of the driveway. "Shoot. We don't need any more delays." The approaching thunderstorm had already dropped the temperature drastically. If they didn't hurry, Leslie would catch pneumonia before they found her. Still, he couldn't ignore the new arrivals in case they had relevant news. If Leslie had already arrived in Independence or found a ride, they'd be wasting valuable time here.

Annoyed, he noticed the person who got out of the car didn't greet him. As the rain increased, he pulled the hood of his weatherproof anorak with the emblem of the rescue team over his head. He hurried toward the person.

"You!" he said. "What are you doing here? Haven't you done enough for one day?"

Paige flinched. But she straightened her shoulders and looked him straight in the face. "That's right. And that's exactly why I'm here. To help."

"We don't need your kind of help here," he said, turning away.

She grabbed him by his sleeve. "Wait!"

Ace turned around in disbelief, staring at the hand holding him.

Paige swallowed and let go of the sleeve. "Please. I didn't mean for any of this to happen. At least let me help make it up to you and everyone."

Ace heard the sincere desperation in her voice; he softened. "All right. Fine. You stay close to me and follow my instructions to the letter. Got it?" Maybe he could prevent all the members of the Carter family from making a fuss when they caught sight of her.

"Okay," she said. "Thank you!"

"You won't have to thank me until Leslie is safely back home," he said.

Without caring if she could keep up with him, he hurried to join the others. Various people gasped audibly when he arrived in front of the house with Paige in tow. He ignored the questioning and indignant looks and gave very last instructions. Then he marched off.

He contacted Tyler via radio. "You're telling me the trail gets lost at the height of Tucker Land?" he asked.

"Yes." Tyler's voice sounded distorted over the radio.

"At the border?" Ace asked.

"No, just on the high ground. But clearly on Paula's land."

"Wait for me there. I'll be there as soon as I can." A loud crash interrupted the conversation. Lightning struck, followed closely by thunder. The thunderstorm was upon them. After a brief pause, waiting for the roar of thunder to subside a bit, he added for good measure, "By the way, Paige is with me. She wanted to help with the search." Before Tyler could reply with what likely would have been a string of cusses, he broke radio contact.

"Come on, let's go. There's no time to lose."

"Did they find her and Dolly?"

"No. Ranger followed the trail, but now he seems to have lost it."

"Why is that?"

"What do I know? Probably by now it's just too wet even for Ranger's nose. Who knows where she went? There's a creek running nearby, too. Maybe she crossed that."

The creek had swollen into a veritable torrent. He could only hope Leslie didn't get too close to the slippery banks. If she landed in the river, the current would sweep her away. Driven by such a horrible scenario, he quickened his steps.

Leslie had to realize that it was not as easy to make her way home as she had thought. In the meantime, it had become pitch dark under the trees. The fog rising from the ground made it impossible to determine which direction she had come from.

"What do you think, Dolly? Left or right?"

Dolly snorted. Her mood was not at its best. From her point of view, the adventure could be over now. She stamped her hoof on the ground and moved in the direction where she knew the stable was.

"That way? All right." She was soaked to the skin. Her teeth chattered uncontrollably. Waiting until the morning to find her way was not an option. By then, she would have frozen into a block of ice.

Leslie was very surprised when she suddenly heard a loud roaring. She stopped. Had she ended up so close to the main road? And why was there so much traffic in the middle of the night? And if there was a lot of traffic, shouldn't she be able to detect headlights? She squinted, straining to see through the darkness.

Dolly was tired of waiting. Determined, she went forward. Leslie had no choice but to follow her if she didn't want to be dragged along by the rope.

The noise grew louder. Leslie put one foot in front of the other. Several times she slipped on the wet ground with the slippery soles of her worn sneakers.

It had rained again. At least the thunderstorm had moved on.

Lightning twitched across the sky and illuminated the surroundings for a moment, but the rumble of thunder was longer in arriving.

Suddenly, the ground dropped steeply, and she lost her footing. Desperately, she held onto Dolly's mane to keep from falling over. Another flash of lightning struck the horizon.

The bright light illuminated the steep embankment and the roaring waters.

Startled, Dolly took a leap backward.

Leslie had to let go of the mane and plunged into the depths.

Tyler knew it was neither the time nor the place to deal with Paige or her unwanted presence. She completely ignored the woman who showed up at their meeting place with Ace.

"Ranger tracked the trail flawlessly and without hesitation to this point. There is some evidence that she sought shelter from the storm under this tree." She paused. "There are some smudged hoof prints here. And on this branch, the bark has been eaten away."

"That could have been a deer, though."

"Maybe. But then there's this gum wrapper. And that probably actually came from Leslie. Unless my sister is also supplying the deer with candy by now."

In the glow of the headlamps, she saw Tyler wink at Ace. He laughed and shook his head in amusement. The drops from his hood flew all around.

"Did you find them?" Paige asked, upset. "Hadn't we better keep looking? A child's life is at stake!"

Tyler gave her a dismissive look. "And whose fault is that?"

Paige stared back. She didn't care what Tyler thought of her. She did care if they were late in finding Leslie.

Finally, Tyler broke eye contact first and turned back to Ace. "I'm going to put Ranger back on their trail now and hope he picks it up again. The conditions are really tough."

"You do that. We'll wait over there so we don't get in your way." He grabbed Paige by the sleeve and dragged her a few feet away from where they had just stood.

The headlamps cast swaths of pale light on the surroundings. The rising haze gave the forest a ghostly touch. A shiver ran down Paige's spine and she suddenly muttered a prayer. She wasn't actually a believer. But in the event there was a God, she finished it.

She watched as Tyler pulled a plastic bag from her jacket pocket and held it open in front of the German shepherd's nose. The dog shoved its muzzle in, pulled it out again, and took off, Tyler following behind at a run.

Paige was about to do the same when Ace took her hand, sending shivers down her spine. What was that all about? He whispered, "Wait. Let Tyler go ahead with Ranger. If she's got a fifty-yard head start, we shouldn't interfere with the dog's work."

She felt fantastic holding his hand, despite the rain and the unfortunate circumstances. His breath, so close to her ear, sent a shiver down her spine, and she was all too aware of Ace's strength. Of all things, her dormant libido had to wake up during a rescue mission in the rain? What a joke!

He let her go.

Paige waited until he took the lead and that way she could see the ground in the glow of his headlamp.

Tyler was out of sight by now, so Ace radioed them. "Are you okay?"

"Moving on," came the reply. "Ranger seems to be single-mindedly pursuing a lead."

"That's good news, isn't it? If she took shelter during the storm, she can't have gotten too far yet."

"That's right. But, Ace, she's running toward Eagle Creek."

"Shoot!"

"Exactly. I'll try to pick up the pace and catch up with them before the river if possible."

"Take care of yourself! We'll be there as soon as we can."

He broke radio contact and quickened his steps.

Paige struggled to keep up with him. Gasping, she asked, "What's at Eagle Creek?"

He gave her a quick look. "You're not going to collapse on me here because of the altitude, are you?"

"Of course not. I've been here too long for that." Still, she tried not to gasp so loudly. An impossible feat. She was simply out of shape. No wonder. Aside from a few walks, she hadn't exercised at all in the last few weeks.

"Eagle Creek is a creek that runs across the bottom of Paula's property. From where we suspect Leslie took shelter from the thunderstorm, it's the most direct route back to the house."

"But that's good news, isn't it? I mean, if Leslie voluntarily turns around and picks the fastest route too?"

"On a nice day, I would agree with you. But with the thunderstorms of the last few days, the creek has grown into a raging, hungry river."

"But then why would she choose that route if she knew it was dangerous?"

"My guess is she's leaving the route planning to Dolly. She doesn't know her way around well enough to find her way home in the darkness, especially with the poor visibility due to the rain."

She had to digest this information first.

"Can't Dolly be relied upon? I mean, I always thought animals have such good instincts." She glanced at him from the side. His mouth was twisted into a grim line.

"Sure. That's confirmed by their choice of route. But the river doesn't play a significant role in Dolly's world. With her four feet, she's all-terrain. Even if she were to fall in, which I highly doubt, she could probably make it to shore relatively unscathed. Whether the same is true for Leslie remains to be seen."

That silenced Paige.

Leslie held on with both hands to the rope attached to Dolly's halter. The pony stood at the edge of the slope, her head lowered, and stuck all four hooves into the embankment.

She realized what the increasingly loud noise meant. Paula once mentioned that surprising, flood-like surges could occur, especially in spring. Apparently, that was also true of the summer ones, too.

While she had tried to climb up immediately after the fall, after several failed attempts that ended with her dangling, she was glad to find some footing. But she couldn't hold on much longer. She could feel the strength in her arms leaving. Her clammy fingers had more and more trouble holding on to the rope.

Tears streamed down her face. As bleak as her immediate future looked, she still didn't want to die. Not until she told Paula she was sorry.

Tyler hurried after Ranger. It was a good sign he was so determined, and she just hoped the two runaways would stick to the dry shore. However, she realized that this was easier said than done.

Again and again she had to leave the path because it was flooded in places. Thanks to her headlamp, she recognized the tough spots early enough.

Ranger had no such problems. Undeterred, he ran through the deep puddles or simply overcame them with a big jump.

Suddenly, he slowed down and barked.

She gripped the long drag line tighter and tried to make out what she was looking at through the rain.

Dolly stood on the edge of a slope, looking down into the river.

What was she looking at, she wondered? And where was Leslie?

Tyler lengthened their strides and reached into her jacket pocket to pull out Ranger's reward.

As soon as they got to the pony, he barked again.

Dolly flinched in place, but didn't move. Strange. Before she forgot, she gave Ranger the now-softened treats.

She moved forward to the edge of the embankment and peeked down, only to see her worst fears confirmed. Leslie was hanging from the rope still attached to Dolly's halter. She moved her head a little so the light from her headlamp fell more directly on Leslie. It looked like she had wrapped the rope around her hands several times. Smart kid.

"Leslie? Can you hear me?" The roar of the waters and the wind swallowed her words. But at least she should see the light, right? Without taking her eyes off Leslie, she pressed a button on the radio and relayed the good news to Ace and the rest of the rescue team that she had found them. She told them their exact location. "Gonna need help here."

Leslie saw the world through a veil. When she noticed the rope was slipping out of her hands more and more, she wrapped it around her hands. She could no longer feel them, but knew they were working. She blinked and raised her head against the light. "Is there anyone there? Help!" she croaked.

"Thank God, you're conscious," Tyler called out. "Hang in there. Help is coming."

"I can't move," Leslie groaned.

Moments later, everyone arrived. The rescue operation was in full swing.

Ace strapped on a climbing harness. A rope was attached to it. Two of his men secured his descent with the added help of a tree, while Tyler soothed Dolly. Once at Leslie's height, he fixed a second climbing harness around the severely hypothermic girl's body with well-practiced moves. A second rope was lowered, which he fixed to her harness.

"Leslie. Can you hear me?" he asked.

She blinked at him unfocused. Better than no reaction, but the greatest speed was required.

"My colleagues will drag you up. You can let go of the rope. We'll hold you."

"I can't."

He could imagine that. She probably had no feeling at all in her cramped fingers. He pressed a button on the radio and relayed the information. They agreed Tyler would untie the rope from the halter as soon as she was level with the lead.

Finally, it was done.

Blankets were passed forward to wrap Leslie up.

Paula picked up Leslie and loaded her into the waiting truck. She was shivering uncontrollably. The tension and cold were taking their toll. Her arms and entire upper body would definitely ache for the next few days. Otherwise, she seemed to have survived the adventure reasonably unscathed. Nate held out his hand without a word. Without protest, Paula dropped her car keys into his hand so that she could join Leslie in the back seat.

"I'm so sorry," she sobbed.

"Shush. There'll be plenty of time for that later. Right now, we need to get you dry and thaw you out."

"What's happening to Dolly?" she said, her teeth chattering. "She needs to get warm and dry, too."

"The track is not passable for a trailer. Tyler's leading them home with Ranger. It's not far now. You'll make it soon. You were on a good trail. If you hadn't fallen, you could've been home in ten minutes." She nodded. "That's where you were going, right? Home?"

Leslie nodded and let her head sink against Paula's shoulder. Paula breathed a sigh of relief. Her eyes met Nate's in the rearview mirror. He smiled, and she smiled back.

Paige followed Tyler, the dog, and the pony from a safe distance. When they arrived at the farm, she tiptoed to her car, unnoticed by the others, and drove away under cover of darkness. The moment belonged to Paula and her family.

CHAPTER SIXTEEN

Leslie held Paula's hands in her own. "I was just scared," she said.

"Of what?" Paula asked, inching closer on Leslie's bed. She'd only had her home for a day, but she was glad Leslie was opening up.

"Of losing all of this," Leslie said. "Of losing you. Whenever I've gotten comfortable...whenever I've become close with someone...that's when the hammer drops."

Paula nodded. "I get it," she said. "But there's no hammers here."

"Just shotguns!"

"And lots of love. From me. From Dolly. From all of our animals." Paula sighed. "And, as you witnessed? The entire town."

"I know. It hit me when I saw everyone. People care."

"They do."

"This is home," Leslie said. "It really feels that way."

"I'm glad."

During the next few days, the storm in Paula's life subsided. Leslie recovered amazingly well from the stress and went back to school after only two days.

She had also taken Nate's suggestion and cautiously broached the subject of a therapist. Leslie, marked by her numerous and usually unpleasant experiences with psychologists who worked with Social Services, had at first reacted skeptically. But when Paula assured her she would have a say in the choice of therapist, she had agreed to consider it. It was a start.

Since the rescue, Ranger had been staying with them temporarily. He hadn't left Leslie's side since, and had even taken Roo and Barns' place in the bed, so Tyler saw fit to leave him there. "Then she can get acquainted with him right away. Next week is already the hearing anyway. She needs him now more than I do."

Nate had proved indispensable. Reluctantly, Paula had to admit she had been very grateful for his presence. Which still puzzled her. She, who had always been so proud of doing everything on her own, was suddenly glad for the presence of a man? She was still very busy trying to reconcile this notion with herself. If Nate noticed her inner struggle, he didn't let on. He brought Shauna over daily so the two girls could talk, but had otherwise maintained a polite distance. Even when, in a fit of unbridled lust and hoping to thus banish him from her thoughts once and for all, she had thrown all her reservations to the wind and suggested a repeat of their nightly outing, he remained distant and politely declined. The jerk. She didn't believe for a moment he didn't want her, too. Probably he just didn't think it was appropriate. Men! She had to choose the only one who had a moral backbone. Frustrated, she tied her long hair into a ponytail and started her quad's engine.

While Paula was biking the pastures, Leslie returned from her first day of school with Shauna in tow. The two had talked it out and made up, which they were both thrilled about. Leslie wanted to show her friend a few tricks Ranger had in store.

"Wouldn't it make more sense to train with Roo and Barns for Parents' Day?"

Leslie laughed. "In principle, yes. Except they can't do it without Paula. They just ignore me. They're both pretty stubborn."

"But they don't leave your side, do they?"

"They do. I'm definitely part of the pack for them. They also like to cuddle with me and love the treats I give them. But they only work for Paula. Fortunately, it's different with Ranger. You'll see for yourself in a minute."

First, they greeted all the dogs, including the lazy ones. Then it was the horse's turn. "Has Dolly recovered well?" asked Shauna with concern.

"I suppose you're glad your darling is back?"

Shauna turned bright red.

Leslie giggled when she saw the horrified look on Shauna's face. "Don't worry. I'm not offended. I'd feel the same way if I were you."

Shauna ducked her head and sheepishly played with Dolly's mane.

Leslie, sensing her uncertainty, changed the subject. "Come on. Let's go outside and play with Ranger."

Next to the pasture, she played through the entire repertoire with Ranger. Sit, down, stay. High five. Giving paw. Slalom through the legs. Falling over dead. Being embarrassed. Jumping up. For the latter, she had him climb on a stool and jump over a fence.

Shauna clapped her hands enthusiastically.

Leslie was almost bursting with pride and let Ranger climb up the ladder to the hayloft. She had only practiced this with him a few times, but like all tasks, Ranger had aced this one. So she led Shauna back into the barn, where she gave the dog a hand signal.

Full of verve he jumped up the steep steps. Everything went well until he was almost at the top. Suddenly one of his paws slipped, as apparently one of the rungs had broken, and he fell to the ground. There he lay for a moment. Paralyzed with shock, the two girls stared at the dog in dismay.

At last, he got up, shook himself once, and stood still on three paws. The left front paw he held in the air. Even after good coaxing and coaxing with treats, he refused to put any weight on the injured limb.

"He must have broken his leg!" How was she going to explain that to Paula? Or Tyler? Not to mention, she couldn't stand it if anything serious happened to the dog.

Shauna, who had often accompanied her father when he was on vet appointments, crouched down next to Ranger and used a little of what she knew. Gently, she took his paw in her hand and carefully moved it back and forth. "I don't think anything is broken."

Leslie asked, "Are you a vet now, too?"

"Hey! I'm just trying to help!"

Leslie took a deep breath and tried to control her panic. "Right," she said when she had calmed down a bit. "I'm sorry about that. Was projecting my fear on you. I'm learning to not do that. But what am I going to do now? Imagine if Paula comes home and the dog is hurt?"

"Why don't we call my dad? Maybe he has time to come over right now. I'm sure he'll know what to do." Shauna shrugged.

"Really, would you?"

"Of course. After all, Paula would do the same thing if she were here."

Half an hour later Nate was on his way to Paula's house. A nervous phone call from his daughter had informed him something was wrong with Ranger.

Paula obviously wasn't home yet, which suited him just fine. It was better if he didn't see Paula too often at the moment. It took him more willpower each time to understand her tempting offers. He knew exactly what she intended by it. But he had other plans for her. Plans that involved a lot more than a few passionate nights in the back of her truck. He knew that if she knew about his plans, she would run away. In that respect, she was like a wild mustang. So, he forced himself to be patient, even if it meant he would take a lot of cold showers for the foreseeable future.

He reached into the back seat, grabbed his doctor's bag, and got out. Barns and Roo greeted him joyfully. Outside the barn, Leslie and Shauna crouched beside Ranger and held him to keep him from joining in the big welcome. Well-mannered as he was, he patiently allowed the two girls to hold him and confined himself to wagging enthusiastically.

"The dog's still alive," he quipped as he got closer, which earned him a dirty look from his daughter.

Leslie completely missed the ironic tone and asked anxiously, "Is he going to die?"

"No, no," he hurried to say. "As I understand Shauna, he hurt his paw?"

"Yes. I wanted to show our latest trick. How he climbs up the ladder to the hayloft. When he was almost at the top he lost his footing and fell."

"Don't worry, I'll look at it right away. Maybe he's just sprained his ankle, as sometimes happens to us. For now, though, you'll have to let him go so I can examine him."

Reluctantly, Leslie released her grip around the dog.

Nate called out to Ranger, and first watched closely how he moved. In the meantime, he didn't spare the paw so much and even put it down again. With a gentle grip, he palpated the injured limb, moving all the joints back and forth, looking for swelling.

As he worked, he explained each of his steps. The girls listened intently and followed his actions with serious eyes. When he could find nothing serious at first glance, he felt for the smaller bones that made up the complex dog's paw. Here it was. As he had hoped, two of the small hand bones had shifted.

"Two bones in Ranger's paw have shifted. If they're not in their proper place, they'll get in the way and hurt him when he steps."

"Does he need a cast?" Leslie asked.

Nate laughed. "No, no. Nothing that dramatic. I'm going to pull on the individual pads of his toes now, hoping that they'll then move back into their proper position."

"Doesn't that hurt him?"

"No. Not at all. It's like when you crack your finger links."

"Really?"

"Watch, then you can see it for yourself. Maybe you can even hear it." Gently, he pulled on each toe. On the third, the typical cracking sound was indeed audible. He released Ranger's paw and waited.

Ranger put the paw down, shook, and ran to join the other two dogs without even a hint of a limp.

"He's all right now," Leslie exclaimed. A glow stretched across her entire face. Shauna gave him an impromptu hug and looked at him like he was the hero of the day.

"There, I'm done here then. Would you like to come home with me now, Shauna?" That would be the perfect solution. Then he wouldn't run into Paula.

But of course, his daughter didn't play along. "Oh, Dad. We were just playing so nicely. And you're not even done with your duty yet," she slyly pointed out. "It's much better if I stay here for a while and eat with Leslie and Paula. You can pick me up after work, as usual."

He conceded defeat. "All right, then. Let's do it your way."

"Thanks, Dad! You're the best."

Inwardly amused at his clever daughter, he had to stifle a grin.

Leslie tugged at his sleeve.

"Yes?"

"Is Ranger okay now?"

"Yeah, you weren't supposed to notice any more of that. But no more dangerous tasks for him. He shouldn't be jumping any higher than out of the car for the next few days. Will you watch out for that?"

"Absolutely! And…could we forget about this incident…*UH*…to Paula?"

He looked at her. "I'm sorry. I can't lie. But if you want, we can tell her together tonight. Would that be an idea?"

Visibly dejected, Leslie nodded.

"I'm going to go now, then. Don't forget your homework."

"Okay, bye, Dad."

He raised his hand in greeting and walked to his car. Behind him he heard the two whispering and giggling. Just like girls. He was glad Shauna had made such a good friend in Leslie. He couldn't imagine if something bad had happened to her when she tried to run away. Shauna would have blamed herself forever!

"Are we still allowed in the barn, grooming Dolly and Rufus?"

Paula raised both eyebrows. "Homework's done?"

The two girls nodded eagerly.

"Well, off you go."

Like lightning, the two disappeared. Paula let her eyes wander over the table. Oh, yes, they should have cleared the table. But the two of them would sweep the stable alley and pick up the horse droppings in the lying area. So, that wasn't a terrible deal. She would make herself some coffee and take her time cleaning up the kitchen. Nate would probably be along soon, too. Although she hadn't really planned on talking to him much when he came to pick up Shauna, she probably wouldn't be able to avoid it tonight.

Having found the girls in unexpectedly subdued spirits when she returned from fence checking, she nudged them until Leslie had burst into tears and confessed everything.

She had then reassured them. In her eyes, the incident had been an unfortunate coincidence, and the girls had acted with presence of mind. She was also pleased that Leslie, after some good coaxing, had finally found the courage to tell her about the accident. She had made her promise that she would call Tyler later to let her know.

Of course, she had been terrified of that, too. But she realized it was necessary.

"Imagine you lend Dolly to Shauna. Then the pony gets hurt in Shauna's care and she doesn't tell you about it. Would you want that?" she asked Leslie.

"No. Of course not."

"See? That's how Tyler feels, too. She loves Ranger just as much as you love him."

Leslie had nodded and put on a brave face.

Paula had already told her sister, so she wouldn't be too shocked when Leslie called. Tyler could be over-anxious about her veteran police dog and was prone to dramatic reactions. She wanted to spare Leslie that after all.

In the two girls' retelling of events, she noticed Nate's kind and prudent behavior toward the children. Leslie, in particular, he had handled her just right, appealing to her sense of responsibility and showing her the consequences.

Reluctantly, she had to admit that he had handled the situation flawlessly, without undermining her authority or making Leslie feel bad.

In her opinion, he actually deserved a pat on the back for that. Well, she certainly wouldn't go that far, she reassured herself. But let him know how much she appreciated his approach, she had to. There was no way around it. Something convinced her it paid to be critical. But that also meant saying the positive things. Otherwise, one risked ending up as an eternal complainer.

Ignoring the nervous knot in her stomach, she rinsed out the empty coffee cup and placed it on the draining rack. She wiped her hands dry on the dishtowel. Relieved, she heard Nate's car approaching.

She took a deep breath, straightened her shoulders, and stepped through the screen door onto the porch.

He got out of the car and smiled. "What gives me the honor of a reception committee?" he asked lightly, hoping to defuse the situation that way.

"You brought this on yourself," she said.

Nate winced.

She started in. "Thanks for your help with Ranger. You did a great job with Leslie. She still feels bad that the dog got hurt because of her, but she's also really proud that she handled the situation and that Ranger is okay now."

"*UH…*" The whole thing was so unexpected that he was actually speechless for a moment. "It was pure luck that it wasn't anything more serious."

"I already realize that. Still, you turned a scary experience into a valuable lesson for her."

She leaned against one of the porch posts and put both hands in her pockets. He didn't have to see how her hands were shaking.

"In any case, I owe you. If you ever need help or an extra cab for Shauna, just reach out."

"Nonsense. You don't owe me anything."

"Yes, I do. I insist."

With a mischievous glint in his eye, he took a few steps closer and casually leaned against the railing next to her.

"All right," he said. "If you insist...I have a wish."

Suspiciously she looked at him. "A wish? It doesn't sound like you need help."

"Ah, but that's not how it works when you owe someone a favor. I'm free to define that favor. And I'd like a date with you. And while you're recovering from the shock that's written all over your face I'm going to go get my daughter. I'll call you tomorrow with details."

Before Paula could protest that she had in no way agreed to his proposal, he was gone. Frustrated, she kicked one of Roo's chew bones across the porch.

Impossible man. How she could even get the idea that he would behave normally was nothing short of a mystery.

Still, she was amused. She couldn't help it. Such masterfully presented shrewdness simply impressed her, since she herself was also quite good at turning situations to her advantage. She just wasn't used to being the target.

CHAPTER SEVENTEEN

With a loud clap, the man dropped the newspaper on the worn plastic table in front of the woman. A cup of coffee promptly spilled over. With a hiss, the cigarette in her hand went out. "Hey, watch it. And get your stuff out of there," she nagged.

Unmoved, the man waddled around the table in his plastic slippers and dropped into the only other chair in the trailer. "Read!" he instructed her, seeing she wanted to use the newspaper to soak up the spilled coffee.

"You know I don't care about that stuff." Lacking a rag, she took the frayed sleeve of her morning coat before immediately lighting another cigarette.

"This is. Your brat is in the *Daily News.*" He tapped the front page with his index finger, then clasped his hands over his sizable belly again. The marks on his scuffed, formerly white undershirt attested it was his favorite posture.

"What are you talking about? I don't have a child," she said.

"Not now. But fourteen years ago, if I remember correctly." He laughed. "Wasn't surprising, either, the way you went with everyone."

She gave him a venomous look. "Maybe it was yours."

He shrugged. "Who knows?"

She reached for the newspaper. "What makes you think it's even talking about my girl? It's not like you've ever seen her. Neither have I, really, come to think of it."

"Look for yourself. She looks like you used to."

"So, she's pretty. That really eliminates you as a possible father. With your mug, I'm sure you would have spoiled everything." The woman stared at the picture. Indeed. The photo could have been from her youth. Had she really once been so young? She stared enviously at the girl who still had her whole life ahead of her. Carelessly, she dropped the newspaper back on the table. "Nice. I've seen it. Did you at least bring beer?"

"No. This is much better." He pushed the paper back toward her. "Read the article. This is our big chance."

"Big chance for what? I didn't want a child then, and I certainly don't want to know one now."

"You know that and I know that. But they don't know that. There's enough dough to be made from this story that we can finally make our way to Florida. We just have to do it right. Read it already."

The woman gave in. She lit another cigarette and grumpily reached for the newspaper. Hopefully, he would give it a rest after that. She didn't like it when her morning routine was interrupted.

"Did you pack Ranger's leash? And his bowl? And food in case it takes longer?"

Paula laughed at Leslie's barrage of anxious questions. "Everything's already in the car. But I sure hope this negotiation ends before Ranger starves."

Leslie hoped so, too, of course. But in her overactive imagination, she saw herself and Ranger stuck in court for hours. At the mercy of endless questions, with no chance to eat anything in between. Her stomach growled at the idea.

"Don't worry. I haven't forgotten about you either. I've made sandwiches, packed fruit and an emergency ration of chocolate, and chilled drinks."

"That won't do us much good in this courthouse if our rations are waiting for us in the car," Leslie muttered, in a bad mood. Her nerves were at a breaking point. Ranger, with his unbeatable sixth sense for such moments, trotted across the kitchen and nestled against her legs. She promptly knelt down and wrapped her arms around his neck.

"I'm so glad you're coming with me today."

Paula was also thrilled about it. Since her own nerves weren't at their best because of worry about Leslie, she was glad for Ranger, who eased the situation a bit. For a moment, she regretted refusing Jaz's offer to go, but no. It was all right the way it was. Leslie and her would manage fine.

"Did you see the clothes I put out for you?" Leslie was still lounging around in her pajamas.

"Do I really have to wear it? I look stupid," Leslie grumbled. Startled, she put her hand over her mouth and cast a furtive glance in Paula's direction.

"Listen, young lady. I'm going to tell you something that I'm sure I'll regret or even revoke in a few months. I want to be happy with you if you think something is good. If you find something stupid, I want to know it too and get upset with you. If I have a different opinion than you, I will also tell you. For example, right now I'm sorry to tell you but you actually have to put on the pleated skirt, blouse, and blazer."

She raised a hand when Leslie tried to interrupt her. "Wait, it's your turn in a minute. I can well understand you feeling weird in those clothes. Mine aren't much better. But it's always an advantage to dress for the occasion. People in court, whether they're a judge, a lawyer, or a juror, just expect formal attire."

She paused, walked over to Leslie, and grabbed her by the arms. "Can also be that we have completely different opinions and even argue about what's right or wrong. I do that with my parents and with my siblings all the time. Do I have to move out because of that?"

Leslie shook her head silently. "Or do they love me or I love them less because of it?"

"No. I don't think so." She was not sure. It was simply outside her range of experience. She was getting used to there being another way. Tentatively, she leaned against Paula and squeezed her before letting her go.

Paula's heart almost sank at this careful demonstration of affection. She felt a lump in her throat. She'd better finish packing the car before she got too sappy.

An hour and a half later, they arrived at the Denver courthouse. It was an impressive construction that reminded Leslie of what Versailles might look like. It had two large wings on either side. The middle was made up of a main building with a beautiful proscenium that was very distinctive. That part looked like it could be right out of Washington, DC. Intimidated, Leslie followed Paula up the front step.

Ranger hurried along as if it were no big deal, his leash taught between them. He looked very official in his service dog vest. *That's probably why none of the security guards questioned his presence*, she bet.

After a brief discussion with their lawyer in the outer hallway, they were led into a holding room. It was hot and stuffy, as if it hadn't been used for a long time, which was nonsense, of course. On the wall hung a painting. To Leslie, the haphazard strokes of color, done in shades of brown, reminded her of a cow patty. The idea made her nervous and she giggled. Paula caught her and winked. This increased the urge to laugh, but at least her heart felt lighter.

Since she was still a minor and a witness for the prosecutor, she did not have to be present in the courtroom for the entire hearing. They would call her directly to the stand with a five minute warning.

Leslie wiped her damp hands inconspicuously on the lining of her jacket while Paula paced up and down like a tiger in a cage. That lifted Leslie's spirits a little. If Paula was a little nervous, she was allowed to be. She smiled at the realization.

"Chocolate anyone?" she interrupted Paula's thoughts and stood in her way.

Surprised, Paula paused and dropped onto one of the plastic chairs lined up along the wall. "Well, I'm a big help to you. Instead of radiating calm and serenity, I fidget more than you do."

"I'm definitely glad you're here. Fidgety or quiet, I couldn't care less."

Paula bobbed her foot and Leslie bit her nails. Ranger shifted from one leg to the other with stoic calm, letting her scratch his fur. Even Leslie noticed. "He sure has it good. Watches out for us and gets pet for it."

"True. He's the best watchdog. He already proved that with Tyler. You want something to drink?"

Leslie shook her head. "Nah. I'm too nervous."

Finally, a female bailiff entered the stuffy room. She briefly informed the two of them about the schedule.

"In ten minutes, the prosecutor will call you to the stand. You know what you have to do?"

Intimidated, Leslie nodded.

Satisfied, the woman nodded and turned to leave.

"And my dog?" Leslie asked.

"Yeah? What about him?"

"He can come, can't he?"

An unexpected smile suddenly made the woman's stern features seem much softer. "But of course, he's allowed to go. That's his job, after all."

Tentatively, Leslie returned the smile. Paula also leaned back, a little more relaxed in her chair.

When the woman had gone, Paula knelt down in front of her protégé and reached for her hands. "You can do it, little one! I'm so proud of you. And remember that you have Ranger on your side should you get scared. That's especially important when the other side's lawyer cross-examines you. I have no idea what he will say, but he will try everything to put you in a terrible light. That's his job."

Leslie, so close to having to appear before the judge, didn't even want to think about it that closely. "I know. We've already discussed all this in the preparation meeting."

Paula felt that there was no harm in recalling various points. But she grudgingly accepted that Leslie would rather avoid that, and swallowed all the admonitions. Trust was the key word. And that only worked both ways. Her job was to trust Leslie to handle this hearing her way.

The time came. With Ranger at her heels, she followed the bailiff into the courtroom and took the stand. She focused on the tips of Ranger's ears to avoid eye contact with her former foster father.

She almost missed the collection of familiar faces in the rows. Everyone was there. Tyler and Pat, Jaz and Jake, Nate and Shauna. *Doesn't she have school?* Leslie wondered. Kat and Sam, Brenda and Stan. Even the Diner Sisters Minnie and Daisy, and Mr. Wilkinson, principal Saunders and her friend Rose were there, too.

Leslie's mouth almost dropped. She had not expected so much support. Until then, she had always been alone. Suddenly she had a vast family. Ranger nudged her and licked her hand. Strangely touched, she clawed her hand into the shepherd's fur. Unexpectedly, her heart felt light. With such a great supporter, what could happen?

She was proven right. Calm and collected, she answered the prosecutor's questions and described daily life in her former foster home. Her answers were clear and consistent. Even the opposing lawyer's attempt to portray her as an ungrateful brat was countered with open and honest answers that left no one in the room untouched.

There was one dicey situation when she described how her former foster father had locked the children out of the house as punishment.

When the defendant heard the story, he rushed toward the witness stand with a yelp. The whole thing happened so unexpectedly that he almost reached them before the bailiffs even realized what was going on.

Leslie could no longer avoid looking at him. The pure hatred that met her eyes made her flinch and recoil in her seat.

Ranger didn't hesitate for a moment, leaping over the fence of the witness stand toward the man and throwing him to the ground. Growling, he remained standing over him until the bailiffs took him into custody.

After the commotion died down, Ranger calmed down and took his seat next to a beaming Leslie. She was so proud of him! And grateful that he had stood up to the man on her behalf.

Her support team thought so, too. No sooner had the judge declared the proceedings adjourned than everyone flocked to her, despite the protests of the numerous security personnel. Since sympathies were clearly on Leslie's side, they seemed to turn a blind eye. Paula reached her first, hugged her in the middle of the hall in front of everyone, and squeezed her tightly.

Leslie was surprised to find that she didn't mind. On the contrary.

Nate caught Paula's glance over Leslie's shoulder and saw that she was fighting tears. He leaned down to Shauna. "Run and congratulate your friend. I'm sure she has a lot to say."

Shauna didn't need to be told twice. She left with Leslie and Ranger, accompanied by her Independence entourage.

Nate took Paula, who was watching Leslie, by the hand and pulled her outside. As soon as they were outside the courtroom, he stopped and pulled her into his arms.

Paula let out a relieved sigh and hugged him. Gratefully, she let herself fall against him, trusting him to hold her. After a few minutes, she reluctantly disentangled herself and said only, "Thank you."

"You're welcome. You looked like you could use a hug."

She stretched and gave him a kiss. Right on the mouth. "And you were absolutely right." With that, she turned away and left him standing.

A surprised smile stretched across his face. Repeatedly, she surprised him. No wonder he had fallen in love with her. Shaking his head at himself, he hurried to catch up with her.

CHAPTER EIGHTEEN

"Do you have the soccer balls? And you're sure we can use the soccer goal posts?" Even though it was fairly early in the morning, Leslie was jumping up and down on the spot.

Paula was glad she had already had her second cup of coffee. Otherwise, so much merriment would have been much more difficult to endure.

Since the trial no longer hung over Leslie like the sword of Damocles, she was a changed girl. Only rarely did she lapse into the closed attitude that had been so typical of her in the past. Instead, she dared to make jokes or even to speak up when something didn't suit her. Just like a normal teen. Paula was glad. She still hoped to find a suitable therapist for her. She didn't fool herself: Experiences that had accumulated over a lifetime would not magically disappear. Better to address the matter while she was in a cooperative mood, rather than wait until she was older. She hoped it would be awhile before that happened.

"The soccer balls are in the pickup's bed. Did you brush your teeth?"

"*Yeah-ha.*" Leslie rolled her eyes to make it clear what she thought of that question. It was probably only a matter of time before it got on her nerves. She still appreciated the flash of confidence.

"Can we go?"

Paula glanced at the clock. It was only ten to seven. It took them twenty minutes to get to school. Good. That would leave them ten minutes to unload the balls and the rest of the equipment. Besides, it probably wasn't bad at all if Leslie and especially the dogs had a little time to calm down.

"Yes, we can." She tossed her the keys. "You go ahead. I'll be right there."

When the little girl had scampered out the door, she dropped into the nearest chair and took a deep breath.

Outside the window, she saw a family of deer grazing. The morning mist rising from the ground was already dissipating. It was going to be another sunny, hot day. Perfect for her drift ball demonstration at the school's sports complex. She was glad she wouldn't have to explain to the athletic director that blue heelers could actually completely plow up a wet field in five minutes while playing push ball. She grinned at the thought.

Absently, she reached for her coffee cup and emptied it in one go. Disgusted, she screwed up her face when she realized the coffee was cold. She stood up, put the cup in the sink, and walked to the car.

They had just turned onto the main road when Paula frowned.

Leslie, still watching the surrounding people closely to expect any mood swings as much as possible, asked nervously, "What's wrong?"

Paula put on her blinker and turned the car around. As she did so, she asked, "Don't you notice anything?"

"No. What should I notice?"

"Well, the silence! Don't you remember what a racket my two boys made when we took them to my parents' house some time ago?"

"Yes, of course I remember."

"Then you should also realize that, despite our excellent preparation, we forgot the most important thing."

Leslie slapped her hand over her head. "Stupid. Of course. But hurry. I don't want to be late."

Paula could relate to that. Every time she visited the school, she immediately felt transported back to her student days. More precisely, to the many occasions when she had to serve detention.

Roo and Barns jumped out of the barn, completely outraged. Leslie had locked them in there after brushing them in the morning.

Actually, she had wanted to shampoo them. But Paula had successfully explained that shampooed ranch dogs were not authentic. She hoped the dogs would appreciate her efforts and behave well in return.

Enthusiastically, the two pointy-eared dogs jumped into the back seat of the pickup truck. With tongues hanging out, they panted down Paula's neck and seemed quite excited about the trip. Odd, actually. Since she rarely took them anywhere, they weren't particularly used to driving. Tractors were something else entirely. Maybe they had seen the soccer balls and thought, *Great, we're going to play!*

Finally, they arrived at the school grounds. Paula was lucky and got the only place in the shade. Good. Then at least it wouldn't be so hot on the way back.

"Will you please leash the dogs and walk them to the sports field? Or is the meeting place somewhere else?" Paula asked, suddenly panicking that she'd missed something on the numerous info sheets.

"No, it's right on schedule. We're on first so you can go back home afterward to make hay or harvest corn." Leslie grinned wryly at her own joke.

"Very well," was all Paula said, thinking it was a perfectly reasonable plan.

Child and dogs set off. Paula tried to keep the first ball from rolling away with her foot while she fished for the other two gym balls in cow colors.

She sweat. Great. She hadn't been in school for five minutes and she was already nervous. Why couldn't she get her hands on that dang cow ball? She was tall and could reach it just fine. She would just need an extra pair of hands. She wanted to curse, but held it in.

A car pulled up next to her. "Do you need help?"

"No," she growled, too busy with the darn balls to turn around. Behind her, she heard a suppressed laugh.

Nate. Awesome. There she was, half standing in the bed of her pickup truck, her head down and her butt in the air. She wouldn't be able to convince him to reconsider her offer in twenty years. *Oh, that's right, he'd rather have a date*, she thought.

When one ball was taken out, she almost lost her balance.

"*OOPS,*" was all Nate said, catching her around the waist with his free hand. Involuntarily, she braced herself against his forearm. Instantly she felt his sinewy muscles tense. She drew in a sharp breath. Then she pushed off and put a safe distance of a good meter between herself and Nate.

"Since you're obviously also a cow-ball whisperer, I'll gladly leave the task to you of herding them to the soccer field. I still urgently need to..." She searched for a halfway plausible excuse. "...talk to someone anyway," she concluded.

Before he could say anything, she fled in the schoolhouse's direction.

His loud laughter was answer enough. When had her control over the situation slipped away like that? Otherwise she had men well under control! She urgently needed to rethink her strategy, she vowed to herself, as she weaved her way through students, mothers, fathers, and teachers.

She met Leslie, who, surrounded by classmates, proudly held court with her two blue heelers on leash. The two dogs sat there majestically while Leslie explained the dogs were not to be touched, unfortunately, because they could not concentrate on their task afterward.

"They are working dogs, you know?" she said.

Paula grinned amusedly to herself. Presumably, as a deputy mother, she should frown disapprovingly now and discuss the subject of "fibbing" later, but honestly, she didn't begrudge Leslie having her moment in the spotlight. If she used the situation in her favor, it was only fair, after the talk she had recently had to endure.

The smell of cut grass and fresh coffee filled the air. The Diner Sisters had recently gained a food truck and had been supplying all the major events with their delicacies ever since. Jaz strolled across the lawn with an oversized croissant in hand and joined Paula.

"Did I just see that correctly, that you assigned our vet to herd cows?"

Paula grimaced. "I wish it were. Hectically fleeing is more like it." She glanced cravingly at the pastry in her friend's hand. *Didn't girlfriends share everything with each other?*

"You and escape?" Jaz offered her a bite.

Paula winced. "I know. Unimaginable, isn't it? Just pathetic. I desperately need a night out among girlfriends and the support of my beloved Jack Daniels to..." she broke off and glanced at Jaz's belly, which was rounding more and more noticeably, "although, you can go ahead and join me for only half the program."

"Oh, I make up for that easily with my wisdom," Jaz said.

Paula snorted.

"What are you doing here anyway? Isn't it still a bit early to practice for parent events? I'm all for early intervention in principle. But this seems a little extreme to me."

Good-naturedly, Jaz nudged Paula. "And it seems to me you need a little relaxation. Why don't you kidnap the handsome vet and have some fun?"

She gritted her teeth. "Already did."

Jaz looked at her. "Really? And why don't I know about it?"

Paula shrugged. "There was just so much else going on." That was a lame excuse if she was honest; there were just so many emotions involved this time that she had wanted no one else to pick them apart. Even if that someone was as understanding as Jaz.

"Why don't you look more cheerful?" Jaz asked.

Paula threw her hands in the air. "Because this stubborn jackass got it into his head that he wanted to go on a date with me. For whatever absurd reason. I don't know why we can't just rip off our clothes like we did last time."

The individual classes were called. Leslie was giving her frantic looks. Grateful for the interruption, Paula squeezed Jaz's arm and pointed at Leslie and the dogs. "I've got to go. We're up first."

"Okay. But just don't think the discussion is over. With or without good old Jack's help, I'm going to get all your secrets out."

"I was afraid of that," Paula muttered, turning to go.

Jaz looked after her and grinned. *Well, well, well. A man had actually dared to set up his own rules.* She was curious to see how the story would continue.

The morning passed in a hustle and bustle of various activities, demonstrations, and occasional dry lectures. It was probably also easier to simulate a herd drive with dogs and balls than to show the rather colorless everyday life of an auditor. Especially if you were by nature a colorless and unimaginative person, like Henry Peters, the father of Henry Junior, who went to Leslie's class. She almost felt sorry for the boy if she hadn't known he was a real show-off.

By the end of the fifteen-minute speech on budgeting, more than half the audience—adults and children alike—had fallen asleep in their chairs. Even the teacher had trouble staying awake.

When Mr. Peters finished speaking, no one reacted at all until the teacher startled out of her trance-like state and began clapping.

One by one, people politely fell in until the speaker bowed his thanks.

"Whew, finally made it," Paula whispered to Leslie, who giggled. In return, they earned disapproving looks from Henry Junior and understanding smiles from bystanders. *Oh well. You could never make everyone happy*, she realized.

Leslie pulled her by the sleeve. "Come on. We're having sloppy joes for dinner."

Paula suppressed a groan. In her memory, sloppy joes were ghastly, soggy rolls, heaped with an indefinable meat and tomato sauce mixture. Only her mother could give such an abomination any flavor or character.

"Why don't you go ahead. Maybe you can find Shauna? I'll see if the dogs have already trashed Miss Saunders' office."

"No need," a voice behind her spoke up. "They're both acting like perfect gentlemen, sleeping snuggled up under my desk."

"Oh, really?"

"Really," Miss Saunders reassured them. "Go ahead and eat. Knock yourselves out."

Robbed of her excuse, Paula let Leslie drag her to the food truck, where they joined the long line. Astonished,

Paula noticed that a strange face stood behind the counter, stirring in a large pot.

"Do you know who that is?" she asked Leslie.

"No. I don't know."

A man waiting in front of them turned and explained, "That's Aileen. The daughter of a cousin of the Diner Sisters. I don't know what you call that kinship."

Lily, who had been in charge of the flowers in the auditorium, stood in line right behind Paula. She pricked up her ears. She had noticed the stranger, too. Unfortunately, the newcomer had enthusiastically hugged Ace earlier. So she probably wasn't playing on her team. That had been expected, unfortunately. But she could still dream.

"I don't know that either. It's exciting though," Paula answered the man.

"The best part is that she seems to be a really superb cook. Even has a degree from a prestigious culinary school."

"Seems to run in the family. Then there's hope that sloppy joes are edible."

"*SHH,*" Leslie went on. "Just don't let Miss Daisy hear you say that. You'll hurt her feelings."

Paula stroked her hair lovingly. Recently, Leslie tolerated such touches better and sometimes even sought her closeness. Now, too, she leaned against Paula for a moment.

At that moment, someone stepped through the door at the back of the truck. It was Paige, with a stack of paper plates in her hand. She stowed them under the counter and immediately began handing out portions.

"Paula, look!" Leslie pointed at Paige, a panicked undertone in her voice.

That was all she needed, Paula thought. Of course, this person had to cast a shadow on her otherwise perfect day. How could the Disney Sisters possibly have given her work? Inwardly, she could only shake her head at so much carelessness. Sometimes she just didn't understand people. Critters were easier. At least they were honest.

"I'm not really hungry," Leslie chirped. "And I'm not sure the dogs are actually okay, either. What if they need to go out? Or thirsty?" There was no mistaking the panic in her voice.

Paula forced herself to calm down. Thank God she had practiced this with horses all her life, and grabbed Leslie's hands. "Leslie. Look at me."

Stubbornly, she kept her eyes on the ground. Very well. The ears would hopefully also work without eye contact.

"That was a terrible thing for Paige to do with that article. I'm still mad at her about it, too. But, and this is really important right now, we're not going to let her ruin our day. You and I have done nothing wrong, only her. So now we're going to go get our food without letting on. Okay?"

Leslie nodded imperceptibly, but still kept her gaze lowered. Paula considered it positive that she relaxed a little.

"Are you guys okay?" Nate had arrived and looked anxiously from Paula to Leslie and back again.

"Yes," she said.

Nate wasn't fooled by her put-upon cheerful tone, but correctly assumed she didn't want to talk about it at the moment. Instead, he turned around, looking for his daughter. When he saw her a few feet away with her classmates, he waved. Shauna said goodbye and skipped toward them.

When she saw Leslie, her face brightened with joy. "I saw your demonstration with the dogs. Yours and Paula's. That was the best thing ever." She clapped her hands.

That seemed to snap Leslie out of her foul mood. In no time, the two were engaged in a lively discussion about whether Roo or Barns was the better driver.

Paula threw Nate a grateful smile. She might be confused about her own relationship with the man. But as far as Leslie was concerned, he invariably had excellent instincts.

"Trouble?" he muttered, inaudible to the children.

Paula pointed her chin at Paige, who was serving food. "Ouch. I can imagine that's a tough situation."

"You can say that again. After all, I was able to convince them to stay here and not flee."

"Progress, no matter how small or how big, is everything."

It was their turn in line. Wordlessly, Paula and Nate accepted the food from Paige and passed it to the children. A little later, she sank down next to Nate on the small stone wall that separated the break area from the sports field. "That's good. Sitting down at last!"

She was not used to standing. It always gave her back pain. Just like shopping trips. Hard, physical work was better.

Suspiciously, Paula surveyed her food. To avoid the soggy bun, she had chosen the option of having the sauce served in half a hollowed-out bell pepper. Carefully, she tasted a bite. And another. And another. "This is delicious," she said in surprise.

"*MMM.* Almost as good as Brenda's," Leslie agreed with her mouth full. She seemed to have recovered quickly from the unwanted encounter and was engaged in a lively conversation.

"Have you found a date for our date yet?" asked Nate casually.

Paula promptly choked and coughed like crazy.

When she calmed down, he lightly commented, "I take it you don't have any suggestions?"

"There's always so much to do during the summer months."

"I know," he said. "I'm a veterinarian, if you can remember."

"Why? Are the animals sick more often in the summer?"

"No. But my main clientele are farmers in the area."

"And ski bunnies," Paula muttered.

He ignored her interjection. Inwardly, however, he was pleased about the hint of jealousy. At least that was how he interpreted her statement.

"Knowing your workload, I arranged for Tyler to babysit our daughters. She'll host a scavenger hunt and keep them entertained."

Paula frowned. *Cheeky, isn't it?* The way he simply had her life all figured out. However, she had to admit it was quite pleasant not to have to decide everything. Even if it was just a simple date.

"And when will this memorable evening take place?"

Nate nodded. "Next Friday. I'll pick you up. Seven o'clock sharp."

CHAPTER NINETEEN

PAIGE LOWERED HER HEAD to the floor and scratched Maybellene's fur, lost in thought. She couldn't tell if she was holding an ear or the tip of a tail, but she didn't care. The dog didn't care either. The main thing was to be cuddled. Somehow it had crept in that Maybellene was spending more and more time with her. If she had to do research on herself now, she would find that the woman in question obviously owned a dog. This insistence that she basically didn't like dogs, other than Maybellene, was getting old. Kat would probably laugh her head off the next time she called her on it.

But actually, she had much more pressing problems. First was her temporary living arrangement. Nadia and Kat were very nice. Really. She mostly stayed out of Sam's way. He was polite but distant. She couldn't blame him for that. Still, the ceiling was about to fall on her head here if she didn't have more contact with other people. After all, that was one reason she enjoyed being a journalist so much.

Then, the prior day had been a disaster. When she had heard that the Diner Sisters were looking for someone to help in the food truck for half a day, she had jumped at the chance and said yes. She knew she had probably only gotten the job because Nadia had stood up for her. But she hadn't cared. The prospect of being back among the people had dispelled all doubts.

However, she had not realized how resentful the inhabitants would be. Apparently, the resentment ran deep. When she came home at the end of her shift, she almost packed all her things and drove away. It didn't matter that she didn't know where she was going. Just gone sounded better than anything else. However, she had made the calculation without Nadia. She had listened attentively with a serious face, even nodded in the right places, only to conclude: "So, now you are running away from your responsibility after all? What a pity. I would not have expected it. But well. Won't be the last time I lose a bet."

With that, Nadia turned and left the room.

That morning, Paige sat on the floor, indecisive, with no idea how to get her life back on track.

She wanted to make some kind of amends about the article. She could sympathize with how uncomfortable it must have been for Leslie at school.

Paige had something like a plan. She just had to finally tackle it. She had licked her wounds long enough.

She noticed Safe Haven's website was a disaster. After she had done her detective work on the unauthorized article, she would devote the evening to optimizing the text and the site. A standard letter seeking support money might also be a good idea.

Then why was she still lying around on the floor, hanging out with the dog that didn't belong to her? she asked herself.

Paige sat up and pulled the computer to her knees. While she was at it, she would immediately write an article about Kat's important work and try to place it somewhere other than the *Daily News*. Maybe she'd sway people's minds in Independence in her favor while doing something good for her new friends.

Humming, Leslie pulled the mail out of the mailbox as she came off the school bus. She was in a good mood. Since the demonstration, the other students, even the bullying girls, treated her with much more respect. She chuckled as she thought of how she'd casually mentioned her personal herding dogs could accompany her to school. Probably that had helped the most. Especially after Roo had chosen that moment to growl.

Without looking at the mail, she jammed the various letters and magazines under her arm and headed for the house. Lucky and Rufus were not in the pasture, she realized with surprise. *I wonder why Paula had brought them in.*

She hoped none were hurt, and quickened her steps. Relieved, she noticed that Nate's car was not in the driveway. So surely there was some innocent explanation for the horses' absence from the pasture. Instead of going into the house, she unceremoniously dropped the mail and her school backpack on the porch steps and walked over to the barn.

The gate was wide open. Inside, Paula was grooming Lucky while listening to some overly loud Brad Paisley music. As she rose from her spot under the horse's belly, she spotted Leslie. "Hey, it's good to have you home. How was school?"

In her best teenage manner, Leslie shrugged indifferently. But she couldn't prevent a broad smile from spreading across her face. "Great! No one pushed me, laughed at me, or otherwise bullied me. The idea of taking the dogs on Parents' Day was really awesome."

Paula laughed. "I also don't think Fridolin would have had the same effect. He's just too affable for that."

"Do you have any plans with the horses?"

"I thought we could go for a ride again. There's been so much going on lately that we haven't gotten to do it at all."

Leslie's face lit up. "Right now?"

"In a minute. Rufus isn't cleaned yet, and afterward you can change and get some more food."

She passed the grooming kit to Leslie. She took it and groomed the old quarter horse's coat with practiced strokes. After removing the dirt, she cleaned the hooves.

Afterward, she hugged him and deeply inhaled the smell of relaxed horse, sun, and meadow. Rufus checked her pockets for treats.

"I don't even know if I have another outfit. These are my school clothes." She dug in her jacket pocket and found a dusty horse cookie. "Here, you rascal."

She slipped one to Lucky, too, who was bubbling soft sounds through his nostrils.

After they finished saddling up, they left the horses tied up and returned to the house for final preparations. Leslie shouldered her backpack, and Paula picked up the stack of letters from the floor.

While Leslie changed, Paula flipped through the mail. Invoices from the feed store, the farm machinery company, one from the guardianship office. *Huh, what did they want again?* There was another, a stained letter. Frowning, she twisted and turned it in her hand. The postmark was from New Mexico. She tore open the envelope using a letter opener.

At first, she didn't understand what she was reading. Shocked, she dropped onto the next best chair. She had no chance to put on a poker face. Great!

Leslie saw that something was wrong and rushed over to her.

"What's the matter? Bad news?" Paula glanced at the letter in her hand. "Honestly, I don't know." She hesitated. Was it right to confront Leslie about it? She didn't really have a choice.

Leslie already wanted to take matters into her own hands and reached for the letter. Just in time, Paula got it out of reach by pulling it away. "The letter is from your biological parents."

Leslie looked at her uncomprehendingly. "From my birth parents?" she echoed. "But how is that possible?"

Paula squirmed uncomfortably. "Apparently they saw the article in the *Daily News,* recognized you since you're the spitting image of your mother, and put one and one together. It seems..."

"That stupid article!" Leslie burst out. "I knew it would ruin everything from the start!" Incensed, she rushed away.

Paula sighed. Her stomach tightened in panic as she got up to look out the window and didn't see Leslie anywhere. Was she going to run away again? Should she go after her?

Torn, she stood motionless in the kitchen for seconds. She dropped back into the chair. She would just trust her now and give her a little time to calm down. If she did run away, she would call Tyler and Ranger for help again. In the meantime, she was going to contemplate the strange letter.

Dear Jane,

You must be wondering to hear from us. We are your parents. You are the spitting image of your mother. When we discovered you in the newspaper, we were thrilled. Our own parents forced us to give you up for adoption. We have been looking for you all our lives. Finally, we have found you. Of course, you will live with us from now on.

Love, Mom and Dad

Jane. What kind of name was that, anyway? About as fanciful as Smith or Brown. No address. Just a cell phone number. Nice, sob story. And it stank to high heaven. Shaking her head, Paula lowered the letter.

It looked like she was going to make a few phone calls before she went looking for Leslie.

Paula stepped into the stable where the saddled horses were still waiting patiently.

"You're two magnificent horses," she praised them and slipped them each an apple. "We'll be off in a minute." They didn't understand the words, but they knew the intent and feelings behind the statement.

Leslie needed the healing effect of a ride more than ever. Paula found her outside in the meadow. She was lying on Dolly's bare back and staring up at the blue sky. Single fleecy clouds adorned the sky. Paula smiled and was relieved. Smart kid.

There was nothing like a dose of horse therapy. She plopped down on the grass next to Dolly and lay on her back as well. While she waited for Leslie to acknowledge her presence, she tried to ignore thoughts of ants and other six-legged meadow dwellers that were surely happily seeking refuge in her tee-shirt.

At last Leslie said, "It's just unfair. We finally got through this stupid court stuff and get official permission for me to live here, and now this." She turned her head to Paula. "Can't I be happy for once?"

Her voice sounded very young, and she looked very vulnerable.

"I'll go through hell to keep you. You belong here. To me and the animals. To this farm and to my heart," Paula said.

"That's amazing to hear," Leslie said. "You know I feel the same."

"Yes, of course you may. And before we go any further, I want to tell you how glad I am to find you here with Dolly safe and inside the pasture fence. For a moment I was worried that you might run away again. As understandable as that would be after such news, I'm very glad you stayed."

Embarrassed, Leslie averted her eyes. That was exactly what had been going through her mind as she had stormed out of the house. In her mind, she had almost been in the next state when she remembered she would scare Paula. She'd fled to Dolly and confided in her. She felt better, as she always did when she had poured out her heart to the little pony with the big personality. But the letter from these unknown people who claimed to be her parents frightened her.

"I won't run away again, I promise," she said. "But this letter...I don't want to leave here, Paula. I want to stay with you. We have it nice together, don't we?" Her brown eyes looked enormous in the youthful face, troubled with worry.

Paula put her hand on Leslie's, which was resting on Dolly's fur. "I will do everything in my power to make it happen." She paused for a moment. Before she continued, there was something she needed to know, and she shied away from the possible answers. "Don't you want to know who your birth parents are? I mean, that would be a perfectly legitimate desire, to want to know them."

"Honestly?"

Paula nodded. "There's no other way, is there?"

"I've managed without them for the last thirteen years. I'll get along without for another thirteen, too. Maybe when I grow up, I will want to know more about her. But now I have enough to do just living my life. They've taken their time finding me for the last thirteen years. Then they can wait until I'm ready."

Once again, Paula was surprised by the depth of the little girl's thoughts. She really didn't let herself be fooled. When she wasn't plagued by self-doubt, she saw the world around her with a startling clarity for her age. She wished she could give Leslie back some of that childlike innocence. But certain things were irreversible.

Her own heart was lifted when she heard Leslie's testimony. In that case, she could also tell her what she had found out.

"It's that the people who wrote this letter and claimed you were their child actually want you to come and live with them."

Leslie peered over at her through Dolly's mane. "Like it would be that easy."

Paula laughed. "That's exactly what I thought when I read that. So I got on the phone and called different people."

"Who?"

"Our social worker who is handling our case. I wanted to know what legal claim these people have on you."

"So?"

"None at all. She meant that if they gave you up for adoption, then they have no right to see you or know where you are. They gave up all rights regarding you. That they know where you are now is an unfortunate coincidence. But since we don't live in the anonymous big city, but in Independence, where everybody knows by ten when Roo's scratched behind his ear at nine, I'm not too worried about that."

Leslie didn't look very reassured, so Paula continued. "The sheriff's office, that is Jake, I informed next. They know about it and are keeping their eyes open."

"Is there any way to find out who these people are? I find it very awkward that some strangers know what I look like while I have no idea who they are. We don't even know their names, after all. I mean, they could approach me in the supermarket and I would assume they were some tourists." She shuddered.

Paula nodded. "That's right. That's also why I called Cole next. Because the people at Social Services can't, or won't, tell us the names of your birth parents. Apparently, you have to be of legal age to request disclosure."

"And Cole is doing what now?"

"Because of his work with the FBI, he has other channels available to him. My brother is very creative when it comes to finding answers." A tactful paraphrase of his talents as a hacker. But Leslie didn't need to know that.

"So, now the sheriff, his deputies, and an FBI agent know." Leslie grinned. "Nothing can happen to me."

Paula, glad that Leslie could already joke about it again, nodded affirmatively. "Not to mention Betty, my shotgun. That's still there, too. Shall we go riding now, finally? The horses have been waiting for quite a while."

"Oh, yes," Leslie said and slid down from Dolly.

They bridled the horses and led them toward the farm.

Leslie would ride Rufus, Paula's old and very reliable horse, while she herself rode Lucky. A little wind had sprung up, driving through the horses' manes and tails and ruffling them.

Paula cast a searching glance at the sky. She didn't want to end up in a storm. In theory, she could check the weather app on her smartphone, but she had left it in the house. No matter. Her own senses never fooled her. She was sure the thunderstorm would be a while in coming. Still, she postponed the trip to the creek until another time and planned the shorter route. A repeat of Leslie's rescue operation in the pouring rain was the last thing she needed.

She glanced at her protégé. The regular riding lessons she had taken on Rufus were doing well, she thought. Leslie sat supplely in the saddle and held the reins with a soft hand.

"You up for a little more speed?"

Leslie's eyes lit up.

Paula laughed. "I'll take that as a yes. Now then, let's gallop. But don't let Rufus get too fast. My youngster here doesn't really need to learn about racing today."

She nodded.

"Well then, let's go."

With a whoop, Leslie gave Rufus the canter aids and strode off.

CHAPTER TWENTY

Paula sat on Rufus at the gate of one of her pastures, cell phone pressed close to her ear. Unfortunately, there was a strong, icy wind, so she had trouble hearing Cole. He had just called. There was news about Leslie's birth parents. "What did you say?"

"I just said you would do well not to have any contact with these people," Cole said.

"And why is that?" she asked.

"They live in a run-down trailer, they're unemployed, they drink too much, they get put in the drunk tank for a night or have to give up their driver's license once in a while because of it," Cole said.

"How nice." Sarcasm dripped from Paula's every word. Even though she was selfishly glad the perfect family wasn't waiting somewhere for Leslie, she still would have liked it if the parents had been at least been somewhat normal. "Good to know, though. Thanks. I'll try to break the news to Leslie as diplomatically as possible."

"Why don't you let me take over?" he asked. "Then it's not on you, as her surrogate mother, bad-mouthing her birth mother. Might be better."

"*HM.* That's right. When are you going to be home again?"

"I don't know. But I can have the conversation with Leslie via video chat tonight, too."

"Oh. I didn't know you guys were in touch?" she asked.

"Sure. What did you think? I'm just not going to get back to her for months?"

She said, "Maybe." That's exactly what Paula had thought. "After all, I only hear from you every few weeks."

"That's different. You're already grown up, and she's not."

"Makes sense." Paula turned a little so the wind wouldn't whistle directly into her cell phone. "Well then, see you tonight."

She didn't wait for his answer. In the meantime, the wind had grown into a real storm. Time to go home. She turned her horse around and let it drop into a steady canter. While Rufus took her to the ranch, her mind kept wandering back to the letter. If these were indeed the kind of people Cole had described, it could really mean only one thing: They were not concerned with Leslie. Probably they had seen the article and recognized an opportunity to profit from the story. But that also meant that the letter had almost certainly not been the last they would hear from them. It was time to clean and load Betty.

She would be right. When Leslie arrived home from school that afternoon with the mail under her arm, there was a new letter. She was careful to slip it under a boring letter from the bank. She would let Paula know later. But not until after she had digested the contents and had an appropriate strategy in place.

"I hear you have a date with Nate tonight?"

"Do I?" asked Paula absently as she looked through the rest of the letters.

"Yes. Your date. With Nate." Leslie chuckled. "That even rhymes."

"It can't be. That's not until the end of July."

"Today is the twenty-eighth," she informed her.

In disbelief, Paula glanced at the weather station, which displayed air pressure, time, and date besides the weather. "It is. Shoot. And what do I do now? I have nothing decent to wear, and I don't have anyone to babysit you. The horses aren't made yet, either."

"Take a deep breath," Leslie said, holding back a grin.

"You think that's funny too, huh?"

"Sure. Now go take a shower. I'll make you some tea and muck out with the horses afterward. Nate will bring Shauna by when he picks you up. So I'm not alone. I've got your emergency number, and you can settle the wardrobe question with Jaz on the phone," Leslie said.

Paula stopped resisting the inevitable date and followed Leslie's instructions to the letter.

Coming down the stairs in her best and tightest jeans, Sunday boots, and a flowy black top, Leslie sat in front of the TV.

"Before I forget, Cole will call tonight via video chat. If you're too tired, just text him and you can do it tomorrow."

"Okay," Leslie said.

Paula went outside to wait.

The wind was still howling hard, but there was no longer a thunderstorm forecast. Apparently, it had passed by the Rockies farther east in the Denver Plateau. She hoped Nate would hurry. The air was noticeably cooler than it had been a few days ago. In her fancy but thin jacket, she would freeze to death if she didn't get to the warm soon. She sighed. She just wasn't cut out for this kind of girly stuff, even if she had to admit that finding the perfect outfit in Leslie's company had been fun. Leslie's cheerfulness and joyful expression had put her in a peaceful mood. She should enjoy the evening in Nate's company and not worry so much for once. And who knows? Maybe after a good meal and a glass of wine, he wouldn't be so ornery. She started whistling as she watched the sun set behind the Rockies, bathing the mountain peaks in a golden light.

Finally, Nate arrived. Shauna jumped out of the car and dashed into the house. Paula stood there open-mouthed, marveling at the classic car. A cherry red Mustang convertible, vintage 1978, if she wasn't mistaken.

"Do you like it?" he asked.

"Like it? Love it!." She stroked the shiny paint and soft leather of the seats almost reverently. "Is this yours?"

Nate grinned boyishly. "Old muscle cars are a weakness of mine."

"It's beautiful!"

He cleared his throat. "Like you. Come. The two girls are getting organized without us. We're going to dinner." He held the driver's door open for her.

Astonished, she looked at him. "I get to drive?"

"Sure thing. You wouldn't have left me alone until I gave you the keys, anyway."

She bit her lower lip lightly and looked at him from the side. "True. But it would have been worth a lot to me, too."

"Indeed. What, exactly?"

She laughed. "Let's put it this way, I can be very creative in achieving a goal." Teasingly, she winked at him and left him to interpret her statement.

His boyish grin returned.

She said, "Well, are you coming now?"

"Yeah, yeah," he muttered.

"Where do you want to go?"

"I thought we'd drive over to Silver Lodge. It's a little longer drive, but they have the best steaks, as I'm sure you know..."

She laughed. Of course she knew that. After all, she was their supplier of beef.

"And you can make some turns."

"Good idea."

She started the engine, delighted in the low rumble, and turned the car around.

The Silver Lodge was a newer place that had opened two or three years ago. In the financial crisis, the then-owner had lost his huge log cabin. Jeff and Jarvis, the current owners, had stepped in and made their dream of a Michelin-starred restaurant a reality. Only organic ingredients went into their cooking, and they took great care to ensure that the animals from which the meat came had had a good life and were not pumped full of drugs and hormones. Both of these were true of Paula's cattle. She sold virtually all of the meat in the local area.

It hadn't taken long for the two of them to show up at her door. And they could really cook. They also had a good relationship with their service staff and paid reasonable wages, so there was always a pleasant atmosphere in the restaurant and the service was impeccable.

Such amazing points meant the Silver Lodge charged high prices. Completely understandable, but therefore mostly out of Paula's budget. All the more reason she was looking forward to eating there.

"Well, that was a fast drive!" she said to Nate as they arrived. "Over too soon."

"Don't be sad. You're welcome to go drive if you want. I've been meaning to try the wine here for a while, anyway."

"You got it. Drink all the wine you want, and I'll drive us both home."

They were given a nice table by the window with a view of the whole valley. "Do you come here often?" Paula asked.

"Mostly just as a vet. Jeff and Jarvis have two Labrador retrievers. Chocolate brown, lovable monsters that eat anything they find."

Paula laughed. "Typical Labrador."

"Exactly. I've dealt with them several times. One time it was really close. The one, Jefferson's his name, had gotten into all the chocolate for dessert. Fortunately, they caught it in time. When he got over it, they were so happy they invited me over for dinner. I've been a fan of the place ever since."

"You really can't beat the food here," Paula said. "Combined with the amazing view, it's almost impossible to top."

Nate reached across the table and brushed a strand of hair from her face.

Spellbound and unable to move, she held still. As always, when Nate touched her, her skin tingled as if electrified, sending shivers all through her.

"Well, with such a beautiful date as you, the place wins again."

Paula lowered her eyes and felt her cheeks grow hot. She snorted, quite unamused, to cover her embarrassment. Something was definitely wrong with her if she was more embarrassed to blush than to snort. Maybe there was some kind of basic course for girls on YouTube? She would find out right away when she got home.

He raised his glass in a toast. "To the successful trial of Leslie."

Relieved he'd changed the subject, she returned the gesture. "I was so proud of her. Ranger was wonderful, too."

"He's something special."

"Yes," Paula said. "That's him."

"So everything's going well with Leslie now? No more runaway attempts?"

"No. Thank goodness, no. Although, a few days ago, it was close."

"What happened?"

"It's a long story."

Nate smiled at her. "I've got time. How about you?"

Paula smirked. "All right."

During the appetizer, a delicious curry soup with coconut milk, she told him what went down. He was glad it all worked out, of course.

"Cole's news has me concerned. Putting it together piece by piece like this, the logical conclusion is that the letter writers want something from us. Probably money. Just today a new letter came in which they rather vehemently insisted on their right to take Leslie. Which of course is not legally tenable at all. I checked with my sources. They seem to think I don't know and are trying to pressure me. But I won't be blackmailed."

"Absolutely not. You're far from a shrinking violet. They have no idea who they're messing with. Is there anything Jake can do about it?"

Paula shrugged. "You know how it is. Until a crime is committed, the police's hands are tied. I just hope now their resources are exhausted with this action." She couldn't shake the ominous feeling, though, that the bio-parents weren't giving up so easily.

After another two hours flew by and they finished a sinfully delicious chocolate mousse, they stepped out into the cool night air. Nate put his hand on the small of her back. Paula leaned against him and put her head back. Above stretched the endless starry sky.

She turned her head a little and kissed him.

Nate kissed her back.

It wasn't until Jarvis, who had stepped out onto the porch for a smoke break, cleared his throat behind them that they let go of each other. "We also have some guest rooms," he noted with a grin.

Paula thought the idea was excellent. Before she could say so, however, Nate shook his head. "Sounds tempting. I hate to be the bad guy, but unfortunately, we both have to get home."

Did they have to? Paula wondered, still a little befuddled by the kiss.

"Our daughters are waiting for us. "

Jarvis nodded in understanding. "Some other time then, maybe."

"Gladly."

Paula winced as her guilty conscience took over. She had forgotten her child. She squinted toward Nate. Had he noticed? So what if he had? After all, Leslie was already thirteen, she had Shauna with her, and the two dogs were looking after her. She worked herself up about it and wondered if Nate was equally nervous. He hadn't spoken up.

On the contrary. He was still talking casually with Jarvis. Only his arm still rested around her shoulder.

Take a deep breath, she ordered herself. At some point, she knew she'd get the hang of this parenting thing and not fall into self-doubt constantly. "All right," she said. "You're right. Let's take off. Now I'm getting nervous."

"Right," he said and they left immediately. "Just let me use the bathroom on the way out."

When Paula sat down in the car, she had time to inspect the interior—to study the dashboard and marvel at the special features—while she waited for Nate. He wasn't too long to join her.

He opened the passenger door. "Sorry, that took longer than I planned. Jarvis can be quite the gossip sometimes." The car's suspension bobbed a little as Nate sat his strong, muscular body in the passenger seat.

"No problem. I've been having the best time exploring your car in the meantime."

"First date and you've already replaced me. With my car to boot." Feigning sadness, he shook his head. "No loyalty at all!"

Paula could hardly contain her laughter. "Say, isn't your car a girl?"

"Sure. It is for me. But I suppose you women see it differently."

She smirked. "You would think so. Maybe it depends on the car, too. But mine all have women's names. Women are just more reliable. And reliability is about the only thing I need from a car. For everything else, I have..." she looked at him, a calculating smile on her face, "...shall I now say *my vet?*"

At his horrified look, her patience wore thin.

He wrinkled his nose.

Her face flushed. "Listen. If you don't want to have anything more to do with me, that's fine. Just tell me before I have a sexual harassment lawsuit on my hands."

Next to her, Nate snorted. "No! That's not it," he laughed at her anger. "I just see myself a little bit more than 'your vet,' is all."

"Well, what else was I supposed to say?" she snapped, irritated. "That you've committed yourself to abstinence overnight? Not wanting sex before marriage and succumbing to my feminine charms? I thought saying 'my vet' was a safe bet. Didn't want to scare you off."

Nate ran his hand through his too-long hair. He turned. "Listen. The problem, if we have one at all, is more that we get along so well. In all areas. And honestly, that's very, very rare, in my opinion, to meet someone who fits you so well. So, I'd like to get that right. Like today. With our first date. If I have my way, I'll have the next few years to enjoy your incredibly beautiful body. Call this thing between us whatever you want. I don't care."

With the last words, he kissed her.

Unconsciously, she ran the tip of her tongue inside his mouth. "And what if I don't want to call it anything?" she asked.

"Then don't," he said. "So long as we're having fun."

"I like fun," she said.

They kissed some more, then stopped.

Driving home, they held hands almost the whole ride, the radio blaring.

The next day, Paula would talk to Jaz and her sister. It couldn't go on so carefree, but she desperately needed female perspectives. What Nate said about keeping it fun sounded very romantic at first, however, she couldn't help feeling his approach wasn't giving the commitment she deserved. *Wow. Do I want a commitment from him and not just fun? Putting myself at risk here. I could get hurt really bad if I let him into my heart.* She smiled listening to his almost-on-key singing, and her heart melted. It was the most fun she'd had in ages.

If I'm going to risk everything, then I darn well should have fun doing it, shouldn't I?

CHAPTER TWENTY-ONE

"Did someone call?" The man let the metal screen door slam shut behind him. His shuffling footsteps made a scraping sound on the linoleum-covered floor.

The woman did not respond to his question and continued to stare at the TV. Some reality show was on. If someone had asked her what she was watching, she would not have been able to answer. The show didn't really interest her. It was simply a means to an end to make the hours of the day go by faster.

"Are you even listening to me?" the man asked angrily, standing in her field of vision so she was forced to look at him.

"No!" she said, stubbing out her cigarette in the overflowing ashtray beside her on an upturned plastic bucket. "You know why? Because you ask the same thing every day. Like a nagging housewife. These people aren't going to call. When are you going to get that through your thick head? They don't care about people like us. That was another one of your drunken ideas. Now get out of my face!" She waved the remote frantically.

The man took a step toward her; he didn't have to go far in the cramped living room.

He punched her right in the face.

"Ow!" she held her cheek. "What was that for? Can't take the truth, can you?" she sneered.

Out of his mind with rage, he grabbed her hair and pulled it until her head was on the back of her neck. Fear showed in her eyes, even though she still grinned. In a sick way, he liked her fighting spirit, even if he had to keep reminding her who the boss of the house was. "Then we'll just have to make sure they take us seriously," he growled. "Got it?"

Reluctantly, she nodded.

To be sure, he jerked again at her hair, which he still had a firm grip on. She cried out. He let go of her and took a step back.

The woman glared at him. All this trouble because of a child she had never wanted. She felt hatred for the girl. She would make the little girl pay if she ever got her hands on her, she swore.

The man got himself a beer and emptied it in one gulp. He squeezed the empty can and carelessly dropped it on the floor. No one cared. His wife watched him, her eyes narrowed calculatingly to narrow slits. Someday she would get back at him. If they managed to actually make money out of the situation with the brat, she'd see to it that he didn't see a dime. In the meantime, she'd listen to whether or not his new plan was worth anything.

"Now listen carefully," he said. "Here's what we're going to do."

Two days after her date with Nate, Paula took a walk over to the McArthy Ranch with her two dogs in tow.

She hadn't gotten around to talking to Jaz, let alone organizing a girls' night out. Every time she tried to pick up the phone, something got in the way. Leslie's homework, a dripping oil line on her tractor, a cow that had gotten very unhappily caught in the fence—the list was endless. Not endless enough for her to have managed to put Nate and his extremely annoying nonchalant behavior out of her mind, though. *He's so yesterday,* she fussed and snorted. She ignored the fact that she had intended to do exactly what he was accusing her of: Go to bed with him a few times until the mutual attraction wore off, then forget him, and continue with her normal, relaxed life.

Determined to get some female advice, she pushed Leslie out the door toward the school bus five minutes early, put on her hat, and headed for Jaz's. Her dogs had been a little confused about the early time of their outing, but happily went along, noses close to the ground, tracking the exciting smells of the previous night.

Jaz was lying on the wooden deck attached to the back of the house, contorting herself in a yoga position. Paula wasn't sure if the human body was meant to assume such a posture. Hers certainly wasn't. She was far too tall and far too stiff for that. How Jaz managed to do that despite her steadily advancing pregnancy was a mystery. Not wanting to be drawn into a spontaneous yoga session, she kept a safe distance and watched.

Jaz assured her that it was all a matter of practice that improved body awareness, which could also affect her riding. Not even that last argument could convince Paula to do yoga regularly.

With Jaz as the newly minted owner of Independence's only yoga studio, she hadn't been able to avoid trying it out a few times. So she knew what she was talking about. Granted, Jaz as a yoga instructor probably did too, but best friend or not, they just saw certain things differently. Which was okay. Rambo, Jaz's black king poodle, came out of the house through his doggie door and greeted Barns and Roo exuberantly. Barns turned away, bored. At least Roo could be persuaded to play a few rounds of chase around the house.

Jaz elegantly unfolded and stretched, then sat up to greet Paula. "Good morning. What brings you here at the crack of dawn?"

"Good morning, too. I need your advice."

Jaz grinned. "Oh yeah. This wouldn't happen to have anything to do with you having dinner with Nate the day before yesterday?"

Paula let herself slide along the wall of the house onto the floor and buried her face in her hands. "Why am I not surprised that you already know about it again?"

"First, because this is Independence," Jaz explained, completely redundantly, "and second, because the Diner Sisters have recently discovered the convenience of the Internet."

Paula blinked out from between her fingers. "The Internet?"

"Yes. Specifically, Facebook."

"No kidding!"

"Oh yes. Apparently Aileen, their niece, gave them a tutorial."

"Is she out of her mind?"

Jaz laughed. "Apparently so, and she didn't realize they were trading information of all kinds."

"And now it's too late."

"I guess you could say that. But now to you. I want details." Expectantly, she leaned forward and rubbed her hands together.

Paula made an attempt to put off the inevitable conversation for a bit. "Can I at least get a cup of coffee with that?"

"I can offer you tea."

Jaz swore by the healing effects of her various teas and didn't drink coffee herself. Paula frowned and fleetingly wondered how it had come about that her best friend was, of all people, a vegetarian who didn't drink coffee.

Seven cups of tea later, Jaz knew everything that had happened between her and Nate in the last few weeks. Lost in thought, she ran her index finger along the edge of her empty cup.

"*HMM*," Jaz said. "I don't really know what to say. Granted, I think he's getting a bit carried away, too. On the other hand, maybe it's not a bad idea for you guys to take it slow. After all, you both have kids to consider."

"I'm not saying he should move in with me. But what Leslie or even Shauna should have to do with my love life is just not clear. I'm not blind or dead just because Leslie lives with me now. It's not like I tried to seduce him in the middle of the living room."

Jaz laughed out loud. "For heaven's sake, girl. I'll never get rid of that picture in my life."

"Oh. But it's true."

Jaz nodded in agreement. "I'd say you just need to up the ante and show him what he's missing."

"And how am I supposed to do that, please?"

"I can think of a few things right off the bat. Come with me. The first thing you need is some new things to wear."

Paula looked down. "What's wrong with my clothes?"

"You're perfect. Only, it's easier to ignore how sexy you are in a shirt, jeans, and boots. And we're changing that now."

Paula doubted it could be done. After all, she couldn't make the stable in a miniskirt and high heels. Besides, she didn't believe that Jaz, who was almost half a head shorter and, above all, much curvier than she, had anything in her wardrobe that would fit her.

Half an hour and much laughter later, she realized she was wrong. Jaz had an inexhaustible supply of comfortable but very form-fitting tops made of stretchy cottons. She could even wear an open shirt over it and take it off on favorable occasions, allowing Nate to enjoy her beautiful back or cleavage, depending on the model. She had to admit she liked the style. It could easily be transformed from serious to sexy and was quite comfortable to boot. Why she hadn't thought of it earlier wasn't clear but she had a best friend for that.

Jaz put away her cell phone. "I've got everything organized. Toby is happy to play your breakfast date at the diner for the next few days. Just as long as the bill is on you."

"How typical." Paula laughed and shook her head. "Toby, of all people. When everyone knows he and I are just good friends and have been since first grade."

"Only Nate doesn't know. At least that's my guess. He's not from around here, after all. I doubt Dr. Grant gave him an introduction to the dynamics of all our residents when he handed over the practice, either."

"Right." After removing all possible obstacles from her mind, she suddenly saw the potential in Jaz's idea. "You're great at scheming. I'll be careful never to get on your bad side."

"I'm sure that's a wise decision." Jaz smiled smugly and a little nastily. A stark contrast to her otherwise even-tempered, sunny disposition.

"Nate won't know what hit him!"

"That's the spirit!"

"I have to admit that I underestimated you. I didn't think you were that sneaky."

"That's a mistake most people make. Only once, though." Jaz winked at her mischievously.

Leslie looked at her watch. Shauna and she wanted to wait for the bus together but she was too late. After throwing a dripping wet sponge at a boy in class and accidentally cold-cocking a teacher, she'd been sent to the principal's office and given detention. Presumably, the buses were gone anyway. Bummer. That meant another walk through the school and back to the secretary's office so she could call Paula to ask her to pick them up. *Today, of all days, when Lucky's owner was finally going to come by.*

The woman had never done that since they started training six months ago. Paula was very curious to see if she would be satisfied with the horse's progress. In any case, today was the worst possible day to need a ride. What if she called someone else from the Carter family? She quickly dismissed that thought. She felt more and more like an actual part of the family, but she still felt too intimidated to make such a call.

She decided to walk. It was only about four miles. It took her about ninety minutes. Paula would be busy with Lucky for the next few hours. If she was lucky, she wouldn't even notice she was late. She would probably assume she was with Shauna. Her guilty conscience kicked in as she thought about how she had taken advantage of Paula's preoccupation last time.

On the other side of the school, the man and woman sat inside their old, battered van. It had seen better days. In many spots, the white paint had peeled off and showed rust.

The man and woman couldn't believe their luck that their target was walking down the street right in front of them. The man snatched the binoculars from the woman's hand and confirmed it was her.

"Go after her. A chance like this is once in a lifetime," he said, handing her the binoculars so he could put the van in drive and roll forward.

"You want me to just drag her into the car?" the woman said.

"No. She'll get in voluntarily. Just tell her some believable story that gets to the heart."

The woman rolled her eyes, but said nothing more. Slowly they approached the girl.

"Drive slowly!" she hissed, pushing open the sliding side door in the back of the van. It would be easier to subdue the child there and pull her inside.

Leslie put one foot in front of the other, lost in thought. She thought about how she could teach Dolly to sit down. Most of the books she had found in the school library recommended practicing lying down first. Dolly was already doing that very reliably on command. It was a matter of breaking down everything into individual steps. Unlike cows, horses always put their front legs up first and only then their hind legs. For a brief moment, it looked like they were sitting. Dolly, of course, did so just like all the other horses. Only with her, it was more a single, fluid movement. She was thinking about how to teach her to pause for breath between her front and hind legs.

She was so preoccupied with her problem that only at the last moment did she notice a van had caught up to her.

She took a step to the side, expecting it to pass.

Instead, the van stopped and the sliding door opened. Surprised, she took a step back. An incredibly fat woman with greasy hair, strands of which were coming loose from a careless ponytail, leaned out of the van. She couldn't get a good look at the person behind the wheel. She suspected it was a man.

"Honey, do you need a ride?" the woman asked.

Puzzled, Leslie paused. "A ride?" She took a step closer. "Where are you going?"

"Wherever you want." When the woman saw Leslie frown in confusion, she added, "A young girl like you shouldn't be walking alone. There's a lot of creeps out here."

Instinctively, Leslie took a step back. The woman's words made sense. But they didn't match the lurking expression in her eyes. Besides, she couldn't remember having seen this car or even the people before. Although, even if Independence was only a small town, she could hardly claim to know all its inhabitants.

Nate drove toward home. He was tired. He hadn't slept well in days since his wonderful date with Paula. He was under the impression it had gone great. Until the end. He believed she'd share his idea about where their relationship was headed. But apparently, he was wrong.

For the past two days, she had been seen at the diner having breakfast with Toby, one of the deputies. *What she sees in him is beyond me. Has to be the uniform.* And every time he saw her, like earlier that afternoon when she had picked up dewormers for her dogs, she looked better. He couldn't even say for sure what it was. His mind drifted to her well-toned upper arms and the outline of her breasts in the skin-tight top she wore under her shirt.

He hadn't realized why he insisted on taking it slow. He would have liked to drag her into the empty treatment room and...

Nate stumbled when he spotted a white, rickety van farther ahead on the street. A girl stood next to it. Was that Leslie? Why was Leslie on the road?

He slowed and glanced at the license plate. New Mexico. A warning light flashed in his head. Hadn't Paula told him that the letter from Leslie's supposed parents had come from New Mexico?

By then, he had almost caught up to the van when two things happened simultaneously. Leslie took a step back so he could clearly see her expression. She looked as if she was not at all comfortable. At the same time, a woman leaned out of the van and tried to reach for the girl.

Nate didn't think twice. He stepped on the gas of his truck and closed the distance between him and the van, violently pressing the horn.

Leslie, who had been paralyzed with fear, was startled and ran for safety. With one leap she turned and hurried back toward the school.

The driver's reaction echoed hers. With Nate's appearance, he stepped on the gas so hard that the woman was thrown back into the interior of the van. They fled.

Nate was tempted to give chase. But first? He had to take care of Leslie. Make sure she was okay.

He turned on the four-wheel drive and drove his truck into the meadow. Hoping Leslie would recognize his car, he honked twice.

Leslie was so panicked, however, that she didn't dare look over her shoulder. Doggedly, she ran on toward the school—toward safety.

Nate drove past her to the parking lot of the school. He assumed she'd recognize him and the truck. He called

Jake. "Someone in a van just tried to snatch Leslie!" he hollered.

"What?" Jake was incredulous. "Where is she? Is she safe? Where are you?"

"I've got eyes on her. She's heading right toward me. I'm in the parking lot at the high school. I'll make sure she's safe," Nate said.

"Where's this van?" Jake asked. "Description of the perps?"

"White, old beat-up van. New Mexico plates," Nate said. "A heavy woman in the back with long, greasy hair was leaning out. Didn't see the driver. They fled up toward the highway. I went after Leslie."

"That's all I need," Jake said. "I'll be at the school just as soon as possible."

Leslie recognized Nate's truck right away in the high school parking lot. She was very glad he had stopped. No telling what might have happened otherwise. Scared, she covered the last few meters to his truck. Somehow she always managed to get herself in hot water, she thought.

He jumped out and opened his arms. "Are you all right?" he asked.

Leslie, suddenly close to tears, nodded. "Yes. Was that you? Did you see what happened?"

"I did," he said, hugging her. "I called Jake. The cops are on it. You're safe."

"Oh, that's good," she said. "Can you take me home?"

"Sure," he said. "I've got you. We've got you. It'll all be okay."

Leslie hoped so.

At the same time, a completely different scene took place in the van. After the woman had struggled to pull herself up, she lunged at the man behind the wheel in a fury. "I almost got her. Almost! But you had to hit the gas just because some law-abiding citizen honked the horn. That was our money you just threw out the window, you idiot!"

The chance to escape her bleak life and her disgusting man seemed far away. Again. She wasn't good at fighting, but what she was good at was yelling. Even so? She swatted him.

He tried to keep the van on track while deflecting her blows. "Stop it! Come on!" She managed to give him some serious boxing hits.

Finally, he had enough and made the van swerve sharply right, then yank it right back onto the road. The sudden sideways movement threw the woman sideways into the passenger seat. Her head hit the windshield so hard, she was left dazed.

"Now look what you've done," she moaned.

"Shut the hell up, woman. At least now we know she's here. It would be ridiculous if we didn't catch her. And if she doesn't come with us voluntarily, we'll just have to use force. Seems like your maternal genes aren't convincing enough." He let out an ugly laugh.

Thus beaten, the woman sank deeper into the seat and held the aching side of her head. Anger filled her. Anger at the man. Anger at the girl who'd destroyed her life.

CHAPTER TWENTY-TWO

"Do you recognize the two people who approached you?"

Jake presented Leslie with a series of pictures. Leslie studied the pictures with the utmost concentration. She set the third aside and picked up the fourth copy when she recognized the woman she nodded. "That was her."

Jake gave Paula a meaningful look. "Are you sure about this?" he asked.

Irritated, Leslie looked up at him. "Of course I'm sure. The woman tried to drag me into her car just a few hours ago."

"And the man?"

"I'm not sure. I didn't really see him. She stood in the sliding door to the cargo area, after all. The area toward the front was open, but his face was in a shadow."

"No wonder," Paula grumbled. "With the size of that woman..."

"The woman *does* appear to be your birth mother," Jake explained.

Leslie shuddered inwardly as she thought about being related to such a frightening person. Hopefully, she would never become like her. She felt an icy chill.

Paula, who had seen how pale Leslie had suddenly become, grabbed her shoulders with both hands. She would definitely need to find a therapist for Leslie. What the little girl had endured couldn't be healthy. "Hey, genes aren't everything."

Leslie gave her a look that made it clear she didn't believe a word she said.

"Yes, it's true," Paula said. "Take horses, for example. In breeding, the rule is that the influence of the stallion on the foal is no more than forty percent. The remaining sixty comes from the mother."

Jake rolled his eyes. "Of course, she brings horses into this."

"And why is that?" Leslie asked.

"As the foal grows up with the mare and spends the imprinting period by her side, it will exhibit more and more of its momma's traits. So, since you haven't spent any significant time in the company of your mother, you're on the safe side."

"Sure. Because my impressionable phase is teeming with shining examples," Leslie returned somberly.

Paula winced, but didn't admit defeat.

"According to your stories, the first two foster homes weren't so bad. Otherwise, you wouldn't be the wonderful person you are today." Leslie nodded. "Not to mention the fact that we humans have it in our power to give our lives a new direction. Every day you can choose anew who you want to be."

"And the man? Is he my father?" She looked at the man's hulking face and hoped that wasn't the case.

"That's highly unlikely," Jake said. "Assuming our information is correct, the two did know each other at the time, but the time frame doesn't add up."

"Okay." Leslie's heart was lifted. After all. "So what happens next?"

"I was about to get to that. Unfortunately, we didn't manage to find them. Let's hope they took the quickest route and won't be back."

"And if they do?" Paula asked.

"In case they show up again, I am instituting a very rigid security protocol. No more spontaneous walks alone, especially on the street."

"I get it."

"What were you thinking, anyway? Walking home? Anything can happen to you there," Paula said.

Leslie winced. "I wouldn't have gone all the way along the road. At Shaffer's Crossing, I would have taken the shortcut through the woods and across the pastures."

"Oh, that makes everything better." Paula's voice dripped with sarcasm. "What if you sprained your ankle? Lying somewhere and no one knows where?"

"So, I'm not allowed to do anything on my own?" hissed Leslie back. "Great. You might as well lock me up then!"

"Of course not," Paula said, a little more calmly. "But I'd like to know where you are, what you're doing. So I know where to start looking when you don't come home. It's quite possible that I would have told you myself today to come home on foot. More likely, though, I would have picked you up."

Leslie sniffled. "That's not what I was trying to do. I knew you had a date with Lucky's owner."

"First of all, you're always more important than one of my horses, Leslie."

"And that's saying something," grumbled Jake.

"Second, I could have called someone." She raised her eyes to Nate, who was waiting patiently, leaning against the wall. "Nate, for example. I'm sure he would have picked you up."

Embarrassed, Leslie stepped from one foot to the other.

"That's a sensible idea with the current situation," Jake intervened. "No going it alone until we're sure the danger has passed. My guess is they were hoping to extort money from Paula. When there was no response from you guys to the letters, I guess they decided to turn up the heat."

Surprised, the two turned to him. "But why?"

Nate pushed himself off the wall and joined them. Paula felt his warmth as he stood next to her. All her senses came to life. If this subtle seduction tactic didn't finally take effect, she would soon be making kidnapping plans of her own, she thought.

Without noticing what was going on in Paula's mind, Nate answered. "It's very simple. In the article, your desire to keep Leslie with you came out very clearly. So they figured that would probably be worth something to you. After you didn't try to make contact the first time to meet the lost birth parents, nor did you do anything to avoid any further contact, they had to come up with something else."

Paula was still confused. "What would they have gotten out of it? Neither one nor the other makes sense to me."

"The former might have had the effect of you giving them money out of pity or obligation. In the second, I think they were speculating on your fear of losing Leslie."

"That I would pay hush money, so to speak, to keep them from going to the authorities."

"It wouldn't do them any good."

"But does Paula know that? If they're extrapolating from themselves to others, they probably assumed she didn't know."

Jake nodded. "Nate summed it up pretty well. In principle, their motivations don't matter either. After today, it's pretty clear they've decided to turn to more extreme measures. So, no more solo excursions for now, got it?"

Paula gave Leslie a stern look. The same look she gave the dogs when they absolutely had to obey. Suitably intimidated, Leslie nodded meekly.

Satisfied that Leslie and Paula, too, had grasped the gravity of the situation, Jake said, "All right, then. If that's everything for now, I need to get on this. See you later. Thanks for your time."

"Of course," Paula said.

"Thanks," Leslie said and made to follow out the door behind him.

Paula caught her by the hood. "Stay right there, young lady. I guess we'll have to work on your short-term memory a little more."

"I just wanted to see Mrs. Miners."

Polly Miners was a former police officer who had actually retired. Since she hadn't been able to stand being at home with her husband without going up the walls, she had knocked on Jake's door again shortly after her retirement and suggested that she come out of retirement and take care of the desk work that was usually chronically left behind anyway. He had hired her on the spot.

Leslie knew her well and also knew that she always had cookies in her desk.

Nate laughed. "I'll leave you two alone now. See you around." He raised his hand.

Paula looked after him. Her hero. Or not hers. She sighed. Why did life have to be so complicated?

"Come on," she said to Leslie. "Let's go home."

Leslie jumped from the window sill where she had sat down when it was clear that she would have to wait. On her way out, she grabbed Paula's hand.

Surprised, Paula looked down at Leslie's lowered head. Someone seemed to have had a fright. All the better. Maybe she'd take the admonitions to heart sooner that way. She squeezed her hand lightly.

"All good?"

Leslie looked up at her shyly. "I think so. How about you?"

"Now that I have you safely with me again, yes."

Leslie smiled and averted her eyes in embarrassment. However, she returned the handshake and did not let go until they were at the car.

As soon as they got home, Paula went to the gun cabinet and pulled out Betty. The rifle was in tip-top shape, freshly cleaned and loaded. She put it next to the kitchen door. From a drawer of noisy odds and ends, she pulled out a red whistle. Then she called Leslie over. "Here's a whistle for you."

"And what am I supposed to do with it? Whistle for the dogs? They'll come without a whistle."

"If you get into an emergency, you can whistle. It's much louder than when you call out and can be heard better."

Leslie looked doubtfully at the plastic part. This thing was going to save her life? She glanced covetously at Betty. The shotgun seemed like a safer option.

Paula, who had seen where her gaze wandered, looked at her sternly.

"I take Betty out of the closet because I want to have her handy. The emphasis is on *me*. You don't touch that rifle. It is loaded and therefore a deadly weapon."

Leslie rolled her eyes. "I get it. I'm not playing cops and robbers with Betty." Reluctantly, she grabbed the whistle and hung it around her neck. "Can I go up now, do homework?"

"Yeah, you do that. I'll cook us something in the meantime."

"How did it go with Lucky?"

Paula was silent for a moment. Then she looked up and said, "The owner canceled at the last minute."

"So everything that had happened this afternoon didn't have to happen?" Leslie said. "You could have still come. Frustrating."

"Well, in the big picture? At least we know they are here and Jake's on it. So it worked out okay," Paula said gently, seeing the stress in Leslie's eyes. "Just try to call someone first next time, okay?"

"I'll try. I promise."

Paige stood in front of the mirror in her Denver hotel room and went through her mental checklist. High heels. Short skirt. Plunging neckline. Lots of makeup. Yep, it was all there. She grabbed her purse and walked purposefully to the elevator.

In fifteen minutes, she had a date with Peter. She planned to glamour him, get him drunk, and get the truth out of him. *Whatever it takes to do that.* She winced inwardly and shuddered. *Well. Maybe not exactly everything.*

When she arrived at the bar, which she had frequented regularly when she worked at the *Daily News*, Peter was already there.

His face lit up when he saw her, and she felt a twinge of guilt. His gaze fell on her breasts just a second later and seemed to be stuck there.

"You look amazing, as always," he said.

She was getting irritated, as she always did around him. She had already known why she had always given him a wide berth in the past. *Awful pervert. Could probably have had a case of sexual harassment against this guy back in the day. Such a creeper.* Keeping in mind the importance of what she was about to do, she swallowed her anger and tried for a pleasant tone.

"Peter. Glad to see you, too. Happy this worked out."

"Me, too," he said to her breasts. His eyes still hadn't lifted. "I knew it was only a matter of time before you softened up."

He stroked his full hair. His pride and joy, it seemed.

"Let's order something to drink. Then we can talk."

"Sure thing. Gin and tonic?" His spell was broken and he looked up. He waved a waiter over. As he was about to place the order, Paige interrupted him.

"We can have gin and tonic later. I'm in the mood for a couple of tequila shots right now." She forced herself to look deep into his eyes. Not so easy when the other person's eyes were glued down. Again. *He's shameless. And he thinks he's actually getting some tonight. Unreal.*

Only when the waitress cleared her throat did he tear his gaze from her breasts and nod. "Tequila. Sure. Good, too. Wow, you don't leave anything burning, do you?"

Paige forced herself to smile.

After the first round, he asked, "What were you toasting?"

Paige giggled, playing along. "Well, here's to us, of course. And to other things."

"To other things, *here-here*!" He smiled.

After three more rounds, Paige noticed Peter no longer pretended to be interested in any part of her anatomy other than her cleavage. Twice she even had to playfully shoo away his wandering hands.

The second thing she noticed, alcohol really did make everything better. In fact, she no longer found the whole situation annoying, but highly amusing. However, she thought it'd be best to replace her next shots with water. Fortunately, Peter had opted for the cheapest, colorless tequila, so that wouldn't be noticeable.

The third thing she noticed, Peter didn't seem to have a huge alcohol tolerance like most journalists. This, of course, shortened her task considerably. Which was good, too. She didn't think she could prevent him from crossing the line much longer.

Paige stood and excused herself. "I have to pee, so don't drink too much without me." She winked at him. That elicited a suggestive grin from him.

"We might as well move on," he suggested.

No, no, no. That was not part of their plan at all. "Oh, later. We have all night. And you still have so much to tell me about your success."

"Of my success?" He stared into his glass in wonder.

The waiter appeared with the next round. Relieved, she leaned forward, stroked his cheek with the fingernail of her index finger and pressed his glass into his hand. "Of course. You're really in good with the boss. He wouldn't know what to do without you."

When Peter heard her words, he nodded as if he had thought about it many times.

Paige took her own glass to the bathroom. Once there, she replaced the contents with water. After washing her hands, she slipped away to the bar and slipped twenty dollars into the waiter's hand. "Can you make my shots with water? I don't feel so good. And my date will be awkward if I don't drink it."

"I can throw this guy out too if he gives you any trouble," the bartender said.

"No, no," she said hastily. "Really. It's all right. I just don't want to drink too much." That was all she needed, a gentleman rushing to her aid. Sweet, actually. Only she didn't need that at all in the situation.

"If you're sure?" His voice sounded doubtful.

She couldn't blame him. To reassure him, she smiled at him confidently. "Don't worry. I'll be all right. I'll go home alone, too."

Back at the table, she and Peter emptied glass number five. Afterward, she leaned toward him. The resulting view of her cleavage seemed to completely overwhelm him. Paige was surprised his tongue didn't fall on the table, like in a cartoon.

"Would you mind ordering us a round of Diet Cokes?" she said, needing him to look away.

"Sure," he said and turned around to scan the bar for their waiter She took the moment to press the button on the recorder hidden in her blazer's inner pocket. She finished just in time for the waiter to come over and for him to order.

He joked with the waiter. "Seems we're slowing down," he said.

"Or just taking a halftime break!" Paige said. "Speaking of shows? My article that appeared in the *Daily News* the other day."

Peter looked at her, suddenly quite alert.

"That was actually yours, wasn't it? I may have come up with the idea. But you delivered the final story."

"Maybe..." he answered cautiously.

She had underestimated him. Would he actually shut her down? Even drunk? Had she started her offensive too soon?

"I'm sure of it. The only thing that surprised me..." She folded her arms under her chest and lifted her cleavage a little. "...was why your name wasn't under the text? But mine was?"

"You have to understand," he said, "that's what I told the boss, too. But he demanded I get the names and take the pictures. Said if I didn't, I'd be out, too." He sat back. "Sorry. Didn't mean it that way. I have all the respect in the world for you."

"You respect me?" she said sugary-sweetly, accompanied by a flirtatious eye-blink, even though she felt quite sick after having her fears confirmed.

"True, and of course I do. It bugs me that it says your name and not mine. On the other hand, maybe you want to show me some appreciation? The article did get your story out there, after all and can help people." Unexpectedly, he bent over and grabbed her breasts.

Disgusted, Paige batted him off. "No! What the hell, Peter?" She grabbed her glass and flung the Diet Coke into his face.

"...the hell?" Peter cried, wiping the sticky soda from his eyes.

Paige stood and pointed. "What you did was illegal. You will hear from my lawyers." She left the restaurant with her head held high.

The nice waiter clapped loudly. As she passed, she threw him a grateful smile.

Back at the hotel, she slipped the beautiful but terribly uncomfortable high heels off her feet and swapped them and her going-out clothes for sweatpants and an old tee-shirt.

As she sat on the bed eating peanuts from the minibar, she planned her next move. She could either drop the tape off at Paula's and let her decide what to do with it, or she could take care of it herself.

Unsure about what the best course of action was, she decided to postpone the decision. Maybe Kat had an idea of what the smartest thing to do would be. She'd call her in the morning. Either way? All hell was about to be unleashed.

CHAPTER TWENTY-THREE

Nate brushed his sweaty hair out of his forehead. He was in the process of doctoring a stubborn calf. While the mother stood there bored—at least that's what she was doing—the little one just wouldn't stay still. "You should have thought about that earlier. Before you ate your way under the fence, dear."

The calf had been so clumsy, it got one leg caught in the wire. Normally Paula helped him, but he had agreed to do it alone so she could pick up the two girls from school.

The timing suited him just fine. Because of the heat, she'd worn a sleeveless, tight tee-shirt that showed off her lean, muscular, tanned arms. Her worn jeans, which stretched like a second skin around her butt and emphasized her long legs, completed the package. He couldn't stop thinking about her.

Out of sheer self-preservation, he had suggested they split up, otherwise, he would've forgotten his good intentions on the spot. Was it only because of what she was wearing that he noticed how attractive she was? *Nah.* He knew better. He had been into her for a long time, no matter what she wore. Somehow he just noticed her figure more. *Absence makes the heart grow fonder.* He shook his head. Ironic he'd sent her away first to avoid temptation, only to go and lust after her. *Maybe I should take a cold shower or something.*

He fastened the end of the bandage with tape. He straightened up, untied the rope from the calf's head, and gave it a friendly pat on its dusty rump. "There you go. Right as rain," he said. With a *MOO* it ran to its mother.

"Get well soon! And don't be stupid around fences, *m'kay?*" Wise words. If only he would consider them himself.

After the whirlwind romance that had brought him and his ex-wife together, which resulted in Shauna, and ended in an even more whirlwind married life, he wanted to approach his next relationship extra carefully. Not as easy as he had thought.

He squinted into the cloudless sky. For days they enjoyed exceptionally high temperatures. Even the usual thunderstorms failed to appear. If rain didn't come soon, the danger of forest fires would increase.

Tired, he stretched his limbs and walked from the pasture back to the house. There he stuck his head under the water tap. *Aah. That feels amazing.* He thought Paula was lucky she had her own spring and direct access to the river because during hot spells it was forbidden to pipe water from the house to outside to water animals.

He grabbed a towel off the porch railing and rubbed his hair reasonably dry when Paula returned with the girls.

They jumped out of the car, threw their backpacks on the porch, and ran to the barn where they turned on the hose they used for the horses. Within seconds they were busy splashing and chasing each other.

He smiled. This is what he wanted for his daughter. A friend who would go through thick and thin with her.

Paula, who had joined him, leaned against him.

"Beautiful, isn't it? How they get along?"

He nodded. "It absolutely is. Want to meet for breakfast at the diner tomorrow? I already know what our odds are."

Paula took a step away. Her green eyes looked at him steadfastly. "I'm sorry. I already have a breakfast date tomorrow." She turned to go.

"Wait!" he hollered, feeling his face flush.

Paula turned, bothered to be interrupted. "What?"

"So...*ah*...yes. I was wondering..." Helplessly, he broke off the sentence. "Are you going out with Toby now?"

"Not that it's any of your business. But yes, my breakfast date is actually with Toby. Unlike other men, he likes what he sees."

That was the problem? She believed he wouldn't want her just because he wanted to take it slow? That was easy to change. *I'll show her once and for all, then.*

Determined, he pulled her to him and kissed her hungrily.

Paula returned his kiss with the same passion.

Until she suddenly broke it off without warning and took a big step back. "Forget it. I'm not doing this anymore. This yo-yo thing where you're kissing me one moment and saying we have to stop kissing the next." She turned and walked toward the house, wiping her mouth with her sleeve.

"Wait."

She paused at the door, her hand on the handle, but did not turn around.

"I have my reasons." That sounded pretty lame, even to him.

"Good for you. Since you can't seem to share them with me, I don't see how that helps."

The screen door and front door slammed shut.

He groaned and tussled his hair. It seemed he'd lost all finesse when it came to women. Could the situation still be saved? Probably not.

He called out to Shauna and said goodbye to Leslie.

"Did you and Paula fight?" Shauna asked. She had suffered a lot when he and Nancy had just been at each other's throats toward the end of their relationship. He was starting up again. He desperately needed to change something. After all, he was the common denominator. While Nancy had enough problems of her own, he really couldn't say that about Paula. He had never met anyone as direct as her.

"No, no," he reassured his daughter. "I just decided something without asking her, even though it was her business, too. That made her angry."

"Well then, Dad, go apologize. Afterward, you can just make up for it and she'll forgive you."

"The logic of children. It sounds so simple coming from you," he said. "Which it probably is. Adults tend to complicate things, don't they?"

"It's so hot in here," the woman lamented, wiping her brow with a dingy paper napkin. The two sat in wait in a new van outside the school. New in the sense of "a different model" than the old one. They had had the presence of mind to ditch the old one in Denver and steal another. The new one was also old, also dented, with seats chewed up, but at least no one had stopped them yet.

"It's hot everywhere," the man growled. "You'd think it would be cooler in the mountains than in New Mexico. But no."

"There's the girl," the woman interrupted.

The man started the engine.

"Shoot. She's getting picked up again. That's no good." Frustrated, she lit a cigarette. "They smelled a rat. We need another plan."

"Now we'll just wait and see. We'll just shadow them for the next few days. Eventually, an opportunity will present itself."

"Great. Sit in this hot van even longer. Eating canned tuna even longer."

"Now don't be like that. It's not like you have the Ritz waiting at home."

"No. But my air conditioner is."

The man didn't know how to respond to that. Instead, he watched Leslie and another girl get into the foster mom Paula's car and drive away.

He followed them from what he bet was a safe distance.

When the truck turned into a driveway in front of them, he drove a little farther, then turned around and parked the car behind some trees. The dirty gray paint provided good camouflage, he was sure. "Now we just have to be patient. Someday, hopefully soon, they'll go somewhere else other than this crazy ranch," he said.

The woman grumbled but had no better idea herself.

A few hours later, they found the child was, indeed, going nowhere. "Waiting for something to happen is worse than jail," the man said.

"You can say that again."

"What do you say we go to the nearest McDonald's and get something to eat?"

"That's definitely better than tuna," she said. "It's in Breckenridge, so we can't be gone long."

"Deal," he said.

After dinner, they drove from Breckenridge back to Independence. They drove past Paula's property. A few miles later, they turned onto a dirt road that led through the woods.

"Now what's that all about?"

He waved a crumpled map from the tourist office. "There are log cabins marked here to serve as shelters for hikers if they're caught in a storm. I've marked two," he leaned over and pointed a thick index finger at the approximate region. "We'll check those out. We can hold the brat at one of those while we wait for the ransom. I'm sure as hell not dragging her to New Mexico."

The woman said nothing. Secretly, she was impressed. He had actually thought of something for once. Sometimes he was quite useful, the man, the asshole. She was glad. Soon she would be rid of him.

"Get ready, Leslie. We're leaving in ten minutes."
"*Yeah*, I'm coming."

Paula grinned. The more teenage airs the little girl showed, the more pleased she was. Normalcy in any form was very welcome. It also didn't really matter if they were ten minutes late.

Tyler had invited them to a cozy girls' night out. Since she knew Leslie's safety was still a sensitive topic, she put the girl on the list of her guests.

Leslie had been happy and asked if she could bring someone with her. Of course, she could. So, they picked Shauna up from her mother's house. Paula hoped that would go smoothly. Unfortunately, that wasn't the case. She bent down to put away dog toys scattered around the living room and checked the water bowl. Roo and Barns were just outside on their annual evening check-up rounds. Before they left, she would call them in. The smell of pine resin was even stronger than usual due to the lingering summer heat. She opened the windows to let in the cooler evening air.

Since Tyler didn't feel like cooking, they met at the diner. Independence could really use a second restaurant or coffee house, Paula thought, not for the first time. Nothing against the Diner Sisters. The food was excellent, and so was the service, but a little variety would still be nice. She just hoped the rumor about the webcams the sisters were supposedly going to put it up for a live stream of the diner actually turned out to be a rumor. It was dangerous to let two women who specialized in meddling in everyone's lives loose onto the Internet. At least that was Paula's opinion.

She shook the sofa cushions and picked up a clump of dog hair off the floor. The animals were wonderful, but the hair was always flying around. Paula wished she had a housekeeper.

At last, Leslie rumbled down the stairs. Grateful for the excuse, she let dog hair be dog hair and grabbed the car keys.

At her observation post in the copse next to the road, the woman elbowed the man in the ribs. "Look! They're going somewhere."

The man, who had been snoring with his mouth open, woke up in one fell swoop.

"Well, what are you waiting for? Start the engine! Otherwise, we'll lose her in the end!"

The woman fumbled with the keys. Finally, she found the right one, and the decrepit van came to life.

Just in time, she turned onto the main road. A few hundred meters ahead, she saw the truck's taillights.

"Slow down. They'll see you," the man ordered the woman as they drove through Independence.

"Where are they going? To church?"

"I don't know. Maybe they're picking somebody up. Stop here, they're stopping."

Together they watched Paula stop in front of a house and jump out. She rang the doorbell. Another woman came out. A heated discussion ensued.

After half an eternity, a little girl came out and followed Paula to the truck, while behind them, the front door slammed. The girl flinched and slipped her hand into Paula's.

"Now she's going to get a second brat?" the woman asked.

"What do you care? You better make sure they don't spot us."

They followed the truck through side streets back to the main road.

"They're turning into a parking lot. What am I supposed to do now?" the woman asked, stressed.

The man lit a cigarette. He would have preferred to drive. Then he wouldn't have had such a fuss. "Keep driving. Slow down. I'll keep an eye on them."

The woman clutched the steering wheel with sweaty hands and drove slowly past the community center.

"Stop. You can stop here."

The woman pulled over to the side of the road.

"I think they're going to get something to eat."

"Reasonable," the woman said. Despite her corpulence, she had been constantly hungry since they had been lying in wait. She longed for her vodka, which she usually chugged like water. They only had lukewarm beer. Sure. The man made sure that *his* favorite drink was plentiful, but he refused to buy vodka, and she was broke. The next check from the state wasn't due for two weeks.

The man's voice snapped. "You can turn around in front of the flower store. Then you drive back to the parking lot and stand there."

"There are too many people there. Are you trying to storm the diner?"

"Stupid cow! Of course not. But maybe there'll finally be an opportunity to catch the brat alone. It's impossible on the farm because of the mutts."

They knew from experience. When they'd driven to the ranch the other day, after Paula and Leslie had left, they found themselves confronted with two extremely irritated dogs, who were not at all pleased to have strangers on their turf.

"I can't imagine. She's sitting on that brat like a mother hen. I don't know what she sees in that kid. How could anyone do that to themselves voluntarily is beyond me." But as long as there was something in it for the woman, that was just fine with her.

"Whew!" Paula dropped into a chair, exhausted. "You won't believe what just happened to me." She straightened up and looked around at the kids. Good. They were already at the dartboards discussing the rules.

"Hello, sis. Tell me." Tyler pressed a glass of beer into her hand, and Jaz handed her a plate of rolls.

"As a rule, I'm the last one to blurt out private things. But this is the last straw."

"You are a stubborn case," Miss Minnie agreed.

"What do you mean?"

"Well, none of us really know what's going on between you and Nate right now. Yet we've all put our money on various developments between you. Only it's no good to us if we have to pull everything out of you."

Paula rolled her eyes and decided to ignore the comment.

"Earlier, when I picked Shauna up from her mother's house, she came out and started calling me names. She would know exactly what I was up to. She'd been watching me make a fool of myself with Nate for a while now. All the new fancy clothes," she nodded to Jaz, "she's talking about the ancient yoga tops you lent me, thanks for that, and she seems threatened by it. But I digress. Anyway, she then gave me a lecture about how Nate would only take advantage of me, and that he'd only put up with me because I play cab driver for Shauna."

She accepted the whiskey cola Miss Minnie handed her. After taking a good swig, she continued with her story. "I then said that she couldn't care less. As far as I knew, she and Nate were separated."

"What did she say?"

"That I wouldn't have a clue. After all, she was Shauna's mother, and if I thought she was going to let her kid get stolen, in addition to my trying to steal her ex-husband, there'd be real trouble."

"Does the woman have reality issues?" This came from Tyler, who had problems with a stalker herself some time ago.

Paula pushed her hair behind her ears before taking another sip of her drink. "Seems so. Anyway, I counted to ten inside, took a deep breath, and tried to be logical with her one last time. How well the kids would get along, and that it's nice to have the two of them be such good friends, and that it only makes sense for me to fill in for Nate once in a while when his job prevents him."

"Did she accept the nanny act from you?" Jaz asked, a big grin on her face.

Paula slumped against the back of the bench. "I'm afraid not. She started throwing every swear word she could think of at me. At least she was very creative with those, by the way. I don't think I've ever been compared to a rutting female moose in my entire life. In any case, that was enough for me."

"Took you long enough," Kat grumbled. "You don't usually take such abuse."

"Well, first of all, I'm trying to do better," she said and lifted her chin. "After all, my best friend always warns me about the devastating effects of karma."

"Oh," Jaz waved it off. "There are always exceptions. With women like that, better to hit them now and ask questions later." She looked at her fingernails. "Saves an enormous amount of time and trouble, in my experience."

Paula laughed. "I kind of missed that part."

"It's a recent development," Jaz admitted.

"And second? Tyler echoed, wanting to know what had happened next.

"Second, yes. I knew Shauna was right behind the door."

"Oh, no," came in unison from the others.

"Yes, so I took a step toward her until she had to look up at me. Nancy's not exactly tall, and I told her if she didn't let Shauna out of the house, I was going to get Betty."

"Does she know who Betty is?" Kat asked.

"No," Paula said. "It doesn't matter if she thinks Betty is my mean grandmother, my gun, or my dangerous dog. Obviously, though, she was suitably rattled. She opened the door a crack and Shauna scurried out, white as a sheet."

"Poor thing," said Lily, who had just joined them.

"You can say that again. When Shauna was in the car and out of earshot, I told Nancy that Nate is a big boy and capable of deciding for himself who he wants to sleep with. Like that. That's when she went quiet."

"So, did he decide to go to bed with you? Were you able to change his mind?"

Paula slumped. "Unfortunately, no. And believe me, I've tried. I don't know what the man wants. A platonic relationship, probably."

"I don't think so, the way he looks at you."

"Then let him freaking act accordingly!" Paula was frustrated.

"Did you ever ask him why?"

"The reasons?" asked Paula perplexed.

"Well, he won't have just decided to slow down. Because unlike you, I don't think the problem is a lack of attraction."

"But then shouldn't he be so overwhelmed with lust that he doesn't have time to think of his reasons at all?"

"*HA*, yes," Tyler sighed.

Paula gave her a dirty look. "Thanks. Nice to see at least one of us getting her money's worth."

Tyler stuck her tongue out at her.

"Children, children," Miss Minnie reprimanded, placing ham croissants and chips on the table. "Meal time."

"Thank you."

"Always happy to." With a sideways glance at Lily, she noted, "Aileen's in the back if you want to talk to her."

Lily would have liked to sink into the ground on the spot. Was there nothing that escaped these two women? She hadn't thought her interest in the other woman was so obvious.

Uncertainly, she glanced around. But no one was paying any attention to her. Apparently, no one else had attached any particular significance to the remark. Only Tyler, with whom she was good friends, but with whom she had never discussed that particular topic, watched her thoughtfully. Finally, she pulled herself together and nodded to Miss Minnie. "Thanks. I might stop by later."

Unnoticed by the adults, who were engrossed in their exciting conversation, Leslie had taken the car keys from Paula's jacket. She brought a horse book for Shauna and promptly left it in the car. "I'll get it for you quickly."

"But not that you're going to get in trouble."

Leslie frowned. "Why would I get in trouble? After all, it'll only take two minutes, and then I'll be back. You can even see the parking lot from her seat by the window. What's the big deal for me?"

"All right, I'll wait here. Then it won't be as noticeable as when we're both suddenly gone."

Leslie stepped out into the lukewarm night air. Normally it cooled down reliably at night. But today it was still over seventy degrees.

Earlier, during the car ride, they had announced on the radio that from now on all open fires were forbidden because of the extreme danger of forest fires. The air even smelled slightly of smoke.

Two counties over, a large area of forest was already burning. Leslie had never witnessed a forest fire firsthand.

She hoped the wind didn't shift and drive the fire closer to them. She couldn't bear to see her new home destroyed. Even if it was just things, she was still very attached to the place. She was also worried about the animals.

Cautiously, she let her eyes wander over the parking lot. She had been very nervous since the incident on the highway, even though she hadn't let on to Shauna earlier. Everything looked calm. Why shouldn't it? The ghastly woman who claimed to be her mother was surely long gone. She gathered all her courage and strolled across the street to the truck.

At the diner, Shauna waited impatiently for Leslie's return. She didn't know why, but she had a bad feeling in her stomach the whole time. Maybe she had eaten something bad. Or maybe it was because of the argument she had overheard between Paula and her mother. Whatever it was, she hoped her friend would hurry.

Ten minutes later, Shauna realized something had gone wrong. She bit her lower lip. What was she supposed to do now? Go outside and look? But it was almost dark out. She didn't dare do that. Then there was really only one option left: to ask Paula.

She walked over to her and whispered in her ear that she missed Leslie.

Confused, Paula asked, "Did she go to the bathroom? Or where is she?"

"She went out for a minute to get a book out of the car for me."

"Out? Alone?" Like lightning, Paula jumped up and yanked open the diner door. She looked from left to right and toward the car, but Leslie was nowhere to be found.

She didn't think twice, and pulled out her phone. She had Jake on the line within seconds.

"Leslie is gone."

"Disappeared how?" Jake asked.

"Well, disappeared. Gone. As if disappeared from the face of the earth."

"Take it easy. Tell me everything in order."

Paula forced herself to calm down and told him what she knew.

When she realized it wasn't much, she waved Shauna over, who was sitting on Kat's lap with wide, anxious eyes.

Rocky and Nikita, who had come along, rested their heads on her thighs. When she saw Paula's gesture, she jumped up and rushed over. "How long has Leslie been gone?"

Shauna shrugged. "Ten minutes, maybe? I just waited a bit. I wasn't sure what was taking her so long."

Paula didn't want to scare her. It wasn't the girl's fault Leslie had disappeared. She passed the information on to Jake. He was going to round up all his deputies and put out an APB on the couple before he got to the diner to discuss what they'd do next.

Paula immediately called Nate. "I'm glad you called," he said cheerfully. Oblivious. "I was just going to call you to—"

"Nate!" Paula interrupted. "Leslie's gone."

CHAPTER TWENTY-FOUR

SATISFIED, THE WOMAN looked down at the unconscious girl on the truck's floor. She had hit her over the head with a can of tuna fish. *Very fitting*, she thought. After all, it was the brat's fault she had been eating little else for a week.

"Are you out of your mind?" the man asked. "I said 'take care of her' not 'kill her'. After all, we still need her!" He gave the woman a rough shove while steering the car with his other hand.

"She's still breathing, so it's fine," the woman said.

The girl was of no further interest to her. It was only a means to an end. Curiously, she looked at the child. That this should be her child was a completely abstract idea that left her completely cold. Except that it had caused her such problems.

She gave the girl another kick.

"Don't do that," the man said, tossing her a bundle of zip ties off the dashboard. "Better tie her up. Don't let her come to again and run away. That brat has already given us more work than she's worth." Disgusted, he spat on the floor.

The woman caught the bundle. "That's just what she needs to do," she said. "Run away! Took long enough already. It'll be another couple of days before we get the cash."

She slipped the plastic straps over Leslie's wrists and cinched them tight. She pulled her toward her rougher than necessary across the corrugated floor of the old van. "Justice for what you've put me through," she said. "And I don't owe you anything. But you owe me."

The diner resembled a command center. The Diner Sisters grasped the gravity of the situation, pushed a few tables together so that everyone could find room, and placed hot coffee in thermos flasks on the table. Just then, Aileen single-handedly brought a tray of still-hot rhubarb muffins from the kitchen. There were already two trays of ham croissants on the table. "Here," she said. "Help yourselves. Hopefully, you'll find her soon."

"Thanks, we hope so too." Jake nodded.

Paula could only give her a grateful look. She was not capable of doing more. Her whole body was tense. If she gave up the slightest bit of tension, she would collapse. Falling was out of the question.

Nate, who had arrived two minutes earlier, was aware. He hugged her but huddled with Jake and Ace, who debated the most sensible course of action.

Paula's temptation had been to just lean on him and start crying. Unfortunately, that wouldn't bring Leslie back. Nothing mattered until the little girl was back home safe and sound.

She didn't know why she'd called Nate in the first place. She felt the need to call him and hear his voice. That he would immediately drop everything to help, she had not expected. However, she had to admit she'd been very relieved when he came.

"You're sure this isn't another runaway attempt?" asked Jake from across the table.

She gritted her teeth, even though her jaw already hurt like hell. "Yes, I'm sure. We've talked about this repeatedly. She had no intention of leaving." Seeking help, she turned to Shauna, who stood next to her father, holding his hand.

"Ask Shauna. She was happy for the first time in a long time. She even began to believe that she was really wanted by me, or us, as the case may be."

"Okay, if you say so."

Pat, who had promptly dropped by at Tyler's call with Ranger in tow, returned from his tour of the parking lot. He held a book and a key. "These two things were in the middle of the road at the exit of the parking lot. It looks like she dropped them."

"That's the book she was going to get for me," Shauna called out.

Paula and Jake exchanged a look. Jake turned to all the helpers. "Listen up, everybody. It looks like Leslie has indeed been kidnapped. Probably by her birth mother and her birth mother's boyfriend."

"I thought the man was her father?" said one of the guests.

"It's not certain he's her father or not. But it doesn't matter. Paula, you should go home."

"I'm going to help out. Not sit around at home and wait for bad news," she defended herself.

"The kidnapping only makes sense if they are trying to extort a ransom. Most likely, they'll contact you with their demands. If you're running around in the woods, they may not be able to contact you."

"I want to find them first. Not wait until they make the first move!"

"I understand that. But we can't blindly search an area of several square kilometers. Who knows if they went across the interstate? They could be halfway to New Mexico by now."

Paula swallowed. She had not even thought of such a possibility.

"We have another problem," Ace said. "As far as we know, the couple doesn't have a place to stay nearby. So the question is, where are they going to take Leslie? If they don't go back to New Mexico."

"Maybe they'll stay in the van?" This suggestion came from Jaz, who put a hand on her stomach.

"Maybe. Or they could find a place to hide in the woods. That's what I would do. If your guess is right about the ransom, they'll have to stick around to receive it. If they've actually taken shelter in the woods, depending on where they are, that could become a real problem."

"What do you mean?" asked Paula.

"The wind has just shifted. At its current strength, the wildfire will reach Independence no later than tomorrow afternoon."

Leslie woke in a daze. Her vision cleared slowly. Her surroundings were black as night. A sliver of light shone through a square cutout across from her. Not light in the sense of lantern light. Just brighter than the rest. It smelled of resin, old dust, and damp earth. Where on Earth was she? And why couldn't she move her hands?

Her heartbeat quickened as she remembered what happened. That horrible woman and the disgusting man had ambushed her. She had gotten the book out of the car for Shauna when a huge shadow appeared out of nowhere. She'd screamed when she recognized him.

She'd dropped the book and was about to run away when a second person came from behind. Then everything went black.

Leslie turned her head a little but stopped immediately as pain exploded behind her forehead and the back of her head. She suppressed a groan.

At that moment, she was alone. But she had no idea if her captors were nearby. She hoped not. Their presence would be more than she could bear.

Whimpering softly, she tried to suppress the rising panic. Was this her punishment for thinking she could be happy with Paula? Her last foster father had kept telling her what a good-for-nothing brat she was, who only caused problems. No wonder no one would want to take her in forever. She should be happy to live without any of them.

She curled up into a little ball, while memories of previous nights spent locked out in the cold overwhelmed her. With no food and no people to keep her company now, only a fox and two raccoons went by occasionally.

Her stomach growled. She had to go to the bathroom. Tears ran down her cheeks. With her bound hands, she tried to wipe her face. Dark thoughts spread like quicksilver throughout her body, threatening to engulf her. Finally, she fell into a fitful sleep from exhaustion.

Without them arranging it, Nate followed Paula home to the ranch in his car. Shauna sat silently beside him. She was clearly shocked by the events of the evening; he would have liked to spare her the experience. What a worry she had to have for her friend. He reached for her small hand and squeezed it gently. "Don't worry, my mouse. I'm sure we'll find her soon."

"You don't know that," she burst out. "No one knows where she is. And everyone pats me on the head and says everything will be okay. I'm not a baby anymore. And life isn't a fairy tale." She turned her head toward the window, away from him.

Wow. She had let him know once again. Always when he least expected it. She was right. Every single word. He cast a sidelong glance at his daughter, who seemed to be growing up very fast. "Not a pony farm," he said in an attempt to lighten the tense mood a bit.

"Huh?"

"They say life is no pony farm. That expression almost fits Leslie better, don't you think?"

She continued to look out the window, but the corners of her mouth twitched.

It was tempting to just drop the subject at this point. But he had vowed to always be as honest as possible with his daughter and to take her feelings seriously. "I understand why you're worried. We all are. You saw how everyone agreed to help with the search. I have every faith that soon someone will find a clue that will lead us to Leslie. It's true, I don't know if everything's going to be okay. But I hope it will. And the odds are with us. What are two out-of-town crooks from New Mexico going to do against a whole bunch of crafty locals?"

"I hope Paula shoots her. She's a really good shot. She and Betty make a great team."

Nate gave his bloodthirsty daughter a surprised look. *Had she been watching Paula during her shooting training?* He'd ask Paula. "Let's focus instead on finding Leslie."

"How? I'm sure I have to stay in the house."

Shauna had picked a great day to try out her fighting spirit. He supposed that was also a variation on dealing with inner helplessness.

He sighed and parked his truck behind Paula's car.

Shauna was out the door in a flash and disappeared onto the porch, where the two blue heelers were already waiting.

He reached into the back seat and pulled a bag forward.

"What are you doing here?" asked Paula as he stepped into the house behind his daughter.

"We thought a little company while you waited might help." He pulled her into his arms. She resisted for a quarter of a second, then relaxed.

"You're right. I'd be climbing the walls stuck here all alone."

"See, I have good ideas once in a while. Have you had dinner yet?"

Paula shook her head. "No. There hasn't been time. After all, we were all going to eat together at the diner. Except for two sips of my Whiskey-cola, I didn't eat anything at all. I didn't even have enough time for a ham croissant."

Nate pulled his arm out from behind his back. "*Ta-ta*: free-range pork loin with applesauce and potatoes."

"I don't know if I can eat anything right now."

"You can," he said and spread the containers on the table. Before placing the last one, he opened the lid and held it under her nose.

"*MMMH*," she gasped. "Who cooked that? I don't even know that recipe."

"See, eating is a good idea after all. The cook, I think, was, Aileen. The niece of the Diner Sisters."

"It certainly sounds delicious."

"I'm sure it is. And you need your energy for Leslie."

"Right. Because sitting around and waiting is so exhausting."

Shauna gave him a look that seemed to say, *See, I told you so!*

He rolled his eyes, which again elicited a smile from his daughter, as intended. Turning to Paula, he said, "True. But if you had to leave in the middle of the night because she was found, and you had a fainting spell at that exact moment, you'd be annoyed."

Paula gave up trying to resist. She would just eat a few bites. And so what? Secretly, she was very glad that the two of them had unceremoniously invited themselves to stay with her. She didn't know how she was going to get through the night ahead.

"So what do we do now?" The man and woman sat in their van in the parking lot of the McDonald's in Breckenridge. She stuffed fries in her mouth while waiting for him to answer. This sitting around waiting was driving her crazy. She missed all her favorite shows. She missed her bed, too.

The man wiped the Big Mac sauce from his face with his hand. "Now we write a letter. If they want her back, they pay. It's that simple."

The woman had her doubts someone would come up with the money for the child. But it was all right. Florida was waiting. "And where do we send the letter?"

"Good question," he said. "Bring it over in person?"

"Have you lost your mind? Unlike you, I don't feel like getting eaten alive. So, the mastermind doesn't have such a clearly thought-out plan after all. Who would have guessed it?" she teased.

"Shut up, woman! How about you contribute something, too? *HMM*? Up until now, I've had to do all the work. If you want to get some of that dough, too, you'd better make a lot more of an effort."

Enraged, she threw the remaining fries, including ketchup, at him.

He ducked and the red sauce hit the window and slowly ran down the glass.

"Without me, there would be no plan at all. No child. No plan!" she screeched.

"And who saw the article in the paper? If it wasn't for me, you'd still be sitting clueless in your trailer rathole."

"Oh, now it's suddenly a rathole? Was that the reason you were drunk every day? Huh?"

They stared angrily at each other. Finally, the man looked away. "Shoot. You're right. We can argue later. Right now, we have to figure out how to get that letter to the woman. And do it fast."

Both were silent. The man lit a cigarette and took a sip of beer.

"A cab," the woman blurted.

"What would we do with a cab?" he asked.

She would have liked to shake him. "We don't need a cab. The letter does. Then the cab driver takes the heat." She was very pleased with herself. This was the ideal solution.

"Have you taken a look around here? This isn't New York. Cabs are in short supply here right now."

The woman shrank into herself. Crap. She had not thought about that.

"I need to sleep for a bit. All this excitement is not good for my heart," he grunted. With one hand, he pulled his cap down over his face, slid deeper into the seat, and closed his eyes.

Filled with disgust, the woman looked at him. His heart. What a mockery. The guy had no heart at all. How could he sleep? It would take forever for them to get their money. There had to be a way.

Suddenly, she knew what she had to do.

Shauna was in bed and sound asleep in Leslie's room.

Nate rifled through Paula's movie collection while she pulled one of Jaz's tea blends from the cupboard. The packet had sat untouched in her cupboard since her birthday, she realized with a guilty conscience. But she felt she could use a little reassurance.

She waited until the water boiled, then poured it over the tea mixture. After two minutes, she took out the bags and sweetened the tea with a spoonful of honey. A cup in each hand, she joined Nate. "Is she asleep?"

Nate nodded. "She was pretty exhausted after all the excitement. I think it helped that she gets to sleep in Leslie's room. It makes her feel close to her."

"I can understand that. I would love to do the same." She stirred her tea with the spoon.

"Where's the chocolate?" asked Nate.

Surprised, Paula looked at him. "The chocolate?"

"Yeah, you know. Brown, sweet, and delicious?"

"Sure. I was just wondering what you wanted with it?"

"*Uh*, food? That's pure energy food!"

Despite her somber mood, Paula had to smile. "In the kitchen, in the cupboard next to the refrigerator."

Nate pushed himself up off the floor with a surprisingly graceful movement for such a large man and disappeared into the kitchen. The dogs followed him, just in case he strayed to the dog cookie jar.

Paula shook her head. Just great. Finally, she had him at home, on the sofa, the ideal opportunity for a seduction attempt, and yet she had no intention whatsoever to do anything about it. With a sigh, she reached for the remote. Time to turn on the local news. Maybe they would report on the fire.

Two hours later, she was woke by the ringing of the telephone. Blinking, she sat up. She'd fallen asleep on Nate's shoulder during the movie. He handed her the phone. "It's Jake."

Wide awake, she answered. "Tell me you have good news."

"How to say it? *HMM*. The kidnappers made contact. The call came from a public pay phone in Breckenridge."

"Thank God!" Paula said. "So they're still around, then." Even though she knew the dangers, she found it reassuring Leslie was nearby. If they were in Breckenridge, that meant they were in the van, too. Her little girl was reasonably safe.

"It seems so. We are to deposit the money, one hundred thousand dollars in small bills, in the big garbage can by the sports field."

"By the sports field?"

"This time they were smarter than I would have thought. The sports field has two access roads, one of which is through the forest. The dumpster is right at the edge of the forest. They can drive there and get away relatively unseen."

"And how do they do the exchange? Are they taking Leslie there or what? Even people with the IQ of a cow patty would know if they did that, they would get caught immediately."

"That's the part that's still a little bit of a headache for me. They said they would get back to me two hours after the cash drop with details."

"Not until two hours later? When is the ransom payment even supposed to happen?" It all sounded very much like a half-baked plan. Not that she cared. It wasn't her problem, as long as she just got Leslie back.

"The instructions are to deposit the money by one in the morning."

"Because I have a hundred thousand lying around at home," Paula couldn't help herself.

Jake laughed. "Honestly? That's what I thought, too. All the better for us. Stupid people make mistakes. Plus, it makes it easier for me to decide how to proceed. We'll grab them right at the drop. I don't want to risk them getting away. Since they're not experienced criminals, I don't think they'll last long being interrogated."

"But Jake," Paula echoed as she remembered the fire. "What if she's not in the van and they take their time telling us where she is?"

The wind had picked up again, driving the fire inexorably in their direction. Their cattle were fortunately in the east pasture on the other side of the river, as was the ranch. But beyond that was miles of forest in danger of going up in flames. If Leslie was anywhere there...

"Now, let's not get carried away. It's our best option."

"What if they don't talk?" repeated Paula.

"They will," her brother said confidently. "It's definitely the safer option than letting them find out there's a majority of paper in the gym bag. Even if they don't check, there's no point relying on them. They're going to run for the hills the quickest way possible."

Paula swallowed. She had no choice but to trust Jake knew what he was doing. She reminded herself he'd been a cop for a long time in Denver, the big city, and knew what he was doing. But it was difficult.

"Why did they actually call you, the sheriff, and not me?" she asked.

"They didn't call me, they called the diner. Whose number is in the phone book, unlike yours? Apparently, they had to get creative when it came to sending the ransom note."

"Well...points for the bad guys. It worked out. I'll ride with you to the sports field."

"You'd better stay where you are. You can't help, anyway." Which translated meant: *You're in the way.*

Frustrated, Paula ended the call. This doing nothing was driving her crazy. Nate sensed her tension. He walked over to her, gently took the phone from her hand, and pulled her up from the sofa.

"What..."

"*SHHH...*"

Had the man really said "Shhh" to her? What did he actually think?

Nate leaned down and kissed her.

Surprised, she looked up at him as he broke away. "What was that?"

He shrugged, an embarrassed smile on his face. "I know the timing stinks to high heaven. On the other hand, I've been fighting the urge to kiss you for days."

Paula raised both eyebrows. "For days? Well, well, well...apparently you aren't as immune as you wanted me to believe."

"Immune? Quite the opposite!"

OOPS, did she just say that out loud? It looked like it. She licked her lips. The timing was really bad. On the other hand, she now had to wait two hours and could do nothing but wait. *Just let yourself go for a moment and forget the fear.*

Paula reached for his shirt and kissed him.

CHAPTER TWENTY-FIVE

PAULA STROKED NATE'S CHEST with her fingertips. It had been nice. But after it was over, she had to turn her worry back to Leslie. She jumped up, gathered her scattered clothes off the sofa, tossed Nate his pants, and walked out of the room to get dressed.

Nate watched her as she literally fled. That had been another great idea of his. Not that he regretted it. It had been inevitable they'd end up in bed, or on the couch. Whether they would actually make it to a real bed someday was still written in the stars, if he interpreted Paula's behavior correctly. He sighed and slipped into his clothes.

When he was dressed, he went to the kitchen and put on some coffee. It was going to be a long night. He got butter, eggs, and bacon and prepared them a midnight snack.

At the same time, in another place in the middle of the forest, Leslie awoke.

Her skull throbbed and her arms tingled unpleasantly through the tight bonds. Her mouth was dry. With difficulty, she straightened up and frantically searched the ground. Maybe they had left her water? Or she might find a water tap? Anything? In the middle of her search, she paused.

Something was different. She tried to be very still and focused all her senses outside. She heard...nothing. The first time she'd wakened after being nabbed, she'd heard various forest sounds. A rustling, the call of an owl, the chirping of a cricket. All that had disappeared. She sniffed and had to cough. The smell of resin, dust, and the damp earth lingered. The acrid smell of smoke permeated it all.

The fire! She was near the forest fire, she realized, and it was getting closer. Adrenaline surged, her spirit awoke. She didn't care if she deserved to live with Paula but she'd do anything to get back to her. *Anything.* That meant fighting to her last breath if need be. Another coughing fit shook her. No way was she just going to give up and let these evil creeps win.

Desperately, she pulled and tugged at her bonds. Using her teeth, she tried to cut the material. Didn't work. She felt hopeless.

Grimly, she gritted her teeth and swallowed the tears. *A plan. I need a plan.*

Her eyes flitted back and forth in the dark room. She could see more as her eyes adjusted to the darkness. The room was empty save for a cot—at least she assumed the oblong, knee-high thing was a cot. She made out a chair and a table against the wall. A closet, maybe, on the other side.

She rolled her head. Her headache throbbed. She moved her legs and pulled them under her. *Can I even stand?* She pushed up along the wall and almost fell.

Bracing herself against the wall, she paused, waiting for the dizziness to subside.

As soon as the world stopped spinning, she felt her way along the wall until she got to the table.

Methodically, she scanned the table with her bound hands. Unfortunately, there was nothing. The table surface was empty.

She coughed, wiped her mouth on her shoulder, and continued her search. Maybe the table had a drawer?

Again, she found nothing. Determined to find a solution, she continued toward the door. Tentatively, she pushed down on the handle. It didn't open. *That would be too easy.* The closet was also locked.

Discouraged, she stopped at the window and peered out. An orange glow caught her attention. What was that, she asked herself, until a moment later she realized with horror that the orange light must be the approaching fire. As if to confirm her suspicions, she was shaken by another coughing fit.

Panic-stricken, she shook the window. Unexpectedly, it gave way and swung open.

She stumbled backward and fell to the floor.

As fast as she could, her hands still tied, she got up and rushed to the window. *I wonder how far down it goes on the other side?*

One look at the orange firelight confirmed what she already knew. No matter what awaited her on the other side, it was definitely better than waiting locked in the cabin until the fire arrived. Then all hope would really be lost...*unless Paula or someone else would come and save me.*

"Do you see anyone who can save you? No. Save yourself! Go on, get out!" she said.

Leslie dragged the chair to the window, climbed up, and jumped head-first through the narrow opening.

She landed on her shoulder but managed to roll and finally stopped at the gnarled trunk of a pine tree. Even though she knew everything would hurt later, her entire body tingled. *Pure adrenaline.*

"AHH!" She took a moment to catch her breath before pushing herself up.

She ran as fast as she could away from the fire that inched closer every second.

Paula sat in the kitchen next to the telephone and stared. Why didn't it ring? It was already a quarter past one.

"Relax. This could take a while. Just because the money is supposed to be dropped by one doesn't mean they're going to pick it up five after one," Nate said. "If they're smart, they'll wait a while to make sure the coast is clear. Here, eat something."

Nate set a plate of eggs and bacon in front of her along with a glass of milk. Absentmindedly, she reached for the fork and shoved a bite into her mouth.

They ate in complete silence. No one felt like making small talk. The worry about Leslie was too great and too present. Paula barely tasted what she ate. It just preoccupied her and kept her from going completely crazy.

Finally, the phone rang. It was Jake. "Yes. Do you have her? Where's Leslie?" she hit him.

"We caught them." He sounded exhausted.

"Oh, thank god. How is Leslie? Was she in the van?"

"Unfortunately, no."

"Where is she?"

Jake did not answer right away.

Paula's guts tightened. "Come on. Tell me."

"They locked her up in one of the cabins on Indian Ridge."

"Well then, what are we waiting for?" she asked.

"The fire. It's already spread to the first cabins. We won't make it in time."

"Oh, yeah?" she said and hung up. She burst into frantic activity. She tugged her shirt over her head and held it under the faucet until it was completely soaked. She did the same with her hair, which she braided into a tight braid and tucked into her shirt. She slipped on her boots and slung a saddlebag over her shoulder. She stowed a first aid kit, a bottle of water, and a flashlight.

"Where are you going?"

"I'm getting Leslie."

He stared at her in disbelief. "Are you out of your mind? How are you going to accomplish what the entire search and rescue team can't?"

"The cabins at Indian Ridge can be reached from here in fifteen minutes. On horseback. Not by car. By car, you'll have to make a circuit several miles long," Paula said. "Besides, everyone's sitting in Independence right now. We're already here." She looked him firmly in the eye. "I have to try, Nate. Imagine if Shauna were in Leslie's place."

He swallowed. "You're right. Give me a horse. I'll go with you."

She put a hand to his cheek and smiled. "Thank you for the offer. But I don't have a second horse I trust to handle the situation. Stay here, watch Shauna, and have the phone ready in case someone calls. I probably won't be able to call. There's no service on the trail."

"That makes me feel so much better," he smiled. "Good luck. Bring our little one home!"

"Will do."

She whistled for the dogs and left the house at a run. She knew it was a risk to take the dogs. She hoped they would be safe in case of emergency.

When she got to the stable and turned on the interior lights, the horses sleepily lifted their heads.

"Let's see if all my training's been worth it!" She heard a snort. "Rufus!" Her old horse growled delightedly when she addressed him. He stepped to the gate, which she opened for him.

After she ran a brush over the saddle as fast as possible, Paula saddled and bridled him. She whispered to him as she used to do before competitions. "Hey, big guy. Today is another big day. We have to give everything we have to get to our girl as soon as possible. What do you think? Can you do it?"

She sat on top of Rufus, rode him outside into the yard. The dogs circled the horse and yelped. After a quick glance back at the house, she gave Rufus the cues to gallop and dashed off.

The first part of the route led across large meadows. She wanted to use them to make quick progress.

As soon as they entered the forest, she would have to slow down.

Ten minutes later, she saw and heard the fire. *Shoot. Hope I'm not too late. At least I have you, Rufus, my friend.*

Undeterred, he trudged forward through the dense undergrowth, ignoring the eerie atmosphere of the forest fire.

Paula had a pretty good idea of which cabin the two kidnappers had hidden Leslie in. Only one was near the gravel road leading high into the mountains. She assumed the two weren't in a hiking mood when they had to hide Leslie.

When the trees cleared a little again, she let Rufus run. He opened up under her and picked up speed. *Such a reliable horse*, she thought with gratitude, and ducked low over the saddle to avoid drooping branches.

Arriving at the cabin, she jumped off, whereupon Rufus stopped as if rooted to the spot. Paula coughed as a gush of hot air and smoke reached her.

She tried to open the door, but to no avail. "Leslie? Are you in there?" Frantically, she pounded on the door. Was she unconscious?

It occurred to her that maybe she should have listened to Jake instead of just hanging up. The barking dogs snapped her out of her thoughts. *Did they find something?* She ran around the corner from where she'd heard the barking.

The window. It was open. The dogs sniffed the ground and kept lifting their noses. *Did Leslie jump?*

Unfortunately, the floor was too dry to detect any conclusive tracks. After another look inside the shack, flashlight be thanked, she was sure that Leslie had been there but had been able to escape through the window.

She spun around and tried to imagine which direction she would run. *Simple, really,* she decided. *Away from the fire.* Not exactly, but roughly in the direction from which Paula had just come. Only, she had not seen her.

That did not bode well. Determined, she shook her head. *Not giving up until I find you. Need to get you safely home and away from this fire. There's no life without you.*

She whistled for Rufus, who immediately trotted toward her. A good ranch horse was worth its weight in gold, she thought, stroking his neck.

Practiced, she swung into the saddle and said to the dogs, "Where's Leslie?"

They had played together countless times at home on the ranch. The dogs were not trained tracking dogs like rangers but she hoped they'd recognize the call of their familiar game and go in search of their beloved friend.

And indeed. They looked at each other, then cast a questioning glance at Paula.

"Go on," she said. "Find her!"

Behind her, not too far away, a tree crashed to the ground.

"Now!"

Off they ran.

She and Rufus followed.

Leslie glanced over her shoulder as she stumbled forward. She just couldn't move fast enough with the shackles on. Running was impossible. Twice, she'd fallen.

Everything hurt. A scratch burned her face. She coughed and had to stop for a moment.

If she only knew where she was, she could head for the river. Unfortunately, she had no clue. The area was completely unfamiliar.

The darkness and the looming fire behind her, steadily approaching, didn't help. The fear surged up like a hungry animal, threatening to devour her. Maybe she should just realize that this was her fate. *No one wants you anyway,* she heard the voices from her past whisper. *Give up, no one cares what happens to you.* Exhausted, she paused. Giving up suddenly seemed to be a very inviting option.

Then she heard a dog barking. Or even two? Could it be...?

She did not finish the thought, but called out. "Here I am! Help!"

Desperately, she believed the wind and the crash of bursting wood, caused by the heat of the fire, swallowed her cries.

The smoke made her eyes water and scratched her throat.

A dog barked again. She let her hands slide down her body. Then she felt something under her sweater. The whistle! It was still there!

She fumbled with her collar until she got hold of the string from which it hung.

She blew into it until she thought her eardrums would burst.

Paula almost cried with relief when she heard the whistle. The dogs heard it, too. Roo and Barns raised their heads and ran barking. She urged Rufus to go faster and followed.

She almost collided with her.

Leslie was leaning against a tree. Her clothes were torn. There was a deep scratch across her cheek and one eye was swollen shut.

Paula jumped from Rufus and embraced her girl.

Leslie wept.

Paula rocked her back and forth and whispered, "Everything will be all right now," into her hair. As she did, the heat grew, and she broke away "We have to keep moving. The fire is getting closer. Can you ride?"

The little girl sniffled one last time, then nodded and held out her bound hands. "If you take them off my hands, absolutely."

Paula pulled the knife out of the sheath on her belt. It was one of those times that really paid off to be a ranch person. She cut through the plastic straps.

Leslie yelped as her hands were free and she felt circulation return.

Paula lifted her up and put her on Rufus.

She grabbed the reins and led the horse and dogs away from the fire, toward the river. Paula put one foot in front of the other. She didn't dare look back. The heat grew. The smoke thickened. They kept on.

She opened one of the saddlebags as she walked and pointed to the water bottle. Leslie drank greedily. When she finished, Paula motioned her to empty the rest over her hair and clothes. Her own clothes had dried. "We're not safe yet," she said. "Come on!"

Fortunately, both she and Rufus and the two faithful dogs knew the area like the back of their hands. Visibility had dropped to zero. Paula relied on her inner compass.

Behind them, a tree crashed to the ground, roaring and hissing from the flames.

Leslie winced. Even Rufus quickened his steps. Poor guy. So much excitement in his old age. She hoped he would come through the strenuous trip all right.

At last, a second sound mingled with the hissing of the flames.

They stepped out of the forest and stood in front of a flat piece of meadow that led down to the river.

Paula looked up at Leslie and put a hand on her thigh. "Look, the water. We're almost there."

Moved, Leslie reached for Paula's hand and squeezed it. "We made it!"

"We did."

They walked the last bit toward the river. Roo and Barns were already there, lying on their stomachs in the shallow water on the bank, cooling down.

Paula helped Leslie, whose limbs were aching, off the horse.

"Lie down with the dogs," she said. "That will ease your pain. I'll let Rufus drink, then we can move on."

"How much longer until we get home?"

Paula smiled. "About half an hour. Once we get to the other side of the river, we can take our time. The river is wide enough that the fire can't jump across."

Relieved, Leslie swayed. With unsteady steps, she covered the stony stretch to the water.

Paula's anger at the two kidnappers rose. She would gladly be alone in a cell with them for half an hour. It reminded her of all the people waiting at home who were worried.

She pulled out her phone and looked at the display. Did she have service?

Yes, she had, she realized with relief. She dialed Nate. He picked up after the first ring. "Paula?"

"I found her. She's fine." She smiled when she heard his voice, and a warm feeling filled her. Nate felt right in her life.

"Thank God!"

"Can you inform the others?"

"Sure. Will do. How close are you?"

Rufus stepped uneasily from one foot to the other. She glanced over her shoulder. The first flames had reached the edge of the forest.

"It's okay. We're going," she assured the horse. After all, it was no use if they made it to the river and then missed the moment to cross.

"What?"

"Oh, nothing. I was just talking to Rufus. We'll be there in thirty minutes."

"Great, I'm waiting for you."

And that's exactly what he would do. Wait for them both. The warm feeling inside her swelled until she was completely filled. Was it love? She didn't know. But she wanted to find out. But first? It was back to the ranch.

A short time later they arrived safely on the other side.

She helped Leslie mount again. "Home?" she asked her daughter.

Leslie smiled broadly. Small branches and leaves had become entangled in her hair. A wide streak of dirt ran across her face. But she beamed as if she had never heard anything more beautiful.

"Home."

EPILOGUE

Paige turned off the engine and took a deep breath. "You can do it. Close your eyes and get through," she said. Fortunately, Maybellene, whom she had taken with Kat's permission for moral support, was the only one within earshot. "You go to that door now and say what you have to say," she added to her own coaching speech. Which was all well and good, but completely moot. Paula would shoot first and ask questions later.

Maybellene sensed her nerves. She left her place in the passenger seat, stood on Paige's thigh, and licked her once across the face. "*EW*. You shouldn't do that," Paige scolded. She had been trying to teach her for days she didn't appreciate such a greeting, to no avail.

She wasn't convincing and found it hard to be stern when Maybellene grinned at her with her black, beady eyes and cute pink tongue.

She opened the door, let the little schipperke dog jump, and got out of the car. Before she could knock, the door opened.

Paula stood, arms folded under her chest, and asked unkindly, "What do you want?"

"What, no Betty?" Paige said. She winced. Wrong words to use when you were trying not to get shot.

"That can easily be changed, don't worry," Paula said. "But I did get a call."

"A call? From whom?"

"From my brother. Sam. He said you were coming over. His recommendation was to listen to what you had to say before I blew you away. So, I'm listening."

Sam had interceded for her? Miracles were happening.

She reached into her shoulder bag and pulled out a thick, padded envelope. She handed it to Paula. She didn't want her to change her mind about listening first and shooting later.

"In this envelope, you will find three things," she blurted out. "One is a taped confession from the editor in charge as well as the journalist who published the story of you and Leslie without permission. They were also the ones who researched and printed your names. That wasn't too difficult, since they knew where I was staying. Since Independence is not exactly a big city, it was easy for them. You know how it is here. One seemingly innocent question and you find out everything about the person from their health to their favorite color."

Paula turned the envelope in her hands. She knew what it was like. But was that excuse enough? Finally, she looked up. "And the other two things?"

"A handwritten apology from both individuals responsible and a check for one hundred thousand dollars."

"A hundred thousand dollars?" exclaimed Paula, almost dropping the envelope in surprise.

Paige nodded. "Granted, it's something akin to hush money. I promised not to go to court."

"What about me?"

Paige shrugged. "Sure. They don't have a deal with you. If you want to spend the money on lawyers..."

"A hundred thousand dollars! What am I going to do with it?"

"It's up to you, of course. But I thought it would be a great grant for Leslie's college fund."

"I can't take it. This is your money." Paula held the envelope out to Paige.

Paige shook her head. "This is my amends. I have not deceived you as you think I have. But I also didn't exercise due caution. And look what that led to." In her mind's eye, all the moments of terror they'd had over Leslie flashed by.

Paula lowered her outstretched hand with the envelope. She peered inside.

"College, you say. That's an excellent idea." She smiled. "Thank you."

"You're welcome," Paige said, turning to leave.

"Where are you off to in such a hurry?"

"Well, home. And from there I have to keep looking. It's hard to live here when all the locals are convinced I'm one of the bad guys." She shrugged and tried to act as indifferent as possible.

"Come on in and have a cup of coffee. Leslie can pet your dog, and you can tell me what you're up to now. Kat told me some interesting things."

Relieved, Paige followed Paula into the house, Maybellene close on her heels. Maybe, just maybe, everything would turn out all right after all.

That afternoon, Paula set out for Nate's house. Paige's visit had reminded her that she had some unfinished business of her own. It was time. Time to talk openly with the man she loved and find out what he thought about it. Maybe he hadn't been entirely wrong in his plan to take things slow between them. They hadn't really talked much. If they did, it was usually about safe topics like the animals, their work, or the two kids. Never about Paula or Nate. Or about Paula *and* Nate. If there really was a Paula and Nate.

On the other hand, she didn't want to miss the small moments. The feeling of connection that came through his physical closeness was just as wonderful as the fireworks that accompanied it. Her fingertips tingled at the memory and she felt hot all over. *Now that's what they mean when they talk about sustainability, isn't it?*

She'd spent the last two weeks with Leslie. After the kidnapping, she took her out of school with Nadine's permission. Considering the traumatic experiences Leslie had gone through and the fact that nothing earth-shattering was taught in the last two weeks before the long summer vacations anyway, it had not been a problem.

They had spent the first few days at home, recovering from the stress of the kidnapping and the fire. Then they packed the saddlebags and rode the horses into the mountains to camp. Leslie on Rufus, who had survived the rescue flawlessly, while she had ridden Lucky, the training horse that would probably soon be hers if the owner didn't pay the outstanding bills.

Roo and Barns were there, of course, and even Dolly came along. The Shetland pony ran along freely and took every opportunity for a stolen feeding break. When the distance became too great, she galloped after them with her short little legs.

They caught fish in the river and hunted rabbits. Leslie learned to shoot and shower under an icy waterfall, slept in a tent, and held marshmallows over the flames at the campfire until they were golden.

The time together in the wilderness with the animals brought them closer together. They talked about their hopes and dreams and built castles in the air. They agreed Paula would apply to adopt her as soon as possible.

A mere formality, Paula secretly thought. To her? Leslie was her daughter, paper or no paper. But for Leslie? It was an important step and Paula was happy to do whatever made Leslie feel more secure. The deep conversations led to an openness between the two of them. That's why Paula hadn't really been surprised when Leslie had asked her about Nate the previous evening.

"Do you like Nate?" the little girl had asked.

"Sure I like him."

"Then why don't you tell him that? Shauna and I would be really happy if you two could finally act normal."

"Normal? Hey!" Paula said. "What would that mean for Shauna and you?"

"We would like to be real sisters."

"Hold it, hold it," she said, and had to laugh after all. "Take it easy with the young horses. Are you saying Nate and I should get married?"

Leslie shrugged. "Why not? You like each other. Shauna and I like each other. What's wrong with that?"

"Yes, really. What is wrong with that?" She shook her head in disbelief. Children's logic. Everything always sounded so simple.

But that's what she wanted to find out. She winced. Maybe not the getting married thing. She definitely wasn't that far along. But Paula and Nate? She wanted to get to the bottom of that.

When she arrived, Nate was wrestling with a behemoth of a dog. They seemed to be fighting over a shoe. A rubber boot, perhaps? She wasn't sure. The two were moving too fast. After all, she was in no hurry, so she leaned against the gate and watched them.

Eventually, Nate gave up and dropped onto his back. "Okay. You win," he said to the giant beast.

The dog, in turn, plopped down on its hindquarters and dropped the hotly contested prey to the ground. An adorable, expansive pink tongue drooped from its broad face. Paula had to stifle a laugh. She walked over to the dog, and picked up the toy. It was a rubber boot. She held it over Nate's face. "Is this what you were looking for?"

Nate opened one eye at the sound of her voice. "Paula? Is it really you?"

"*Uh*, yeah? Why? Have you been having hallucinations lately that you're not sure about, or what's going on?" She looked around in confusion.

He closed his eyes.

It was quite nice to lie in the sun and just listen to her voice. She had dropped off the face of the earth after the kidnapping. Though he knew from Jake she was fine. He also understood the need to retreat and spend time with Leslie after such a horrific experience.

But he would have liked to have seen her, to talk to her, to hold her...and yes, even sleep with her, if he was honest. This artificial distance had been a decidedly stupid idea on his part. Why couldn't they do both? Get to know each other slowly while still enjoying the closeness of the other? Especially when the approach came from someone like Paula, who wasn't so quick to let anyone in. Not for nothing, but she was considered the prickliest member of the Carter clan. He'd picked up that much of the family dynamic.

Thanks to the concerned town gossips! How must she have felt when she'd taken a chance on him and he'd so carelessly rejected her affections? He had had a lot of time to think about it all. He was shocked she sought him out again.

"Hello, Earth to Nate?"

When he still didn't answer, she dropped to her knees beside him and put two fingers to his carotid artery to feel his pulse. Was he about to pass out?

He laughed. "Stop it. That tickles."

She gave him a good punch in the shoulder. "What do you think you're doing? I'm already worried here and you're just taking a nap?"

He put one of his muscular arms around her and pulled her down to lie on his chest.

She could get used to that, Paula thought.

"You were absolutely right."

Astonished, she looked at him. "Was I now? I'm always glad to hear that, of course. But what exactly are you talking about?"

"Getting to know a girl slowly is completely overrated," he said, kissing her.

If it had been up to Paula, the kiss would have never ended.

Nessie, however, had other plans. The young, impetuous Newfoundland girl was eager to join in the cuddle and pushed her snout between the two.

Laughing, they let go of each other.

Paula tickled the velvety soft floppy ears. "Do you feel neglected, little one?"

Nate snorted. "Little one. Don't make me laugh. She's a shoe-eating monster!"

"How did you find this dog, of all things?"

"How you come to any of your dogs as a veterinarian, that's how. Someone dropped him off and never picked him up. What was I supposed to do?"

"Yes, what then?" She laughed. "Obviously, I would have acted in exactly the same way." She stroked the dog, which had rolled onto its back and stretched out on all fours.

Nate stared her directly in the eyes and she felt happy and seen. Maybe a little tired. But very content, at peace with herself and the world. He reached out and touched her lightly on the shoulder.

"What are you doing here, anyway? As far as I can tell, you don't have a sick animal or Leslie with you. So what brings you to me?"

Paula stood up and looked him in the eye. She spotted the gold flecks around his iris that captivated her every time. "I'm here because a very wise person told me I should have a conversation with you about us."

"About us? Is there such a thing as 'us'?"

"I think so. What do you think? I'm willing to take a slower pace, too." She wrinkled her nose. "I have to admit, though, that don't-touch rule doesn't work very well for me." She narrowed her eyes. "But I'll try to behave myself."

Nate smiled and pulled her close until her body nestled perfectly against his. Their noses touched. "Oh, I've heard compromise is a wonderful thing," he said.

"So, let's just do both," she said.

"Sounds like a plan."

They laughed and kissed and laughed some more, their hearts light, their lives full, their thoughts racing with the millions of promises and possibilities of tomorrow.

THANK YOU FOR READING!

Readers like you are my daily motivation to write.

If you enjoyed my story, it would mean a lot if you could leave a review on your preferred book platforms. This actively supports my writing, as it is one of the few ways for me as an author to draw attention to my craft.

If you are a NetGalley member, you can review advanced reader copies of my upcoming titles before they are released.

CONNECT WITH ME

I love hearing from my valued readers, so please reach out to me directly via email or social media:

 MAIL@VIRGINIAFOX.COM

 @FOX_VIRGINIA

 BooksVirginiaFox

www.VirginiaFox.com

JOIN ME!

*Don't miss the next book
in the Rocky Mountain Romances series!*

CHAPTER ONE

Avery Wilkinson shifted from one foot to the other, bored. She worked undercover for five months. It felt like half an eternity. Often, she found it hard to remember where fiction ended and reality began. She scratched the right side of her head, which was half-shaved. On the left side, her long black hair fell smoothly down to her shoulders, cut in irregular steps. She had dyed the tips bright red. Her eyes were generously framed with black kohl makeup. Anything to maintain her cover as a young punk rocker. Soon she would be too old for the role. But at the moment, thanks to her flawless skin and slender, almost boyish physique, no one suspected a thing.

When she raised her arm, the rivets of her black leather jacket clinked together with a metallic tinkle. Miss Marple, her traveling rat who lived inside her jacket and was also an employee of the DEA—the U.S. Drug Enforcement Administration—just like her, stuck her nose out and blinked at her with black beady eyes.

She stroked Miss Marple's head and fed her a sunflower seed from the bag in her pocket.

"You still have to wait. It's not time." The rat grabbed the seed and disappeared back into the jacket. Good thing it was two sizes too big.

In recent month, Avery had managed to infiltrate the Monsanto clan, a family with mafia connections. Her specialties were money laundering and drugs. So far, the DEA had not managed to prove any of this in regard to the Monsantos.

That's where Avery and Miss Marple came in. Miss Marple was trained like a drug-sniffing dog. Except she didn't know sit, down, and heel, of course. Good manners came naturally to the rat, so there was no need for extra practice. Originally from the Netherlands, she'd been kicked out of the police's test program because her hit rate was too low.

Avery suspected the problem was more that Miss Marple was very sensitive and, unlike many of her peers, enjoyed human contact. If you locked her up and brought her out only to train, she really resented you. In any case, Avery was extremely satisfied with her little helper's work; so far, she'd never been let down. Trained in four different scents, Miss Marple's repertoire could be expanded at will. If everything went smoothly, she'd be able to prove her good nose again.

After a thorough analysis of the Monsanto brothers, it emerged that the whole family had a big heart for street children. Probably because they had worked their way up from the streets themselves. Ironic, really, that they were also dealing drugs, which were often the reason kids ended up on the streets.

Avery thought about her friend Paula back home in Independence, Colorado, who fostered one such runaway for the past year. *I wonder how they're doing over the past few months.* As exciting as her job was, she was getting tired of the daily charade. Just being herself seemed more tempting to her every day. If she even remembered who she was at all.

She shooed away her bad thoughts and focused on the conversation between Tony and Alberto. Tony had taken her under his wing after their first encounter and treated her like his little sister. The other three brothers didn't go quite that far, but at least they tolerated her as if she were Tony's little hobby.

It was fine with Avery. As long as no one wanted to get in her pants and she got the opportunity to do her job, she didn't care about anything else.

Little sister or not, Tony had long been very careful about where he took her or what conversations he let her overhear. She had perfected the brash emo-punk-rocker-teenager act and spread a convincing *I-don't-care-about-anything-maybe-I'll-die-today* mood, so Tony came to the conclusion she was completely harmless. In principle, she was. Almost. Except for her black belt in karate. And the knife in her boot. And Miss Marple.

Miss Marple was always along for the ride. Tony tried to convince her rats were unsanitary and disgusting. But he soon realized Avery wasn't going anywhere without her rat. So, he grudgingly accepted the rodent.

For the first time, he had taken her to a business meeting with his brother. The office was on the top floor of a large warehouse on the San Diego waterfront.

Avery would have loved to send Miss Marple on a tour of the long corridors with the wooden pallets but Tony insisted she come with him to the office. He impressed upon her to stay with him. Too bad. It would have been a once-in-a-lifetime opportunity.

Suddenly her ears pricked up. They were talking about a delivery that was supposed to arrive. They spoke only of "the goods." No one specified what exactly.

"You have to be here at ten o'clock sharp. Five minutes later and they'll be gone," Alberto said to Tony. Poor Tony. Even in a gangster family, being the youngest wasn't easy. She didn't know if she was suffering from a weird version of Stockholm syndrome, but she actually felt some sympathy for him. She sighed. The world was rarely exclusively black or white, after all. Noisily, she popped her gum bubble.

"Are we finally done here?" she asked in the brash manner she'd perfected over the past few months.

"In a minute, honey. I still have work to do."

Inwardly, she shuddered at the mention of his nickname for her. But she soon realized that he wanted to express his affection for her in a strange way. So, she had no choice but to live with it. Anything that confirmed her suspect's perception of her role, she had to accept willy-nilly. Well. Almost anything. That's why she was so grateful he seemed to have only brotherly feelings for her.

"Can I at least walk around a little?" She tried her luck.

"No way," Alberto said.

She would have to keep an eye on Alberto. He was the most perceptive of the family. He was the only one around whom she regularly had an uneasy feeling. She would catch him studying her, as if he couldn't quite figure her out. Smart guy. Inconvenient for her, and she had no illusions. Blood was definitely thicker than water in these circles. Especially if the water turned out to be a snitch.

She contorted her face into a convincing expression of a pouting teenager and let herself slide along the wall to the floor. Out of sheer boredom and to upset Alberto, she took Miss Marple out of her jacket and sat her on the floor.

The rat sat on its hind legs and sniffed the air with interest. She liked strange places and always blossomed when she got the opportunity to go exploring.

Alberto seemed annoyed when he saw the rodent, but decided he didn't want to waste his energy on them both. He turned back to his brother.

"Make sure you're on time," he urged him. When he turned away, Tony rolled his eyes and winked at her.

She bit her lips and had to stifle a laugh. Sometimes he could be quite charming.

"You receive the goods, check them, and have them supplied to the designated containers. You have five men available for that. And leave your appendage at home," he instructed him with a nod in their direction.

Avery took note of this without any reaction. It wasn't difficult, either, because Miss Marple was sitting under Alberto's desk, sounding the alarm. She clicked the small tin frog, which made a click. That was a signal to Miss Marple. Fortunately, none of the brothers had the faintest clue what clicker training was. Otherwise, the whole thing would have been much more difficult.

The rat ran back to her and picked up another sunflower seed as a reward. She was not surprised Miss Marple had found something. She suspected that Alberto had either money or cocaine in the desk. Both in quantities too small to be of any use to her investigation.

This was more than just a small amount of narcotics for personal use. That would only get him a slap on the wrist, a fine, and maybe a few hours of community service. *Probably not even that, with the lawyers he could afford,* she thought.

After Alberto had asked Tony to leave her at home, she had no choice but to put away her little protector. She held out her jacket to Miss Marple and let the rat slip into her safe den. Hopefully, they'd be done soon. If she had to be back by ten, she didn't have much time to make the necessary preparations.

Cole checked his pistol. Everything was in order and ready to go, he noted, and slid it back into his holster. He picked up the heavy Kevlar vest and strapped it on. Last, he grabbed the phones and microphone and was ready for action. A raid was planned on one of the warehouses near the docks. According to his supervisor, the FBI had received a tip that a major shipment was due to arrive there tonight. Info about the nature of the shipment had been vague. It could be anything from drugs to guns or women to stolen art.

He didn't like assignments where you didn't know exactly where you stood. With such incomplete information, it was difficult to assess risks such as the expected propensity for violence.

His partner Ali, who everyone called Big A because of his size, knew his attitude toward such missions and slapped him on the shoulders as he passed. That was meant to be encouraging. But when Big A gave out such pats on the back, normal men went down on their knees, even though Cole himself was also quite tall and broad-shouldered.

"It'll be a piece of cake. You'll see. We'll be in and out in twenty minutes. If we're lucky, and with a big haul."

"Right. As if it was ever that simple," Cole muttered in a bad mood. He didn't know what was wrong with him. After several years of undercover assignments and subsequent burnout, he'd switched to inside work as a computer specialist, commonly known as a hacker. That had been intellectually very exciting, but after a while, he missed the adrenaline rush of working on the street.

His boss obviously didn't trust his mental stability. What had the FBI psychologist told him? Were the sessions not confidential? But he had complied with his request for fieldwork to the extent he was allowed to sit in on team assignments. Yay. He would much rather work and solve actual cases from start to finish with Ali as a two-person team. It didn't look like he was going to get the chance to do that anytime soon.

The director of operations called them. He jumped up and took his seat in the large, nondescript FBI van. He leaned his head against the headrest and closed his eyes, mentally going over the course of the raid one more time.

Half an hour later, the time had come. Everyone stood at their assigned position. By means of hand signals, they coordinated access.

After a few minutes, the raid was over. Big A held the leader, Tony Monsanto, at bay. The fellow, he couldn't be much older than twenty-five. He started sweating profusely when he saw Cole push his own prisoner forward with one hand on the collar. His captive fought like a lion and let a torrent of obscenities rain down. Impressive, the kid's vocabulary.

"What about the others?"

"The others are all employees of the freighter," Big A said. "We've shipped them back to their boat until we know what we're dealing with here."

"It's all a big misunderstanding," Tony whined.

"I'm sure it is. But let's let the prosecutor decide that, don't you think?" said Big A.

Cole pushed his prisoner, whom he had surprised and caught hiding behind the container, into the light. Time to take a closer look at this person.

"Let her go," Tony said. "She has nothing to do with the business side of our family."

Cole turned his prisoner around, which resulted in another barrage of curses. Creative, he had to admit. He was about to comment when he saw the face and froze. The night had suddenly become much more interesting when it dawned on him who he was holding in his hands. *But what the hell was she doing here? In this outfit?*

The woman in his hands disagreed and was not interested in his questions. For a second, a warning flashed in her eyes. Before he had time to interpret it, however, the expression disappeared and she spat in his face.

Stunned, he stared at her and silently wiped the spittle away.

"Maria, don't do that. You'll only get yourself into trouble," Tony shouted. "Just talk to the policeman and you'll be back home in bed in no time, where you should have stayed from the start."

Avery ignored the speech addressed to her alter ego, Maria. She was just fighting for survival in the Monsanto family. Time to show some loyalty. So she kicked Cole in the shin with the toe of her heavy motorcycle boots. Not with all her might, but in such a way that he had no choice but to wince.

"Hey! That's enough of that!"

Across the room, Big A grinned as he saw the prisoner, a girl at that, beating Cole.

Avery, on the other hand, reached the end of her rope. If she wanted to have the slightest chance of keeping her cover, Cole had to finally do something. Arrest her, preferably. Hell, as far as she knew, he'd been undercover himself for years. He should know how the game was played.

"Cuff me already, you ass!" she hissed at him between clenched teeth.

That seemed to snap him out of his confusion. With a curse of his own, he roughly turned her around and twisted both arms behind her back. She hoped Miss Marple survived all the turbulence in her jacket unscathed, poor thing.

While Cole locked the handcuffs around her wrists, he leaned over and murmured in her ear, "If you'd said something, I would have brought handcuffs last time."

He was referring to their last run-in in Independence when his sister had been kidnapped and she, as a profiler, and he, as a computer expert, had helped to recover her. The great relief and, yes, of course, the undeniable, highly explosive attraction between them, had led to them ending up in bed together after a successful rescue. And not for the first time. Furious he had brought up the subject at this most inopportune time, she stomped on his foot.

He suppressed a yelp and pulled on the handcuffs. "Behave!"

"In your dreams," she said, glaring at him over her shoulder. Miss Marple picked this moment to get some fresh air and wriggled out of her collar.

Startled, Cole jumped back a large step. Just in time, he remembered he had better not let go of his prisoner. "What the hell is that?"

He was already about to reach for the rodent to hurl it into the nearest corner when Avery began to sob heartbreakingly and, above all, loudly. Miss Marple, sensing the impending danger, quickly disappeared back into her hiding place.

"Hey, what are you doing with her? I'm reporting you for the disproportionate use of force. It's not necessary to scare my sister like that and treat her roughly."

Cole gritted his teeth and refrained from telling Tony off. Instead, he raised an eyebrow and asked, "Your sister? Is that what they call it these days?"

Tony stared at him.

Cole ignored him. "You can explain that to the D.A. Let's go!" He pushed Maria/Avery out of the warehouse and toward the squad car.

Finally, Avery thought with relief and almost sank into Cole's arms. But stubbornly, she found her last reserves of strength. There was no reason to let any weakness show. Not a good idea in an environment dominated by testosterone, as she'd learned early on.

"Sister? A handcuff fetish? Anything else you wanted to tell me?" he asked, the amusement in his voice flawlessly audible.

"Do me a favor."

"What now?"

"Just be quiet."

AUTHOR'S NOTE

Leslie's story, unfortunately, is not uncommon. Time and again, children fall through gaps in a system that is supposed to protect them. On the other hand, there are very dedicated employees who do their best every day to help children in difficult situations. Many thanks to all those who carry out such a respectable profession.

MISS DAISY'S RECIPES

Jaz' Sweet Potato Soup (Vegan)

INGREDIENTS

1 onion

2 carrots

1 leek

2 sweet potatoes, peeled

1 chili pepper

½ cup white wine

Vegetable broth

Salt

Cayenne pepper

Thyme

Olive oil

INSTRUCTIONS

Clean the vegetables. Depending on your heat tolerance, remove the seeds from the chili pepper (less spicy) or leave them in (very spicy, depending on the type of chili).

Sauté vegetables in olive oil. Deglaze with white wine. Let the wine boil down.

Fill up pan with vegetable broth. I always use enough so that the vegetables are just covered. Depending on whether you prefer soups thicker or thinner, you can adjust the amount.

Simmer for 15–20 minutes. Check if vegetables (especially sweet potatoes) are soft. Once they are, puree with a hand blender. The consistency can be adjusted here again with some vegetable broth (unfortunately only towards "liquid").

Season with salt, pepper, and other spices to taste.

The soup can be refined with cream or crème fraîche (or, of course, the corresponding vegetable product), but also tastes very good without. If you have fresh thyme sprigs, you can decorate the soup bowls with them.

Paula's Mac & Cheese

There is of course the Mac & Cheese version from the pasta package, but homemade, it tastes much better!

THIS RECIPE IS INTENDED FOR 6 PEOPLE.

INGREDIENTS

½ cup butter

2½ cups breadcrumbs, coarse

1 onion, chopped

4 tsp. sea salt (or more, applies to all spices: to taste)

½ tsp. black pepper (or also, cayenne pepper)

Nutmeg

½ cup flour

4¼ cups milk

1 lb. macaroni

6 oz. sharp cheddar (or another spicy cheese, e.g., Gruyère), coarsely grated

6 oz. Gouda (or another mild cheese, e.g., shortly ripened Manchego, Edam), coarsely grated

3½ oz. Parmesan cheese, grated (or also Grana Padano, Sbrinz...)

INSTRUCTIONS

Preheat oven to 400°F.

Melt butter in a large saucepan.

Add 2 tbsp. of the melted butter to a bowl and mix with the breadcrumbs. Season with salt and pepper; mix well again. Set aside.

Add onions, salt, and pepper to the rest of the melted butter in saucepan and cook slowly over moderate heat until the onions are softened, but not browned.

In a pot, cook pasta until al dente (that is, a few minutes less than it says on the package). This prevents the dish from becoming mushy after further cooking in the oven. Once the pasta is done, drain the cooking water and rinse briefly with cold water in colander. Set aside.

Gradually add flour to butter and onion mixture in the saucepan, stirring constantly, until it thickens into a paste.

In the saucepan gradually add the cold milk, stirring constantly. The mixture will thicken immediately, especially in the beginning. Do not be tempted to add all the milk at once.

When the milk has been completely added, and the béchamel sauce is thickened and smooth, season with nutmeg and salt.

Stir the cheese into the béchamel sauce until melted but set aside a little of the Parmesan for topping.

Add the pasta to the saucepan and mix well.

Pour the mixture into a baking dish, sprinkle with breadcrumb mixture and Parmesan, and bake for about 25 minutes until breadcrumbs are lightly browned. Let cool for 5 minutes before serving.

Miss Daisy's Sloppy Joes (Refined by Aileen)

*The diner has always been known for its delicious home cooking.
However, Aileen, who recently joined the sisters team,
has become influential in the cooking.*

INGREDIENTS

1⅓ organic ground beef

1 onion, chopped

2 cloves of garlic, pressed

1 green bell pepper, chopped

3½ oz. mushrooms, sliced

1 large can of tomatoes

2 tbsp. acacia honey (optional, I usually leave it out)

5 tbsp. ketchup

2 tbsp. Worcestershire sauce

½ tbsp. Dijon mustard

½ tbsp. yellow mustard

1 tbsp. organic apple cider vinegar

1 tbsp. chili, ground

1 tsp. cumin

Cayenne pepper

1^{7}/$_{8}$ cups vegetable broth

Sea salt

2 tbsp. olive oil

INSTRUCTIONS

Sauté onions in olive oil. Add the peppers and mushrooms, salt a little, and sauté. If you want to add other vegetables like carrots or celery, you can add them here as well.

Add the meat and brown briefly; then lower the temperature and add the garlic.

Deglaze with the apple cider vinegar. Let it boil down a little.

Add tomatoes including juice and remaining ingredients.

Cover and simmer at low temperature for two to three hours. If too much liquid remains at the end, remove the lid for the last 15–25 minutes.

Traditionally, the meat sauce is served with a hamburger bun.

However, you can also serve it with the following: avocado slices, sweet potato fries (see Volume 3, *Rocky Mountain Dogs* for recipe) or as a stuffing for portobello mushrooms, large zucchini, hollowed-out squash, tomatoes, or peppers. Then bake the stuffed vegetables in the oven at 400°F (feel free to sprinkle a little cheese on top) to soften them as well (duration 10–25 minutes, depending on the type of vegetable).

Aileen's Lemon Cheesecake Muffins

(Makes 12 Muffins)

*Aileen's specialty is muffins, cupcakes,
and similar sweet delicacies.
The base consists of homemade oat cookies.*

INGREDIENTS

OAT COOKIES:

⅓ cup soft butter

⅓ cup brown cane sugar

1 pinch of salt (if using spelt flour, 2 pinches of salt)

1 egg

½ tsp. vanilla extract

1½ cups oat bran

¼ cup spelt flour (wheat also works, of course)

2 tsp. cinnamon

⅛ cup butter

LEMON CHEESECAKE FILLING:

$^{7}/_{8}$ cup low fat cottage cheese

3½ oz. cream cheese

⅓ cup sugar

1 lemon (organic), washed, zest and juice

1 egg

¼ cup corn starch

INSTRUCTIONS

OAT COOKIES:

Preheat oven to 350°F.

Beat soft butter, sugar, and salt until fluffy. Mix in the egg and vanilla extract.

In a separate bowl, mix oats, flour, baking powder, and cinnamon. Add to butter-sugar mixture and stir briefly until everything is well-blended.

Divide batter into 24 balls of dough placed on a baking sheet lined with parchment paper, spacing them apart and flattening slightly.

Bake cookies in the center of the oven for 13 minutes at 350°F.

Let cool on a cooling rack.

Once cooled, process the cookies into fine crumbs with a pastry blender. Melt the butter and mix with the crumbs. Divide the mixture for the base into 12 muffin cups, pressing down firmly. Refrigerate.

LEMON CHEESECAKE FILLING:

Preheat oven to 350°F.

Mix all ingredients together until smooth. Spread on the prepared oat cookie bases.

Bake in the middle of the oven for 30 minutes. Take out.

Let cool and serve dusted with powdered sugar.

TO SAVE TIME: If you don't feel like making the oatmeal cookies yourself, you can use speculaas cookies for the base. The procedure remains the same.

By the way, I discovered this recipe on Sia's Soulfood Foodblog. Visit her blog for more great recipes.

BOOK CLUB QUESTIONS

1. In the story, Paula often hides her feelings for Nate by being mean or curt with him. Why do you think she does this? Is this something that happens in real life?

2. Paige the intrepid reporter is scared of dogs and is lost after losing her job at the *Daily News*. Others try to help her by hooking her up with a dog of her own. Do you think this was a smart decision? Could it have backfired? Why or why not?

3. There seems to be a major theme in Rocky Mountain Kid that sometimes family doesn't always have to be strictly those who we are related to by blood. Do you agree with this? In real life, can you think of any examples of this in your own or other people's lives?

4. Leslie has been through a lot as a second-time foster child. Do you think she's a good role model for kids in similar situations?

5. Many characters suffer unrequited love for long periods of time in the story. Some act upon it earlier than others, while others never do. What ramifications have they had from this in their lives?

6. Service Animals have been controversial, as many have taken advantage of designating their pets as such

to gain special privileges while traveling and in other areas. But for many, they can be life-changing. In Rocky Mountain Kid, several make huge differences to their caregivers. Who were some of your favorites and why? Do you think Leslie bringing Ranger to court was ultimately a good or bad idea?

7. The media is represented as a big baddie. Their actions set into place several major plot points that have serious consequences for some of the characters, even endangering their lives. Is this something that still happens today? Is it realistic? Or have things gotten better?

8. A big contrast is made between living a country life and a big city life. Often, country life is portrayed as being more genuine, real, and honest. Do you think this is true?

ROCKY MOUNTAIN ROMANCES

Rocky Mountain Yoga

Rocky Mountain Star

Rocky Mountain Dogs

Rocky Mountain Kid

Rocky Mountain Secrets

COLLECT THE ENTIRE SERIES!

ABOUT THE AUTHOR

AUTHOR, MOTHER, HORSE WHISPERER, and part-time healthy food cook, Virginia Fox is a woman who cares deeply about family, animals, the environment, and friendships.

Creative from a young age, she turned her love of books into a prolific career as a writer. Her German-language Rocky Mountain series saw every volume enter the Top 50 of the Kindle charts on day one of launch. Now the bestselling Rocky Mountain Romances series breaks onto the US scene.

Virginia Fox lives on a small ranch near Zurich with her family, her Australian cattle dog, and two moody tomcats. When she isn't writing, she delights in caring for her horses and cooking for her family. Discover more on her website:

WWW.VIRGINIAFOX.COM

www.ingramcontent.com/pod-product-compliance
Lightning Source LLC
Chambersburg PA
CBHW070609300726
48975CB00006B/1762